Witch Is How Dreams Became Reality

Published by Implode Publishing Ltd
© Implode Publishing Ltd 2019

Chapter 1

It was Monday morning, and I'd left the house earlier than usual. It wasn't that I particularly needed to be at work early, but I couldn't stand to hear another one of Jack's lame jokes about my tap dancing, or my drenching in the water tank. My cunning plan to escape TenPinCon had backfired big time, but for one reason and one reason only.

Grandma!

I was determined to get my revenge on her, but that would be a whole lot easier said than done.

Still, at least TenPinCon was behind me now. There was no reason I should ever have to think about it again.

"Morning, Jill." The cucumber hand puppet in the toll booth took my cash.

"Morning." I willed the barrier to lift so I could be on my way.

"I had no idea you were so talented." Mr Ivers popped his head up. "I thought you should have won that talent contest."

Oh no! "You saw it, then?"

"Of course. It made unmissable TV. How they voted that sword swallower above you and your tap dancing, I'll never know. You should have registered an objection."

"I was happy with second place."

"I've always wanted to learn to dance. I don't suppose you'd consider giving me lessons, would you?"

"I'm sorry, I'm really—"

"I'd pay of course."

"I was going to say that I'm really too busy at the moment."

1

"Maybe at a later date when things quieten down?"

"Maybe, we'll see."

"I hope so. I can't help but feel that I'd be very good at it."

He started to bob up and down, and although I couldn't see his feet, I assumed he was attempting to tap dance.

"The barrier, please, Mr Ivers. I am in rather a hurry."

"You won't forget about the lessons, will you?"

"Of course not."

***

At least the office would be a safe haven. Mrs V wasn't the kind of person to watch trivial news items such as the coverage of TenPinCon.

"Morning, Jill." She was knitting. "Did you see the local news this morning?"

Oh bum! "No, and before you ask, I'm not giving tap dancing lessons."

"Sorry? I don't understand."

"You said you'd been watching the local news?"

"I meant that awful car crash. You must have heard about it?"

"No, I haven't seen the news today."

"A young couple. They'd just got married and were on the way to the reception in the limousine when it crashed. They were both killed outright."

"That's terrible. It just goes to show that when your time's up, your time's up."

"Quite. What was that you were saying about tap-dancing lessons?"

"Err, nothing. It doesn't matter. Do you think you could

rustle up a coffee for me? I left the house without having one this morning."

"That's not like you."

"Jack was getting on my nerves."

"Oh dear. I hope you didn't leave without making up. You never know what might happen. Just look at that poor couple."

"We haven't fallen out; he was just being a bit of a pain. It was nothing serious. Will you bring my coffee through?"

"Of course, dear."

Winky was rolling back and forth on my desk, and he was laughing so hard there were tears in his eye.

"You have to see this." He pointed to the screen. "It's the funniest thing I've seen all year."

"What are you watching?" I had bad vibes even before I reached the desk.

"Watch!"

On-screen, there was an image of me on the stage at TenPinCon, perched on a chair above the water tank.

"I don't want to watch."

"Wait! Look!"

On screen, the last of the tenpins was knocked over, and the chair threw me forward into the water.

"Turn it off!"

He ignored me and instead rewound the footage, and this time, played it in slow motion.

"Is that your grandmother standing in front of the tank?"

"Yes, she was the one who 'volunteered' me for the ducking stool."

3

"You must have done something to upset her. What did you do?"

"Nothing. Much. That water was freezing."

He rewound the footage and played it again. "Too funny."

"That's enough." I snatched the mouse and closed down the browser. "I don't want to hear another word about it."

"Fair enough." He jumped off the sofa. "I can see you're upset."

"Do you promise not to mention it again?"

"You have my word." He disappeared under the sofa, but quickly reappeared.

Wearing tap shoes!

"That's not funny!"

"What do you think?" He tapped his way across the room. "Fred Astaire, eat your heart out."

Thankfully, the tap dancing seemed to wear Winky out, and twenty minutes later, he was fast asleep under the sofa. Maybe now, I could finally forget about the tap dancing and the soaking.

My phone rang; it was Kathy.

"Have you dried off yet, Jill?"

"Did you call for anything in particular?"

"Not really. I just wanted to say how impressed Pete and I were at the way you threw yourself into TenPinCon. You're usually such a misery guts when you go anywhere."

"Gee, thanks."

"You know what I mean. You aren't normally one to volunteer for stuff. I still can't believe you kept the tap-dancing quiet. I was saying to Pete that I should get you to give me lessons. It'd be a great way to get fit."

"I really am busy this morning, Kathy."

"Sorry, I just thought you'd like to know that the kids had a wonderful time on Saturday."

"Yeah, it seemed like it."

"Lizzie wants to take up tap dancing too."

"I suppose Mikey wants to as well?"

"No, all he can talk about at the moment is dogs. He wants one, but we've told him he can't have one because there's no one in the house during the daytime, and it wouldn't be fair to leave a dog alone for such long periods."

"How did he take that?"

"Not very well, as you can imagine. It seems that his two best friends both have dogs. We've told him he can have a pet, but that it will have to be something that can be left alone during the daytime. I think we may have talked him around."

"Sorry, but I really do have to get going."

"Okay. Catch you later."

***

My first new client of the week was a Mrs Forrest who had called earlier that morning, in a bit of a flap.

In her late forties or maybe early fifties, she looked like the kind of woman who would normally wear a lot of makeup but hadn't bothered that day.

"Can I get you a drink, Mrs Forrest?"

"Sorry? No, I'd rather get started."

"As you wish. What brings you here today?"

"It's about my son, Laurence. He's been arrested for murder."

"Who is he supposed to have killed?"

"They say he murdered Alison—his wife, but he would never do anything like that. He wouldn't hurt a flea."

"When was he arrested?"

"Last Friday. I've been looking after Adam since then."

"And Adam is—?"

"Laurence's son; my grandson. He's only three. He doesn't have any idea what's going on, the poor little lamb."

"Does he know his mother is dead?"

"Not yet, no. Fortunately, he was staying at our house the night it happened."

"Is it usual for the boy to stay at your house?"

"Yes, he stays with us most Fridays, so that Laurence and Alison can have a little time to themselves."

"Do you feel up to talking me through what happened?"

"Not really, but I'll do my best." She took a few moments to gather herself. "Like I said, it happened last Friday. From what I can make out, Laurence and Alison had had an argument, and Laurence had stormed out. He went for a walk to try and calm down. When he returned to the apartment, a couple of hours later, he found Alison—." That seemed to tip Mrs Forrest over the edge, and she began to cry.

"Here." I passed her the box of tissues I kept for such occasions. "Take your time. There's no hurry. Are you sure you wouldn't like a drink?"

She shook her head. "I'll be okay in a minute."

I waited until she was ready to continue.

"Laurence called the police, and then he called me."

"How did Alison die?"

"She was beaten around the head. Laurence was hysterical on the phone. He just kept saying *she's dead* and *there's blood everywhere*. I didn't know what to do. I just kept thinking about Adam, who was upstairs just a few yards away. The poor little boy had lost his mummy."

"Has Laurence been charged?"

"Yes, just when I thought the nightmare couldn't get any worse, I heard he'd been charged with Alison's murder."

"Did he confess?"

"No! Why would he do that? He didn't kill Alison."

"I understand that, but sometimes people in these situations are so confused that they'll—"

"Well, he didn't. The police seem to have just decided he murdered her."

"On what evidence?"

"I don't know. No one will tell me anything."

"When did you last speak to Laurence?"

"Yesterday."

"How was he?"

"How do you think? He's devastated by Alison's death, he's worried about Adam, and he's scared of what is going to happen to him. Can you help me, Mrs Maxwell?"

"Yes, of course. And please call me Jill."

"Thank you, Jill. I didn't know what to do. It was a neighbour who suggested I contact a private investigator, and I found your name online."

"Do you feel up to answering a few more questions, Mrs Forrest?"

"Of course. And it's Sheila."

1

"Okay, Sheila. Let's start with your son's apartment. I'll need to take a look around there."

"The police won't let me go inside. I tried yesterday, but they turned me away. They said it should be released in a few days."

"Let me know as soon as it is. What does your son do?"

"He's a manager at an electrical retailer. That reminds me, I don't imagine anyone has told them that he won't be in."

"Don't worry about that just now. What about Alison? What did she do?"

"She was a solicitor at West & Partners. Family law."

"Do you know any of Alison's close friends?"

"She has a few, but the only one I know by name is Rachel Somers. They were work colleagues."

"Okay. You mentioned that there had been an argument on the night that Alison was murdered."

"It was nothing. All couples argue, don't they?"

"Of course. But how was the marriage generally? Any problems that you were aware of?"

"No. They were really happy together, particularly since Adam arrived."

"You're sure about that? This will work best if you're completely honest with me."

"I'm positive. I'd have known if anything was wrong."

"Okay." I could see she was getting more and more upset, so I decided not to push it any further.

***

"Coo-ee, Jill." Harold, the pigeon, was peering through the open window.

"Morning, Harold. Were you looking for Winky? He's fast asleep under the sofa."

"Actually, it was you I wanted to talk to."

"Oh?"

"First, though, I'd like to introduce you to my missus." He glanced along the ledge. "Ida, come here. Don't be shy. Jill doesn't bite."

Moments later, a slightly smaller pigeon edged into view.

"Hello, Ida," I said.

"Hi. I'm very pleased to meet you."

"I hear we've been neighbours for some time. I had no idea you were living there."

"We may not be for much longer," Harold said.

"Oh? Why's that? Do you have a new place lined up?"

"We wouldn't be moving through choice, Jill."

"Why then?"

"We heard on the pigeonvine that the landlord of this building is having those awful spike things put on all of the ledges."

"Really? That's the first I've heard of it. Are you sure?"

"My source is usually reliable. Don't get me wrong, Jill, we understand why two-leggeds feel the need to install those spikes, but most pigeons are like us, very house-proud. It's just the inconsiderate minority that give the rest of us a bad name. This whole business has got Ida really upset."

"I love it here," she said. "It's the nicest spot we've ever lived. I can't bear the thought of having to move after we've spent so long getting it just as we like it."

"I really am sorry to hear about this, but I'm still having difficulty in believing my landlord would do it. He hates

9

spending money on anything."

Not long after Harold and Ida left, I had to shut the window because the heavens had opened.

"I hate this weather." Winky crawled out from under the sofa. "It does nothing but rain around here."

"Think yourself lucky that you're in a cosy, warm office. Poor old Harold and Ida are outside in all weathers."

"It doesn't seem to bother them." He stretched.

"They were here while you were asleep. They're worried they might have to find a new home."

"Why? You didn't threaten to start charging them rent, did you?"

"Of course I didn't. What do you take me for?"

"I know what you're like. Anything to make a quick buck."

"That's rich coming from you. They've heard the landlord is having spikes installed on the window ledges around the building."

"Macabre? Are they sure? That man's as tight as a duck's—"

"That's what I said, but Harold was adamant it's true."

"In that case, you'd better do something about it."

"Me? What can I do?"

"You're a witch, aren't you? You'll think of something."

"The spikes thing might not even be true. I'll wait until I've heard it direct from the horse's mouth."

Mrs V popped her head around the door. "Jill, while you were on the phone, Mr Macabre called. He's coming to see you tomorrow."

Apparently, the horse had something he wanted to tell me.

Chapter 2

I'd said that I'd pop over to Aunt Lucy's later that afternoon but seeing as I had nothing spoiling at that moment, I thought I might as well pay her a visit now. And besides, Winky had just put on his tap shoes again. There was a limit to how much of the soft-shoe shuffle I could take in one day.

I'd expected to find her in the kitchen, but instead, I heard the sound of the TV coming from the lounge. Aunt Lucy was so engrossed in whatever it was she was watching that she didn't even notice me walk into the room.

"Aunt Lucy?"

"Jill?" She jumped. "I didn't realise you were there."

"What's that you're watching?"

"Come and sit next to me. It's Candle Place. You must have heard of it?"

"I can't say that I have."

"It's Candlefield's longest running daytime soap. I watch it every day if I can."

"I wouldn't have had you down as a soap fan."

"I'm not normally, but I love this." She pointed to the screen. "Michael has just asked Rosemary to marry him. She's so beautiful, isn't she?"

"I guess. Shall I go and put the kettle on?"

"I do hope she says yes. Michael loves her so much."

This was a whole new side to Aunt Lucy that I hadn't seen before. She was so engrossed in the soap she hadn't even heard me ask about the tea, but I decided to make it anyway.

I was still waiting for the kettle to boil when she came to

join me in the kitchen.

"I'm sorry about that, Jill, but it was so exciting. I've been waiting for Michael to pop the question for months."

"Did Rosemary say yes?"

"The credits rolled before she could answer. I'll have to wait until tomorrow to find out. The suspense is going to kill me."

"How are the twins and the little ones?"

"All fine. The girls were around here yesterday."

"For lunch?"

"Actually, no." She began to grin like a Cheshire cat. "I think you were very brave."

"Me? What do you mean?"

"To volunteer to take that ducking."

Oh great! Was there anyone who didn't know?

"How did you hear about that?"

"Grandma came around to show us the video she'd recorded."

"*Us?* Have the twins seen it too?"

"Yes, it was Grandma who invited them over."

"I don't suppose she told you she was the one who 'volunteered' me for that soaking, did she?"

"No, she never mentioned that."

"I'm going to get my revenge on that woman if it's the last thing I do."

"Be careful, Jill. She has a habit of having the last laugh."

"The water in that tank was freezing. It's a wonder I didn't catch my death."

"What about the tap dancing?"

"That was Grandma too."

"Oh dear. Whatever did you do to upset her?"

"I don't want to talk about it. Let's change the subject."

"Okay. We're getting new neighbours."

"Is Grandma moving out?"

"No such luck." Aunt Lucy put a hand to her mouth. "That's an awful thing for me to say, isn't it?"

"Not really. I couldn't imagine having to live next door to her. I take it you mean the house on the other side?"

"Yes. They're moving in tomorrow."

"You've met them, then?"

"I have. It's two sisters."

"That's a little unusual, isn't it? Are they elderly?"

"No. Quite young, actually. I spoke to one of them yesterday. Her name is Pea. She seems nice."

"Pea?"

"I assume it's short for something."

"Did you warn them about Grandma?"

"No, I didn't want to scare them away."

"How's Lester?"

"He's fine. Much more relaxed now they've done away with that horrible bonus scheme."

"Have they scrapped it?"

"Yes, thank goodness. After what happened with that awful Dunston man, his bosses realised that it was incentivising the wrong kind of behaviour."

"Jill!" Rhymes came 'speeding' through the door.

"Hi, little guy."

"When will I get my trophy?"

"I'm going to collect it on Friday night."

"I can't wait."

"Me neither."

I'd just finished my tea when I received a phone call from Mad.

13

"Hey, Mad, how goes it?"

"Great, thanks. Are you busy? Do you have time to meet up?"

"Right now? Are you in Washbridge?"

"Yeah."

"How long for?"

"The foreseeable future."

"How come?"

"I landed a promotion."

"That's great. Where do you want to meet? Coffee Games?"

"I thought you might like to come over to see my new place."

"Definitely. Where is it?"

"Do you know the apartments they built in the old sock factory?"

"On Colbourn Drive? Yeah, I know it."

"I'm on the top floor."

"Okay. I'll be there in a few minutes."

***

It had been a while since I'd visited the apartment block where Mad was now living. Susan Hall, the only decent reporter The Bugle had ever employed, had lived there for a while. Fortunately for her, but unfortunately for local journalism, she'd moved back to London.

Mad must have seen me arrive because she was waiting in her doorway when I stepped out of the lift.

"What do you think?" Mad showed me inside.

"I've always liked these apartments. How many people are you sharing with?"

"I'm not. It's just me."

"How many bedrooms are there?"

"Just the two. It's one of the smaller apartments in the block."

"Even so, it must be costing you an arm and a leg."

"I can just about afford it with the promotion."

"How come you didn't tell me you were coming back?"

"It all happened so quickly. One of the controllers decided to take early retirement, and they offered me his job. I was gobsmacked. There are many others with bags more experience than me."

"They must think you can do the job."

"I guess so."

"Are you going to be based in Washbridge permanently?"

"Yeah, I'll be splitting my time between here and GT. I have a small flat-cum-office over there, but it's nothing like this place."

"What did your mum have to say about you coming back?"

Mad frowned. "I haven't actually got around to telling her yet."

"Why not?"

"I wanted the chance to get settled in before she came over here."

"You have to tell her."

"I will. Soon. Would you like a drink?"

"Not for me, thanks. I've just had a cup of tea at Aunt Lucy's. What exactly will you be doing in your new role?"

"It's not that much different to what I've always done, except I'll be controlling a small team of ghost hunters. It's all a bit daunting, to tell you the truth."

15

"You'll be great at it."

"I'm hoping you might be able to help me out from time to time."

"Of course. Likewise, I might need your help occasionally."

"No problem. Just say the word."

"I really do like this place. Have you met any of your neighbours yet?"

"A few of them, yes. From what I can gather, they're all sups."

"I used to know a few people who lived here, but they might have moved on by now. There was a vampire called Dorothy. Is she still here?"

"I don't know. If she is, I haven't met her yet."

"And a werewolf. I'm trying to remember his name?"

"Was it Charlie?"

"That's him."

"Yeah, I've met Charlie. He's a love. He helped to carry my stuff upstairs because the lift was out of commission on the day I moved in. Do you know his flatmate, Neil? He fancies himself as a bit of a ladies' man."

"Yeah." I nodded. "The last I heard, he was working in a fancy-dress shop."

"And then there's the ghost."

"I didn't realise there was one."

"Mr Tobias Fotheringham."

"Who?"

"Socky for short. He used to own the sock factory. He lives with Charlie and Neil, but I got the impression he was hoping to move in with me."

"Is he a looker?"

"Not really." She laughed. "He's a gazillion years old

and has a wooden leg. I don't know how those guys put up with him, clomping around all night long."

When the time came for me to leave, Mad walked me to the lift, only to find an out of order notice stuck on the doors.

"It was working when I arrived."

"It's useless. It breaks down all the time."

"Oh well, the exercise will do me good. Bye, Mad, and don't forget to tell Deli you're back."

"I won't."

When I reached the first floor, I bumped into two familiar faces: Charlie and Dorothy.

"Hey, Jill," Dorothy said. "What are you doing here?"

"I've just been to see a friend of mine who's moved into an apartment on the top floor."

"Do you mean Mad?" Charlie said.

"Yeah."

"She's a ghost hunter, isn't she?" Dorothy put down one of her shopping bags.

"That's right. She's a good sort. She'll make a good neighbour. What are you two doing now? Are you still at the bookshop, Dorothy?"

"No. I have my own business now."

"Doing what?"

"It's probably best you don't know." She grinned.

"Fair enough. What about you, Charlie? Are you still at the gym?"

"He's a full-time model now," Dorothy got in before he could speak.

"Really? That's great. Do you enjoy it?"

"Yeah." He blushed. "It doesn't really feel like work,

though."

"What about your other flatmates?"

"Flatmate. Singular." Dorothy corrected me. "It's just us two and Neil."

"Is he still at the fancy dress shop?"

"When he's not doing his magician act, yeah."

"Didn't you get anyone to take Susan's place?"

"We've had a couple of people, but they didn't last very long."

"Humans?"

"No way! The landlord foisted another one on us, but we soon got rid of him. We've had two witches, actually, but they didn't work out."

"How come?"

"They talked too much and were too opinionated," Dorothy said.

Charlie grinned, and I got the distinct impression that he might have had a different take on the matter, but he wasn't going to voice his opinion while Dorothy was there.

"Okay, well it was nice to see you both again. I'd better get going."

***

I was just about to head back to the office when I got a phone call from Belladonna.

"I'm ready, Jill."

"Ready? Ready for what?"

"For you to do your thing. You know—change my identity."

"I thought I'd explained. I can't do that until you've

moved into your new place."

"I have. I moved in over the weekend."

"That was quick! How did you manage that?"

"It wasn't easy, but I want to get back to work at the creche, so I pulled out all the stops. This place isn't great, but I can always find somewhere better later. So, what do you say, can we do this?"

"Sure. Give me your address, and I'll magic myself over there now."

Oh dear.

When Belladonna had said her new place wasn't great, she hadn't been kidding. She now lived in a one-bedroom flat above a cheese shop.

"Come in, Jill. You'll have to excuse the mess. I haven't had the chance to unpack yet."

"This could have waited until you were settled in."

"No, it couldn't. I want to get back to the creche as soon as possible, and besides, I'm scared that if I put it off for too long, I might lose my nerve."

"Are you absolutely sure you want to go ahead with this?"

"Definitely."

"And you know that there's no going back once it's done?"

"Yes, you made that very clear. There's just one thing."

"What's that?"

"Do I get any kind of say in what the 'new' me will look like? Can I choose my hair colour? That kind of thing?"

"I'm afraid not. This spell took me ages to put together, and it isn't anywhere as sophisticated as that."

"What will I look like, then?"

"The spell will use random images from my mind to create the new you. Even I have no idea how that will turn out."

"That's even more scary than I thought."

"Unfortunately, it's the only way to do it. But it's entirely up to you whether or not you want to go through with this."

"I do. Let's do it now before I change my mind."

"Okay. Go and sit in that chair."

"Is this going to hurt?"

"Of course not. You won't feel a thing. Well, maybe a little tingle, but that's all."

"How long will it take?"

"A matter of seconds, and when it's done, you'll be Jemima. Are you ready?"

"Yeah. Let's do it."

Without a shadow of a doubt, the spell was one of the most complicated I'd ever put together, and although I didn't say anything to Belladonna, I was a little nervous.

"Okay, here goes."

Moments later, the woman in front of me had been transformed into a totally new person. And, although I say so myself, the end-result was quite stunning.

"Can I open my eyes yet?" Even her voice was different.

"Just a minute." I passed her a hand mirror. "Okay, you can open them now."

"Wow!" Jemima touched her 'new' face. "I'm beautiful." She stood up and walked over to the full-length mirror attached to the back of the bedroom door. "It's amazing, Jill. Thank you."

"My pleasure."

"When can I go back to the creche?"

"Don't you think you should take a few days to get used to the new you?"

"No, I want to get back to work straight away."

"Are you sure?"

"Positive."

"Okay, then." I took out my phone and made a call.

"Cuppy C. Amber speaking."

"Amber, it's Jill. I'm just checking if it would be alright for Jemima to start work in the creche tomorrow."

"Who? Oh, you mean Bella—"

"Shush! Her name is Jemima now."

"Sorry. I didn't think she'd be ready to start back for a while yet."

"Well she is, and she's raring to go. So, what do you say? Can she start tomorrow?"

"Why not? Those kids have been running Pearl and I ragged."

"Tomorrow it is, then." I gave Jemima the thumbs up.

Chapter 3

I was about to enter the office building when a clown came rushing out and ran straight into me. The impact caused me to drop my bag, spilling its contents all over the pavement.

"I'm so dreadfully sorry," he mumbled, as he knelt down to help me pick everything up.

"It's okay. Nothing broken."

"Sorry again," he said, once we'd got everything back in the bag. And then he hurried away.

Armi was in the outer office.

"Look, Jill." Mrs V gushed. "Armi has finished your cuckoo clock."

Sure enough, there on her desk was the ugliest clock you ever did see.

"It's lovely. Thanks."

"I've fitted it with the Tweetling3619," Armi said. "I was very fortunate to get hold of one."

"That was lucky." I tried to look suitably grateful.

Mrs V checked her watch. "If you hang on a couple of minutes, you'll see it in action."

"Great!"

The three of us stared at the clock as the seconds counted down.

When the minute hand reached the hour, the little door flew open, and out popped the bird.

"Is that a cuckoo?" I said.

"Of course it's a cuckoo." Mrs V gave me a look. "What do you think it is?"

"I—err—it looks a little like a chicken."

"Of course it doesn't. It's quite obviously a cuckoo."

"Not just any cuckoo," Armi chipped in. "The Tweetling3619."

"Where will you put it?" Mrs V said.

I was *so* very tempted. "I—err—I thought I'd—"

"After all the work Armi has put into it, I hope you'll give it pride of place in your lounge."

"Of course. I wouldn't dream of putting it anywhere else. Thank you, Armi."

"The pleasure was all mine."

Never had a truer word been spoken.

There were huge piles of books on the floor in my office. What was Winky up to now? There was no sign of him, and I assumed he must have nipped out, but then a couple of the books moved, and I realised he was ensconced in the middle of the mountain of books.

"What are all these?" I said.

"Last time I checked, they were books."

"I know they're books, but what are they doing all over the floor, and why are there so many of them?"

"I'm cramming."

"For what?"

"Cat Genius. It's the premier feline TV quiz programme."

"And you've applied to take part?"

"Applied and been accepted. My heat is being recorded next week."

"What do you stand to win?"

"The overall winner gets a thousand pounds."

"A grand?"

"Yes, but I'm not in it for the money. I'm in it for the

prestige. I'll need you to take me to the studio."

"Okay. I wouldn't mind watching that being recorded."

"It's strictly cats only."

"Do you seriously expect me to ferry you around when I'm not allowed to come inside to see the show?"

"Yeah."

"And if I say no?"

"I'll sulk and make your life a misery for a week."

"Okay, but only if I get a share of your winnings."

"Ten percent."

"Twenty."

"Five."

"Hang on. You started at ten."

"Ten it is, then."

"What? Oh, okay then. Ten per cent of whatever you win."

"Done."

"I have been." Again.

"That's an ugly thing out there in the outer office."

"The cuckoo clock?"

"No, I meant Arnie."

"Don't be awful. *Armi* is lovely. I do wish he hadn't made me that dreadful cuckoo clock, though."

"You could always accidentally drop it out of the window."

"I'd never get away with it. Mrs V would kill me."

"It looks like you'll have to give it pride of place in your lounge, then." He shuddered. "Can you imagine having to look at that ugly thing all day?"

"The clock isn't that bad."

"I was talking about the old bag lady."

"Between you and me, that clock is never going to see

the inside of my lounge."

"So you *are* going to throw it out of the window."

"No, I'm not. It might hit someone and injure them. I'm going to put it in the spare bedroom, and then forget all about it."

***

Mid-afternoon, I had an unexpected visitor.

"Jill," Mrs V said in a whisper. "I have a Mr Tunes out there."

"The new sign man? I wasn't expecting him, was I?"

"No. He said he was in the area, so he popped in on the off chance."

"Okay, you'd better send him through."

"I should warn you, he talks like that other man, Mr Song."

"In a sing-songy voice, you mean?"

"Yes. Why do you suppose they do that?"

"It's hard to imagine. Perhaps it's taught as part of the signage course."

"I'll send him through."

Terry Tunes was several years younger than Sid Song, and if I wasn't mistaken, he was a baritone whereas Sid had been more of a tenor.

"Thank you for seeing me."

"No problem. Have you come to tell me the replacement sign is ready?"

"I'm afraid not. As you can imagine, things have been rather hectic since we took over Sid's order book. In fact, the reason for my visit is to try and clarify your requirements."

"I thought that was all sorted already."

"Unfortunately, Sid's paperwork leaves a lot to be desired. I'm sure it all made perfect sense to him, but for someone trying to pick it up—well, let's just say it's rather challenging. If you could clarify a few points, I'll be able to get things moving."

"Okay, what do you want to know?"

He put on his reading glasses and then took a folded sheet of paper out of his pocket.

"First, can you confirm the name to go on the sign. I have Jill and Max Well, but I can't help but feel that's a mistake."

"There is no Max."

"What happened to him? Did he leave?"

"There never was a Max. I used to be Jill Gooder, then I got married and changed my name to Jill Maxwell. When I tried to explain that to Sid, he misunderstood and thought I'd said Jill *and* Max Well."

"I see." Terry smiled. "Next question: Do you still sweat?"

"I beg your pardon?"

Before he could respond he was distracted by Winky who had just fallen off the sofa, laughing.

"Is your cat alright?"

"He's fine." But he wouldn't be when I got my hands on him later.

"It's just that one of the notes says Jill Maxwell – I Sweat."

"That's another mix-up. There used to be a fitness club just along the corridor. They were actually called I-Sweat. They were nothing to do with me or my business."

"Okay, that makes sense. I thought it was a rather

strange thing to put on a sign."

"Anything else?"

"Are you still a clown?"

"No. After I-Sweat moved out, a clown school moved in. Again, they're nothing to do with me."

"A clown school?" His face lit up. "I must check that out. I love clowns, don't you?"

"With a passion. Look, it might be best if I write down exactly what I want on the sign." I grabbed his scrap of paper, and jotted down the following:

Jill Maxwell
Private Investigator

"And is that two signs or just the one?"

"Just the one."

"You could probably save yourself a little money if instead of Private Investigator you simply had P.I."

"Definitely not. I've already been down that particular cul-de-sac."

"Okay, then. I'm all set to go."

"And you know how big it has to be?"

"Two centimetres narrower than the last one supplied."

"Correct. Any idea when I should get it?"

"A couple of weeks ought to do it."

"Okay, but if you can get it finished any quicker, I'd be very grateful."

"I'll do my best." He stood up. "You have an awful lot of books. Are you studying for something?"

"I — err, no. I'm actually going to be taking part in a TV quiz programme."

"How exciting. Which one?"

"Err, Brain — err — drain. Braindrain."

"I don't think I've seen that."

"It's new. It hasn't aired yet."

"I'll keep a lookout for it. Good luck."

"Thanks."

"Braindrain?" Winky climbed back onto the sofa. "Is that the best you could come up with?"

"You need to move those books."

"Not until after my heat. I still have lots of studying to do." He laughed. "You should have your own TV show. You could call it Where's My Sign?"

"It really shouldn't be this difficult. All I want is a simple sign. Do other people have all this trouble?"

"Nah, it's just you."

***

I was in the outer office, listening to Mrs V wax lyrical about her favourite songsmith, Brian Lion, who was apparently touring the UK, and due to perform in Washbridge the following week.

"You must have heard of him, Jill. He's one of the country's leading singer/songwriters."

"I haven't."

"I can't wait to see him. You must know his big hit, My Caravan Knows Secrets."

"I've never heard of it."

"What about The Carrots Are Lonely Now?"

"That's a joke, right?" I laughed.

"Certainly not." And to prove it, she began to warble said song.

Now, I'll be the first to admit I'm not the world's

greatest singer, but compared to Mrs V, I have the voice of an angel. Fortunately, I was rescued from that awful racket by the sudden appearance of Kimmy, who was clearly upset.

"Kimmy?" I took her hand. "What's wrong."

"It's Sneezy when I'm in costume," she sobbed.

"Sorry. What's happened, Sneezy?"

"It's that awful PomPom again." She took off her red nose, so that she could blow her real one.

"What's he done now?"

"Come and see."

"Okay." I turned to Mrs V. "I shall probably go straight home after I've finished with these clowns."

Ignoring Mrs V's disapproving look, I followed Sneezy down the corridor to Clown.

"Come through to the main classroom, Jill. Breezy is taking a class in there. Or at least, he's trying to."

The students, seated at rows of desks, were all in clown costume. At the head of the classroom, was Breezy, who was clearly agitated about something.

"Thank you for coming, Jill." He walked over to join us by the door.

"Sneezy said you've been having more trouble from PomPom."

"We certainly have." He gestured towards the class. "See for yourself."

Up to that point, I'd been doing my best not to look at the student clowns.

"What exactly is it I'm supposed to be looking at?"

"Their bow ties of course."

"They're all spinning around. Is that part of today's lesson?"

29

"No, it most certainly isn't. They started to spin about ten minutes ago, and nothing anyone does will stop them."

"And you think PomPom is behind it?"

"I'd bet my life on it. How are the students expected to study with that distraction?"

"It can't be easy."

"It's impossible. I'm going to have to cancel today's lessons."

"This isn't an isolated incident," Sneezy chipped in. "Tell Jill what happened on Friday."

"The buttonhole flowers wouldn't stop spraying water. The floor was awash."

"Have you spoken to PomPom, Breezy?"

"I rang him on Friday, and he denied all knowledge of it, but I could tell he was lying."

"You have to help us, Jill," Sneezy said. "If this carries on, we'll be out of business within three months."

"Okay. Leave it with me. I'll pay our Mr PomPom a visit."

***

Just as I'd hoped, I arrived home before Jack. If he'd been in, and he'd seen the cuckoo clock, he would have insisted that we put it up in the lounge. Having worked in the same room as one of those awful things once before, there was no way I was going to put myself through that torture again.

The spare bedroom had been practically empty after Jack had kindly donated his furniture to Lizzie, but it had already started to fill up again. Where did all these boxes come from? I emptied one of them, put the cuckoo clock at the bottom, and then replaced everything.

Phew! Crisis averted.

I'd no sooner got downstairs when there was a knock at the door.

"Hi, Britt."

"I'm sorry to bother you, Jill, but I was just wondering if you happen to have seen Lovely?"

"Not for a couple of days."

"She didn't come home last night, which isn't like her at all. I'm really worried."

"I'm sure she'll be fine."

"Do you think I should put up some missing posters?"

"Perhaps not just yet. Maybe if she hasn't come back by the morning."

"Okay. You'll let me know if you see her, won't you?"

"Of course. And don't worry. I'm sure she'll be fine."

Jack had sent me a text to say he'd be a little late, so I'd got dinner started in order that it would be ready soon after he arrived home.

What do you mean, you're surprised I didn't just order in takeaway? Sheesh, anyone would think I never cooked a meal.

"Something smells nice," Jack said when he walked through the door. "Did you order takeaway?"

"No, I didn't. I've been slaving over a hot stove for the last hour."

"Thank you." He gave me a kiss. "What is it?"

"It was going to be a roast dinner."

"*Was?*"

"Now it's just the dinner. I forgot to put the meat in."

"Never mind. I'll just have more potatoes."

"Hmm."

"Don't tell me you forgot to put in the potatoes too?"

"Of course I didn't. It's just that when I called at the Corner Shop, Little Jack was all out of them."

"No potatoes, then?"

"We do have a few."

"Thank goodness."

"Two each."

"Oh well. That's better than nothing." He took something out of his pocket. "When our numbers come up, we'll be able to dine out every week."

"What are those?"

"Tickets for the Washbridge Lottery. Here, this one is for you. Put it somewhere safe."

"We won't win. I never win with those things."

"We might. By the way, I don't suppose you've seen my Hundred Best Strikes book anywhere, have you?"

"I didn't realise you were interested in industrial relations."

"Not that kind of strike. It's about ten-pin bowling."

"Oh, right." Yawn. "No, I haven't seen it."

"I reckon it must be in one of those boxes in the spare bedroom. I'll take a look after dinner."

"No!"

"Pardon?"

"I meant that you don't need to do that. You've had a long day. I'll go up there and look for it."

"That's very sweet of you."

"Nothing's too good for my darling husband."

Chapter 4

"Seriously, Jack, I'm telling you, it was *so* weird."

"Ninety-nine percent of your life is weird. I'm the only sane part of it."

My husband could be so annoying at times. There was I, trying to tell him about the weird dreams I'd had, and he was more interested in his stupid bowling book.

"Number thirty-two is a real doozy." He held up the book so I could get a better look.

"How can one strike be any better than another? They all knock down the same number of pins, don't they?"

"You wouldn't understand." He shoved a spoonful of muesli into his mouth.

"But there was a giant squirrel in my dream."

"Nice."

"He wanted to talk to me about storage solutions."

"That's interesting."

"For his nuts."

"Hmm."

"You're not listening to a word I say, are you?"

"Fascinating."

"I'm going to empty that bowl of muesli over your head."

"Amazing." He looked up. "Hold on. What did you just say?"

"Oh, hello. You are here, then?"

"Yes, but number thirty-nine is—"

"Incredible, yeah, I get it. Just wait until you want to tell me about *your* dreams."

"I'm sorry." He closed the book. "I promise I'm listening now. You were saying something about a nutty rabbit?"

"He was a squirrel; a giant one. And he was asking me about storage solutions for his nuts."

"That is pretty weird."

"I know. What do you think it means?"

"Probably that you've been eating too many custard creams just before you go to bed."

I stood up from the table. "There's no point in talking to you if you aren't going to take it seriously."

"How am I supposed to take a giant squirrel talking about storage solutions seriously?"

Men!

***

Jack didn't have to go into work until later, so I was the first to leave the house.

"Jill!" Kimmy came hurrying across the road.

"Morning. I haven't had the chance to do anything about PomPom yet."

"That's okay. That isn't what I wanted to talk to you about."

"Oh?"

"I wondered if you'd seen our little fluffykins?"

"Bruiser? No, not for a while."

"Oh dear. We haven't seen him for a couple of days, and we're starting to get a little worried."

"I'm sure he'll be okay. He's a big lad; he can look after himself."

"I used to think that too, but something seems to have spooked him. He's been very quiet recently."

"I'm sure he'll turn up soon. Winky often disappears for

days at a time." Usually on a microlite. "But he always comes back." More's the pity.

What? Of course I'm joking.

"I do hope you're right, Jill. You'll let us know if you happen to see him, won't you?"

"Of course."

I'd considered telling her that Lovely was missing too, but I figured that might make her worry even more. It was probably just a coincidence anyway.

***

The carrot, AKA Mr Ivers, took my money at the toll booth.

"Morning, Jill." Before I could drive away, the man himself popped his head up.

"Morning. Don't you ever get bored of the vegetable hand puppets?"

"Never! I love these little guys. They're my best friends."

I didn't know whether to laugh or cry at that. "That's nice."

"I shouldn't really be telling you this, but I have an exclusive interview in the next issue of my newsletter."

"Probably best not to tell me, then. I wouldn't want you to break any kind of embargo."

"It's okay. It's my newsletter, after all, so I get to make the rules."

"Still, I don't think —"

"You'll never guess who it is that I've interviewed."

"I have no idea. Is it a Hollywood A-lister?"

"The next best thing."

35

"I give up."

"You saw Red Storm, didn't you?"

"Most of it."

"What did you think of the stunts?"

"The ones I saw were pretty impressive. Is your interviewee a stunt man?"

"Not exactly."

"You're going to have to tell me."

"Vince Watts is second cousin to the stunt co-ordinator."

"*Second* cousin? Are they close?"

"No, they've never met."

"That's certainly some scoop you've landed yourself."

"I know. I'm expecting subscriptions to increase dramatically."

***

"Morning, Mrs V."

"Morning, dear. Did Jack like it?"

"Sorry?"

"The clock? What did Jack think of it?"

"He loves it. In fact, he stayed back this morning so he could hear it chirp."

"*Chirp*?"

"I mean, cuckoo."

"Did he have any problems putting it up?"

"No. Jack's quite the handyman when he puts his mind to it."

"Would you like a cup of tea?"

"Yes, please. I had a really weird dream last night. There was this—"

"Me too. Someone had cut me in half. I blame Armi and his magic tricks."

"Right. Anyway, there was this giant—"

"Did I tell you that my cousin Agatha has moved into the area?"

"No, I don't think you mentioned it."

"I haven't seen her in years. To tell you the truth, she's always been a bit weird."

"Talking of weird, in my dream there was this giant—"

"She used to collect mops. I'm not sure if she still does, though."

"Bring my tea through, would you?"

Sheesh! Was no one interested in my weird dream?

"Hey, Winky, do you want to hear about my dream?"

"No." He had his head buried in a book.

"You've started early with the reading."

"I've been at it since four this morning."

"You're taking this very seriously."

"What do you expect? Winky doesn't do anything by half measures."

Especially not the third person references.

I'd just finished my cup of tea when my landlord, Martin Macabre, arrived.

"Do I have to make him a drink?" Mrs V disliked the man almost as much as I did.

"No. I don't want to give him an excuse to stay any longer than is strictly necessary. Give me a couple of minutes, and then show him in, will you?"

"Okay, dear."

"Winky, the landlord is here."

"So?"

"Get behind the screen, and don't make a sound."

"What about my studies?"

"They'll just have to wait."

"If I don't win the quiz, it'll be your fault."

"I can live with that."

"Morning, Mr Macabre."

"Good morning, Mrs Maxwell. May I have a seat?"

"Sure. Help yourself."

"You haven't started selling books, have you? You know that would be against the terms of your lease."

"No, I haven't. They're all mine."

"Really? I wouldn't have had you down as the studious type."

"Was there something you wanted?"

"I see you still don't have a sign?"

"That's because you made me take it down."

"It was too wide, as you're well aware."

"Yes, I know, and the replacement is being made as we speak."

"It seems to be taking a long time."

"The man who was making it, Sid Song, was killed when one of his signs fell on him."

"That's unfortunate."

Steady on there with the sympathy. "His death has meant the order is delayed slightly, but I'm assured I'll have it within a couple of weeks. Is that what you wanted to see me about?"

"No. I wanted to talk pigeons."

"What about them?"

"There have been complaints."

"From the pigeons?"

"No, not from the – oh, I see. A joke? Very funny. Some of the other occupants of the building have complained about the mess that the pigeons are making."

"I can't say I've noticed it."

"Hmm." He looked around the room. "I suppose some people notice these things more than others."

"What are you planning to do?"

"In the next few days, anti-pigeon measures will be taken."

"What does that mean, exactly?"

"Strips of spikes will be installed on all the window ledges to stop the birds from nesting there."

"Isn't that a little cruel? What about those pigeons who have already made their homes there?"

"There are plenty more window ledges in Washbridge."

"Still, it doesn't seem fair to simply throw them out of the homes that they may have had for years."

"Are you some kind of pigeon-fancier?"

"No, I just think it's a little uncaring."

"Nevertheless, it's going to happen. I'm just here to give you advance warning."

As soon as Macabre had left, Winky re-emerged from behind the screen.

"You can't let him do that! What about Harold and Ida?"

"There's nothing I can do about it."

The sound of someone crying caught our attention.

"It's going to be okay, Ida." Harold had his wing around his wife. "We'll find somewhere else."

"But I love it here, Harold," she sobbed. "I thought we'd

spend the rest of our lives here."

"See!" Winky said. "Are you going to stand by and allow this to happen?"

"I really don't see what I can do."

"It's not Jill's fault, Winky," Harold said. "You can't blame her."

He was right, so why did I feel so guilty?

Thirty minutes later, I was still feeling bad about the pigeons when Mrs V popped her head around the door.

"I have Mr Billy Gotnuts here."

"Who?"

"He does have an appointment."

"Oh? Okay, you'd better show him in."

And she did.

"Good morning, Mrs Maxwell."

I didn't respond. I couldn't. I was too shocked to be face to face with a giant squirrel. Eventually, though, I managed to splutter, "You—you are—"

"Late? I know. The traffic was terrible." He took a seat opposite me.

"What can I do for you, Mr—err—"

"Gotnuts. I'd like to discuss storage solutions with you."

"Earth to Jill!" Winky shouted. "Are you with us?"

I looked over at him, and then back at the chair opposite me. It was empty.

"Did you see him?"

"Who?"

"The squirrel?"

"Where?" He glanced all around the floor.

"The giant one who was seated opposite me?"

"You looked like you were in some kind of daze. Have you been smoking those funny ciggies?"

"No, I haven't." I hurried through to the outer office. "Where did he go, Mrs V?"

"Mr Macabre? He didn't say."

"Not Mr Macabre. Billy Gotnuts."

"Who?"

"The squirrel?"

"Are you feeling alright, Jill?"

"Yeah, no, I think so."

"Do you think you should go home?"

"No, I'm fine."

But was I?

Thirty minutes later, and I was still finding it difficult to focus on anything. All I could think about was Billy Gotnuts. What exactly had happened? Had I drifted off to sleep at my desk? It was the only thing that made any sense. But it was still the morning, and I hadn't felt at all tired.

"Aren't you going to answer that?" Winky said.

It was only then that I realised my phone was ringing. "Hello?"

"Jill, it's Amber. You need to get over here."

"What's wrong? It doesn't have anything to do with a squirrel, does it?"

"*Squirrel*? What are you talking about?"

"Never mind. What's up?"

"You'd better come and see for yourself."

"Okay. I'm on my way."

Hopefully, whatever it was would take my mind off the squirrel.

***

"What were you thinking, Jill?" Amber said.

"What have I done now?"

"It's Belladonna. I mean, Jemima."

"Hasn't she turned up?"

"Yes, she was here bang on time as usual."

"Nothing bad has happened to the kids, has it?"

"No, of course not. Mindy's up in the creche with them."

"Where's Jemima?"

"Come with me." Amber asked one of the other assistants to watch the tearoom, and then she led me into the back.

"Hi, Jill." Jemima was in the stockroom.

"Would someone like to tell me what is going on?"

"This!" Amber pointed to Jemima's face. "*This* is what's going on."

"You're talking in riddles. I told you that she'd look different. That was the whole point of the exercise."

"I know that, but you didn't say she'd look like this." Once again, she pointed to Jemima's face. "Don't you recognise her?"

"Of course I recognise her. I was the one who changed her appearance, remember?"

"And you decided to make her the spitting image of Rebecca Milestone?"

"Who?"

"Rosemary."

"I thought you said Rebecca?"

"I did. Rebecca Milestone plays Rosemary in Candle

Place."

"Isn't that the soap opera your mum watches?"

"Practically everyone in Candlefield watches it."

I looked again at Jemima, and that's when it struck me. She was the spitting image of the woman I'd seen on TV when I'd visited Aunt Lucy's.

"Well?" Amber demanded.

"The soap was on TV at Aunt Lucy's just before I went to Jemima's to cast the spell. Her face must have been in my sub-conscious." I turned to Jemima. "Why didn't you say anything yesterday?"

"I didn't know. I never watch soaps—I find them so boring. The first I knew about it was when someone asked for my autograph on my walk over here this morning. I thought they were just messing around, so I ignored them."

"It's a good job there was no one else in the shop when she arrived," Amber said. "If anyone had seen her, word would have spread like wildfire."

"What can I say?" I shrugged. "I'm sorry."

"What are you going to do about it?"

"Can you change me back to how I used to be?" Jemima said.

"I can't. I told you that before I cast the spell."

"You have to do something!" Amber said.

"Okay, okay. I'll just have to change your appearance again."

"Not to a soap star this time!" Amber was well and truly on my case.

"You aren't helping. Why don't you leave the two of us alone, so I can concentrate?"

Somewhat begrudgingly, Amber did as I asked.

43

"I really liked my new face, too." Jemima sighed.

"I'm sure your *new* new one will be just as good. Are you ready?"

"I guess so."

"Okay. Take two."

When I left Cuppy C, Jemima was back at work in the creche. Fortunately, she seemed just as happy with her second new face as she had been with Rosemary's. Amber was much happier too now that she and Pearl could focus on the tearoom and cake shop, and no longer had to cover the creche.

Chapter 5

Back in the human world, I'd arranged to meet Rachel Somers who was a friend and work colleague of Alison Forrest. They both worked as solicitors at West & Partners: Alison in family law, Rachel in probate. We met at a small coffee shop called Best Coffee Ever, which was just around the corner from the offices of West & Partners. The shop's name made a very bold claim, and unfortunately, it was one that proved to be unfounded. My Americano was at best average, and certainly not good enough to justify the price tag. Rachel had opted for a green tea.

"What do you think of the coffee?" she said.

"It's certainly not the best ever."

"Not even close. That's why I always have tea."

"Thanks for sparing me your time today."

"No problem. I still can't believe that Alison has gone."

"Had you known her long?"

"We started at West's in the same week, and we hit it off straight away."

"How would you describe her?"

"A little quiet until you got to know her, but once her guard was down, she was good fun." Rachel hesitated. "Until recently that is."

"What changed?"

"Just lately, she'd been much quieter than usual. Little things seemed to stress her much more than they would normally."

"Do you have any idea why?"

"I'm not sure if I should say any more about that."

"Why not?"

"I know that Laurence is supposed to have killed Alison, but I don't believe it. He's a good guy. He always struck me as a gentle man. Certainly not the kind of man who would do something like this. I don't want to say anything that might make matters worse for him."

"Telling the truth can never be a bad thing."

"I suppose not. The thing is, Alison had said a few things recently that made me think she and Laurence weren't as happy as they once were."

"Such as?"

"She wanted more kids, and she was angry because Laurence seemed to have gone cool on the idea. And she complained a few times that he was always working late."

"Did she think he was seeing someone else?"

"She didn't say so. Not in so many words, anyway."

"When was the last time you saw her?"

"On the day she was murdered, but only to say hello to."

"And did she seem okay?"

"As far as I could tell, but like I said, I only passed her in the corridor."

"Laurence's mother gave me your name. Yours was the only name she could bring to mind when I asked about Alison's friends. Did she have any other close friends you think I should speak to?"

"Alison and I had the occasional night out when Laurence was away on business. She'd sometimes invite some of her other friends along." Rachel took out her phone. "There's Susan Shields and Craig Mann. I have their numbers if you'd like them?"

Rachel Somers' account of Alison and Laurence's

marriage was at odds with the version told to me by Sheila Forrest. Had Sheila deliberately held back the truth in order to protect her son, or was she oblivious to the problems in their marriage? Then again, there was always the possibility that Rachel was reading more into it than there actually was.

I now had the contact details for two other close friends of Alison. Hopefully, talking to them would give me a clearer idea of the state of the marriage.

***

As I walked back to the office, I bumped into Deli. Normally, whenever I saw her, she was larger than life and twice as loud. Today, though, she had her head bowed, and could only manage a half-hearted greeting.

"Hi, Jill."

"Is everything okay, Deli? You seem a little subdued."

"Is there any wonder?"

"Sorry? Has something happened I should know about?"

"Your *grandmother* has happened."

Oh bum! What had she done now? "Grandma?"

"I thought you might have tipped me off to her plans, Jill."

"I'm sorry, but I have no idea what you're talking about."

"The beauty salon of course."

"I'm still no wiser. Has she done something to your shop?"

"No. She's going to open her own beauty salon, two doors down from Nailed-It."

47

"Are you sure? She's never mentioned anything to me about a beauty salon."

"See for yourself." She pointed. "The shopfitters are already in there. I was just beginning to think we were making progress, and now this happens. Why couldn't she have opened her shop somewhere else? Why did it have to be so close to mine?"

"I'm sure you'll be okay. You have first-mover advantage."

"I have *what*?"

"It means you were here first, and you've already built up a customer base."

"Yes, but your grandmother is so good at marketing and stuff. Just look at the promotions she's run recently. How am I supposed to compete with that?"

"Try not to worry too much. At least Mad is back here to stay now. You must be pleased about that?"

"Back? Since when?"

Oh bum!

"I—err—"

"Jill?"

"I assumed you knew."

"I had no idea. When did she come back?"

I could have killed Mad. Why hadn't she told her mother? "She's only just moved back here."

"Where's she living?"

"I—err—"

"Tell me, Jill. I'm her mother. I have a right to know."

"She has an apartment in the old sock factory on Colbourn Drive."

"That place is really posh. How can she afford to live there?"

"You really should ask her that yourself."

"Don't worry, I intend to." She started down the street. "Right now."

As soon as Deli was out of sight, I gave Mad a call.

"Mad, I thought I'd better warn you that your mother is on her way over there."

"You told her I was back?"

"I assumed she knew. Why haven't you told her?"

"I was getting around to it. What did she say?"

"She's not best pleased. She was already in a bad mood before I told her about you."

"What's Nails done to upset her now?"

"It's not him this time. My grandmother is apparently going to open a beauty salon two doors down from your mum's place."

"Oh dear."

"I'm sorry if I've dropped you in it."

"It's not your fault. I should have let her know I was back. Okay, I'd better go and prepare myself."

"Good luck."

"Thanks."

I decided to drop into Ever to see Grandma. I still had a bone to pick with her about what she'd done at TenPinCon.

Julie, the head Everette, was on duty, and looking exceptionally pleased with life. No mean feat for someone who had to put up with Grandma for long periods of time.

"Morning, Jill. What do you think?"

"Of what?"

"Multi-colour day, what else?"

"Of course." I glanced around looking for any kind of clue as to what she was talking about but found none. "Remind me again what that is."

"Instead of all of us wearing the same colour uniforms, each of the Everettes gets to choose which colour they want to wear. It's never been so colourful in here."

"Of course. I should have realised. And you went for—"

"Blue, of course. I think it suits me best."

"It definitely does. Is my grandmother in?"

"Yes, she's in her office."

"Okay. Catch you later."

Grandma was cutting her nails. Her *toenails*.

"If it isn't my tap-dancing granddaughter."

"Do you have to do that on the desk?"

"You could cut them for me if you like?"

"No, thanks."

"To what do I owe the pleasure of your company?"

"I've got a number of things I want to discuss with you."

"Fire away." She'd just finished the nails on one foot and had made a start on the other.

"That's very distracting, you know."

"You'd better be quick because when I've finished this, I'm heading across the road to check on the shopfitters. If I don't keep an eye on them, they're liable to slack off."

"That's one of the things I wanted to talk to you about. Deli reckons you're opening a beauty salon."

"She's right. If things go according to plan, Ever Beauty will open in about three weeks."

"You've never mentioned any of this before."

"Oh sorry. I didn't realise I had to run my plans by

you."

"You don't, but I thought you might have at least said something. Why did you choose to open the shop so close to Nailed-It?"

"Nailed what?"

"Deli's beauty salon?"

"Do me a favour." She cackled. "That place is no more than a down-market nail bar."

"She does eyebrow threading, too."

"Very badly from what I hear."

"And spray tans."

"How is that orange sister of yours by the way?"

"It's still Deli's livelihood."

"And your point is?"

"That you could have chosen somewhere else to open your salon."

"I could have, but I didn't. Now, is there anything else?"

"I just wanted to say that I'm not very happy about what you did at TenPinCon."

"I don't know what you're talking about."

"You know very well what I mean. The talent contest and the water tank."

"That was so funny." She took out her phone. "I have photos. Would you like to see them?"

"No, I wouldn't. I don't know how you could be so horrible."

"Don't come the innocent. You know exactly why I did it. After you'd lectured me about the importance of not using magic, you went and did exactly that."

"Yes, but that was —"

"*Different*? I don't think so. You didn't want to stay at

the convention, so you used magic to escape for a few hours. Isn't that what happened?"

"Well, yes but—"

"I rest my case." Grandma had finished her pedicure. "Is that everything?"

"Err, yes, I suppose so."

"Before I throw these away, would you like the clippings?"

"What?" Just the thought of it made the bile rise in my throat. "No! Why would I want your nail clippings?"

"It would be something to remember me by when I'm gone."

"That's disgusting."

"Please yourself. I'll put them in my pie tonight, then."

"Please tell me you're joking."

"Of course I'm joking. Who puts toenail clippings into a pie?"

"Thank goodness for that."

"A stew, though. That's a different matter."

I had no idea if she was still joking or not, but I made a mental note never to eat a stew that Grandma had prepared.

"Bye, then."

"Before you go, Jill, what do you think of my multi-colour day?" she cackled again.

"I think the way you treat the Everettes over their uniforms is despicable."

"Why? They all seem perfectly happy with them."

"That's because they're under the impression that they're wearing their favourite colours when in fact they all still look like canaries."

"I assume we'll see you at Lucy's on Saturday?"

"What's happening on Saturday?"

"Dearie me. Do you really not know?"

"Is it someone's birthday?"

"No. It's Witchgiving of course."

"What's that?"

"Are you serious?"

"I've never heard of it."

"It's when families gather together to celebrate their witch heritage."

"I don't remember it happening last year."

"That's because it's only held every four years. I trust you'll be there?"

"Err, yes, I guess so."

By the time I left Ever, the heavens had opened, and wouldn't you know it, I didn't have my umbrella with me.

Great! Just great!

"You're soaked, Jill," Mrs V said.

"I—err—" I gasped.

"And out of breath by the look of it. What have you been doing?"

When I eventually caught my breath, I said, "I had to run all the way from the high street."

"You should have taken your umbrella with you."

"That's great advice. I wish I'd thought of that."

"There's no need to get snippy with me."

"Sorry. I didn't mean it."

"You should buy some of these new lottery tickets. One of the prizes is a romantic weekend in Paris."

"Jack's already bought some. I don't know why he bothered, though. I never win anything."

"You never know. Maybe this time your luck will

change."

"You look like a drowned rat," Winky said.
"I know. It's coming down in buckets out there. And don't tell me I should have taken my umbrella."
"I'm fed up with this weather."
"There's not much you can do about it."
"You could book a holiday."
"Jack and I can't afford a holiday this year."
"You could always get a second job to pay for it."
"And you can take a hike. Even if we could afford a holiday, you wouldn't be invited along."
"I guess I'll just have to make my own arrangements, then."
"Looks that way."

Winky was still looking forlornly out at the rain when my phone rang.
"Jill, it's Desdemona Nightowl."
"Headmistress?"
"*Temporary* headmistress." She corrected me.
"How are things at CASS?"
"Slowly getting back to normal. I'm hoping to persuade Philomena Eastwest to come out of retirement."
"Do you think she will?"
"I hope so, but I should know for sure within the next couple of days. I had hoped that I'd be able to talk Reginald into coming back too, but he tells me he has a new job at a hotel in Candlefield."
"Even so, I'm surprised he doesn't want to return to the school."
"I got the feeling he does, but he doesn't feel he can let

down the friend who gave him the opportunity. I've told him that I'll hold his job open for a month in case he changes his mind. The main reason for my call was to check that you'll be coming over on Thursday to take your class as usual."

"Of course, and now that Maligarth has gone, I'm actually looking forward to it again."

"Excellent. Pop in and see me when you're over here, would you?"

"Sure. I'll see you on Thursday."

"A cruise," Winky said.

"Sorry?"

"I fancy a cruise."

"Good luck with that. Those things cost a small fortune."

"I can see it now. Sitting on the deck, sunbathing and watching the ocean."

"Dream on, buddy."

Chapter 6

I called Red Nose and asked to speak to Raymond Higgins.

"Mr Higgins?"

"Please call me PomPom. Everyone does."

"Okay, PomPom, my name is Trudy Lewchuse."

"Is that your clown name?"

"No, it's my given name."

"How do you spell that?"

"L-E-W-C-H-U-S-E."

"Sorry, I thought you said *loose shoes*."

"That's right. Trudy Lewchuse."

"How can I help?"

"I wonder if I could come to see you. I need to hire a number of clowns."

"Of course. I'm free right now."

"Unfortunately, I'm not. Are you available tomorrow? Preferably in the morning."

"Yes. What time?"

"How about ten?"

"Ten will be fine."

"Excellent. I'll see you then Mr—err, I mean, PomPom."

***

I couldn't understand why Aunt Lucy hadn't mentioned Witchgiving to me. Surely, she wouldn't have excluded me from such an important family gathering. Maybe she'd just forgotten.

There was only one way to find out.

"Aunt Lucy! It's me!" I called from the hallway.

"I'm upstairs, Jill. Lil has left me a little present in her nappy. Why don't you put the kettle on, and I'll be down in a minute? Unless you'd prefer to see to Lil?"

"Err no, that's okay. I'll put the kettle on."

By the time she joined me, the drinks were on the kitchen table.

"She fell asleep while I was changing her, so I've put her down. I'm sure those little ones do it on purpose. They wait until I've just put a clean nappy on and then decide to fill it. Biscuit, Jill?"

"Err, no thanks. I'll be having dinner soon. What's that noise? Has someone got the radio on?"

"It's our new neighbours."

"The sisters? Have they moved in?"

"Yes, this morning. I don't think it's the radio, though. I think it's them singing."

"It's a little loud, isn't it? Are you going to have a word with them about it?"

"It's their first day in their new house, so I'll see how things go before I say anything. And besides, it's not an unpleasant sound. The twins tell me they have their creche lady back."

"Yes, fingers crossed it all works out okay."

"Have you caught up with Grandma yet?"

"Yes, I was at Ever earlier."

"Did you give her a hard time about what happened at the weekend?"

"I tried, but it didn't do any good. The main reason I went to see her was to ask about the beauty salon she's planning on opening."

"That's news to me."

"And me. The first I heard about it was when Deli told

me."

"*Deli?*"

"Mad's mother. She already has a beauty salon on the high street. As you can imagine, she wasn't thrilled to learn of Grandma's plans."

"She'll soon have taken over the whole high street."

"I know." I hesitated, unsure how best to approach the subject of Witchgiving. I would need to be diplomatic. "Why haven't you invited me to Witchgiving?"

"Grandma told you, I assume?"

"Yes. She seemed surprised I didn't know about it."

"To be honest, Jill, I was trying to spare you from the misery of it. I loathe Witchgiving and I know the twins do too. If it wasn't for your grandmother, we wouldn't even bother."

"What's so bad about it?"

"It's all so boring. We sit around, wearing traditional witch costumes, eating dinner."

"That doesn't sound all that bad. Except for the costume part."

"Yes, but custom dictates that we're only allowed to eat traditional witch food."

"What does that include?"

"Nothing to whet your appetite. It's all very bland and boring. There's no cake and the only drink allowed is Witch Claw cider."

"Cider's okay."

"Trust me, Witch Claw cider isn't. It's horrible. And you haven't heard the worst part yet. We have to spend the whole evening discussing spells and potions. It's deadly boring."

"And there was I, thinking that I was missing out."

"You're welcome to come if you like."

"Of course she's coming!" Grandma walked into the kitchen.

"Were you eavesdropping, Mother?" Aunt Lucy scowled.

"It's just as well I was. To hear you describe Witchgiving, anyone would think it was awful."

"It is. It's dreadful."

"Don't listen to her, Jill. Witchgiving is a longstanding tradition celebrated by all witches, and I expect you to be there."

"I might already be doing something on Saturday."

"Cancel it. If you don't come, I'll track you down and drag you here. Understood?"

"I—err—"

"Good." Pleasantries over, she disappeared.

"It seems you will be coming to Witchgiving, after all." Aunt Lucy shrugged.

"It looks that way."

Barry suddenly came charging into the room.

"Jill! I didn't know you were here. I was asleep."

"Hi, boy. How are you?"

"Dolly took him for a long walk, didn't she, Barry?" Aunt Lucy gave him a pat.

"We went to the park. I love the park."

"So I hear. Did Babs go with you?"

"Yes. I love Babs too."

"I know you do. And have you drawn any more pictures? I really liked the one you gave to me."

"I've retired from that."

"Why? Your exhibition was a runaway success."

"I think it's best to retire on a high."

"Surely another three or four pictures wouldn't hurt."

"No, I've made my mind up, and besides, I need to focus on the contest."

"What contest?"

"I hadn't got around to telling you about that," Aunt Lucy chipped in. "Barry wants to enter the Candlefield Talented Pets Competition."

"Doing what?"

"I haven't decided yet," Barry said. "What do *you* think I should do?"

"I don't know. Can you play a musical instrument?"

Aunt Lucy gave me a look. "He's a dog, Jill. Of course he can't play a musical instrument."

"If he can hold an art exhibition, why is playing a musical instrument such an outrageous idea?"

"I suggested he should dance."

"Actually, that's not a bad idea. What do you think, Barry?"

"I'd like to, but I might need someone to teach me."

"Jill will help you, won't you, Jill?" Aunt Lucy was grinning from ear to ear.

"Will you, Jill?" Barry spun around in excitement. "Please say you'll teach me to dance."

"Err, well, I suppose—"

"That's settled then." Aunt Lucy gave him another pat. "Off you go and get some rest now."

"Okay. Thanks for saying you'll help me with the dancing, Jill."

"My pleasure."

Once he was out of the room, I turned my glare on Aunt Lucy.

"What?"

"Don't come the innocent. You really dropped me in it there."

"The exercise will do you good."

"I'm not so sure about that. Anyway, I'd better get going. If I don't see you before, I'll be over for Witchgiving."

"Okay, see you then."

***

It was Kathy's day off (the lazy so and so was always skiving), and she'd asked me to call in on my way home.

"How come you're never at work?"

"Yes, Jill. I'm fine. Thanks for asking."

"So? How do you manage it?"

"It's called the art of delegation. Not something a control freak like you would know anything about."

"There you go again with the *control freak* thing. I don't know where people get that idea from."

"Tell me again how that office manager of yours worked out."

"That was different. How are Peter and the kids?"

"Pete's working way too hard, but he's enjoying every moment of it. And the kids are great; their rooms are tidier than ever. I don't know what's come over them, but whatever it is I couldn't be happier about it. Do you want a drink?"

"No, thanks. I've just had one at Aunt Lucy's."

"I didn't realise you'd been to see her. Does that mean you had the day off too?"

"Err, yeah. Well part of it, anyway."

"How is she?"

"Fine. Her new neighbours moved in today."

"That brings me nicely to the main reason I asked you over. I have big news! *Really* big news!"

"You're not pregnant again, are you?"

"No, of course not. My two are more than enough for me. We're moving house."

"How come? Where to?"

"The businesses are both doing really well, and we have much more cash coming in now. The kids were both at their friends' houses the other day, so Pete and I went out for a meal. While we were driving back, we happened to spot a house for sale in Middle Wash."

"And you decided to buy it? Just like that?"

"More or less. We didn't have an appointment to view, but we knocked on the door, and they let us take a look around. It's gorgeous, Jill. And so much bigger than this place. We put in an offer yesterday and it's been accepted. I'm so excited."

"Middle Wash? The houses there are really expensive."

"They are usually, but we fell lucky. The asking price was ten percent less than we'd expected it to be."

"Are you sure it's okay? It's not about to fall down, is it?"

"We've seen the full survey. There were no faults highlighted whatsoever."

"Why are they selling it so cheaply, then?"

"The current owners want a quick sale. They're a lovely couple."

"Congratulations, I guess."

"I asked you to come over so that I can take you to see the house."

"Right now?"

"Yeah. I've spoken to Mr and Mrs Hedges, and they say we're welcome to pop over any time. Are you up for it?"

"Sure. Why not?"

Kathy talked non-stop on the way to Middle Wash. Understandably, she was thrilled at the prospect of moving to a new house. And when we pulled up outside 21 Moreland Crescent, I could see why. The detached house, which was twice the size of her current one, was beautiful with a delightful enclosed garden.

"What do you think, Jill? Isn't it wonderful?"

"It's lovely."

"It's even better inside. Come and see."

The current owners must have seen us arrive because they opened the door when we were only halfway up the drive.

"This is Jill, my sister. I brought her to have a look at the house. I hope you don't mind?"

"Of course not." The woman beamed at me. "I'm Holly, and this is my husband, Hugh."

"Nice to meet you both. You must be sad to be leaving this lovely house?"

"Sad? Err, yes, we're very sad, aren't we Hugh?"

"Devastated." Hugh was at least a foot taller than his wife. "Totally devastated."

Curiously, neither of them looked even the tiniest bit upset. Maybe they were putting on a brave face for our benefit.

The Hedges allowed Kathy and me to look around by ourselves.

"This will be Lizzie's bedroom. That's going to be Mikey's. And this one will be ours."

"It's enormous."

"I know. We'll have a spare bedroom too. Pete and I will be able to use that as an office."

I looked out of the window. "The back garden is huge."

"Pete fell in love with it as soon as he saw it."

"I still don't get why they dropped the price. Surely with a property of this calibre they didn't need to."

"Shush! Don't let them hear you say that. I don't want them to change their minds before we've exchanged contracts."

If there was anything wrong with the property, I certainly didn't spot it during my tour of the house and garden. It was about as perfect as perfect could be, and I could see why Kathy was so excited about it.

"Tell me honestly, Jill." Kathy was still buzzing on the drive back to her house. "What do you think of it?"

"It's lovely, but it'll take a lot of cleaning."

"Pete and I have already talked about that. We're going to pay for a weekly clean."

"Isn't that a bit extravagant?"

"Not really. Didn't you used to have a cleaner once upon a time?"

"Yeah, but it was more trouble than it was worth."

"What did you think of the kitchen? I love that island."

"That oven looked complicated. Or are you going to employ a cook too?"

"You're not jealous, are you?"

"Of course not. I love our house."

***

When I arrived home, Britt and Kimmy were both out on the street.

"What are you two up to?"

"We're putting these up." Kimmy held out a sheet of paper, which turned out to be a missing poster for Lovely and Bruiser.

"They're both still missing, then?"

"We're really worried now, Jill," Britt said. "They've been gone for so long."

"I'm sure they'll be okay."

"Do you think someone might have taken them?" Kimmy said. "You hear about pets being stolen, don't you?"

"I wouldn't have thought so. Neither of them is a pedigree, are they?"

"That doesn't mean they aren't precious to us," Kimmy snapped.

"I know, I didn't mean—err—it's just that it's usually the more valuable pets that are stolen."

"Sorry, Jill. I didn't mean to bite your head off. We're just so worried."

"That's okay. I understand. I hope they turn up soon."

***

Jack arrived home an hour later.

"I'm back!"

"In here."

"You've started dinner?"

"Why wouldn't I?"

"Isn't it my turn?"

"What does it matter? I'm happy to do it."

65

"What's going on, Jill?"

"Nothing. Why?"

"It takes me all my time to get you to make dinner when it *is* your turn."

"It's no trouble. Why don't you go and get changed? When you come down, it should be ready."

He took a seat at the kitchen table. "What's this all about?"

"Nothing. I called at Kathy's on the way home."

"What did she have to say?"

"Not much. Just that they're buying a new house; it's in Middle Wash. She took me to see it. It's beautiful, and huge."

"That explains the dinner."

"I don't know what you mean."

"We can't afford to move to a bigger house."

"But this place is so small."

"It's perfectly big enough for the two of us."

"But her new house is really beautiful."

"It's not happening, Jill." He stood up and started for the door.

"Where do you think you're going?"

"To get changed."

"No, you don't." I passed him the apron. "It's your turn to make dinner."

Chapter 7

The next morning when I came downstairs, Jack was standing by the kitchen sink, staring out of the back window.

"Budge over." I made a show of squeezing past him on my way to the fridge. "This kitchen is so small."

"We're not moving house."

"I never mentioned moving house."

"You didn't need to. You were dropping not so subtle hints all last night."

"You should have seen Kathy's new place, Jack. It's beautiful."

"I'm sure it is, and I'm very pleased for Peter and Kathy. But they do have two kids, so they need more room."

"Your bowling paraphernalia takes up as much space as a couple of kids."

"If we win the national lottery, I promise we'll buy a new house."

"We don't even do it. Talking of lotteries, what's first prize in the Washbridge lottery?"

"No one knows; it's a tightly held secret."

"What's the betting it'll be something really pathetic? Like a free pass for the deckchairs in the parks."

We took our tea through to the lounge.

"What are those posters on the lampposts?" Jack pointed out of the window.

"Britt and Kimmy put them up yesterday. Their cats have gone missing."

"Both of them?"

"Yeah."

"What do you reckon has happened to them?"

"I don't know. At first, I assumed they'd just gone walkabout, but it's a bit weird that they both disappeared at the same time."

"Do you reckon we might have a catnapper in the neighbourhood?" Jack sounded genuinely concerned.

"It's possible, I suppose, but neither of them is a pedigree, so it's not like they're valuable."

"You should investigate."

"I'm too busy to spend my time looking for missing cats. If you're so concerned, why don't you look for them?"

***

I'd broken my own rule not to use magic to travel around the human world way too often recently. For that reason, and because I fancied a drive, I elected to take the car to Red Nose who were based in the centre of Manchester.

On the drive over, I was still thinking about Kathy's new house. I knew Jack was right: We didn't need a bigger place, and we certainly couldn't afford one. Kathy and I had always been competitive, and pathetic as it was, I didn't like the idea that she was doing better than I was. But instead of moaning and groaning to Jack, I knew I should be focussing on expanding the business.

Either that or divorce Jack and find myself a rich man.

What? Of course I'm joking. Sheesh!

Red Nose shared an office building with the Society of

Bottle Top Manufacturers. I made a mental note to mention it to Norman the next time I saw him.

I'd just walked into reception when a gush of water hit me in the eyes.

"Good morning, and welcome to Red Nose," said a squeaky female voice.

"Morning." Once I'd wiped the water from my eyes, I came face to face with the receptionist who was dressed as a clown.

"I'm Petunia." She sprayed some more water at me, but I was ready this time, and managed to duck to one side.

"I'm Trudy Lewchuse. I have an appointment with PomPom."

She checked her computer. "Oh yes. Have a seat please, and I'll let him know you're here."

"Thanks." Before sitting down, I checked for whoopee cushions. You can never be too careful.

I'd expected PomPom to be dressed as a clown, but he was wearing a sharp, double-breasted suit, and looked more like a city lawyer than the owner of a clown school.

"Trudy, nice to meet you." He had a surprisingly firm handshake. "I'm sorry for the mix-up with your name when we spoke on the phone yesterday. I imagine you must get that a lot. Please come with me."

The walls of his office were lined with photos of clowns.

"Those are some of our students who went on to do great things. You see that one? That's Topo. You may have heard of him?"

"I don't think so."

"He had his own show on cable TV in the USA for a while. Take a seat, Trudy."

69

"Thanks. Am I right in thinking that you combine the clown school with the talent agency?"

"That's right. It's pretty much fifty-fifty. As you might expect, a percentage of those who come through the school sign up with the agency afterwards."

"And how is business?"

"Excellent. Everyone loves clowns, don't they?"

Not everyone. "Absolutely. What's not to love?"

"You mentioned on the phone that you were looking to hire a number of clowns?"

"That's right. I'm putting together a stage production that will be touring the country for about six months. I'm going to need at least a dozen clowns."

"How exciting! Might I ask what the production is?"

"I'm afraid that's still under wraps at the moment. I'm sure you understand."

"Of course."

"I was given the name of two companies that might be able to help in my quest. Yours and one called Clown who are based in Washbridge."

"*Clown*? Really? You do realise they're a new business? They don't have our track record."

"Still, I've heard very good things about them. I'm planning to hold auditions early next week. I'm hoping that you'd be prepared to send some of your clowns along. I'll be asking Clown to do the same."

"Do you intend to pick a number of clowns from each company?"

"No, I think that will overcomplicate matters. I'll offer contracts to the clowns from whichever company puts on the best performance. Would that be something that would interest you?"

"Absolutely, although you could save yourself a lot of time and expense if you simply signed up with Red Nose today."

"That may be true, but I'd prefer to be sure."

"That's your prerogative, obviously. When and where is the audition?"

"That's still being finalised. Is it okay if I email you the details in the next couple of days?"

"Of course."

***

Back at the office, Mrs V was looking very pleased with herself.

"What do you think, Jill?" She held out her hands.

"New gloves? They're very colourful. Did you knit them?"

"I did, but these aren't just any old gloves. These are special."

"How's that?"

"Look." She pulled the tip off one of the glove's fingers. "What do you think?"

"I — err — "

While I was still struggling to make sense of what I'd just seen, she pulled off the tips of the other fingers and thumbs.

"Voila!" She beamed.

"I don't get it."

"They're convertible. You can wear them as either conventional gloves or fingerless."

"Right. How do you stop the fingertips from dropping off when you don't want them to?"

"Velcro, of course. I think I may have found a gap in the market."

"Is there likely to be a lot of demand for convertible gloves?"

"Who wouldn't want a pair of these? Do you think I should apply for a patent? I wouldn't want anyone to steal my idea."

"I don't think that's very likely."

"I also need to come up with a catchy name for them. Do you have any suggestions?"

Plenty, but none I thought she'd appreciate. "I'll give it some thought."

Winky was on the sofa, reading a glossy brochure. "Useless."

"What is?" As was often the case, I had no idea what he was talking about.

"That's my suggestion for what the old bag lady should call those stupid gloves of hers."

"That's rather harsh."

"Are you going to tell me you think they're any more useful than a chocolate fireguard?"

"It's hard to imagine who'd want to buy a pair."

"No one, that's who. The woman's a liability. It's time you got rid of her and brought back Jules."

"Jules has another job now."

"I should start up a petition."

"To bring back Jules? Who's going to sign that?"

"Everyone who reads this stuff for a start. I bet they'd all be glad to see the back of the old bag lady."

"I have no idea what you're talking about. And what's that brochure you're reading?"

"See for yourself." He threw it to me.

"Feline Cruises? Is this a joke?"

"I told you that I'd had enough of the rain."

I should have been surprised that there was such a thing as feline cruises, but I'd reached the point where nothing shocked me anymore.

I flicked through the pages of the brochure. "These are expensive."

"I have a little put away for a rainy day." He laughed. "And it's pouring down right now."

"Have you seen this? Don't you think this a bit weird?"

"Seen what?"

"The departure point for all the cruises is Nottingham."

"What's so strange about that?"

"It's in the centre of the country. It's nowhere near the coast."

"So? I imagine we'll travel by coach to the port."

"I suppose so. Are you seriously thinking of booking one of these?"

"Darn tootin'."

"Who says that?"

"I just did. Didn't you hear me?"

"I wish I could afford a nice holiday." I sighed. "Or a big house."

"Like your sister's, you mean?"

"How do you know about that?"

"Winky knows everything."

"Come on. How do you know?"

"Willy the Wire told me."

"Who's he?"

"He lives a couple of doors down from that sibling of yours. He keeps me up to speed on all their gossip."

"He won't be able to do that after Kathy has moved."

"No, but Buster the Brains will. He lives next door to their new house."

"Is he like some kind of genius?"

"No, he's a bit slow on the uptake. The nickname is ironic."

"Jill!" Harold appeared in the window. "They're here!"

"Who's here?"

"The men with the spikes. Look!" He used his wing to point to a van parked on the street, directly outside the building.

"Don't worry. I'll go and have a word with them."

"Do you think you can stop them? Ida is heartbroken."

"I'll do my best."

Words can't describe the disgust that I felt when I saw the side of the van. The name, Pigeon Purge, was bad enough, but the image of cartoon pigeons skewered on spikes was beyond the pale.

"Good, ain't it, love?" The man somehow managed to speak without dropping the cigarette wedged in the corner of his mouth. He was wearing navy blue overalls with 'Pigeon Purge' on the back.

"I find it all rather distasteful."

"That's cos you ain't got no sense of humour."

Another man, wearing identical overalls, climbed out of the van. "Hello, gorgeous."

"I assume you and your colleague are here at the request of Mr Macabre?"

"That we are. You'll be pleased to hear that we're going to get rid of all your flying rats. We'll be starting on Thursday."

"I assume you mean the pigeons."

"Yep. When we're done, there won't be one left on this building."

"That's what I wanted to talk to you about." I pointed to my office. "That's my office there."

"The one with the cat in the window?"

"Err, that's not a real cat. It's a—err—an ornament."

"It just moved."

"Yeah, it's a—err—mechanical ornament."

"It's waving at us now."

"Never mind that. I wanted to ask you not to install those horrid spikes of yours along that section of ledge, either side of my office."

"If we leave it clear, all the pigeons will make a beeline for it."

"Still, I'd prefer you left it alone."

"Sorry, love, we have our reputation to think of. How would it look if we only did half a job?"

"No one need ever know."

"We'd know, and that's enough."

"But you can't put the spikes on there."

"Why not?"

"I—err—never mind."

It was obvious that I'd never be able to persuade them to leave the ledge alone, so I'd just have to break the bad news to Harold.

By the time I got back to my office, Ida had joined him outside the window. He had his wing around her and was trying to console her. "It's going to be okay, love. Jill said she's going to sort it out for us."

Oh bum!

Ida saw me through her tears. "What happened, Jill?

75

Are we going to lose our home?"

"I – err – "

"Of course we aren't, are we, Jill?" Harold said.

All eyes were on me now. I felt terrible, but what could I do? I'd done my best. I'd just have to be brutally honest. There was no point in trying to sugarcoat it. So of course, I said, "Don't worry, you won't lose your home. I managed to persuade them not to put spikes on this ledge."

Both of their little faces lit up, and they hugged one another.

"Thank you so much, Jill." Ida began to cry again, but this time with tears of happiness.

"If there's ever anything we can do for you, just say the word," Harold said, and then he led Ida away.

"How on earth did you pull that off?" Winky said.

"I haven't worked that out yet."

"What do you mean? You just told Harold and Ida that you had."

"I know what I said. What else was I supposed to do? You saw their pathetic little faces."

"You do realise if you don't manage to get it sorted now, that it will hit them a hundred times harder."

No pressure then.

Twenty minutes later, Mrs V brought me a cup of tea. She was sporting the new gloves. "I think I've come up with a name for them, Jill."

"Oh?"

"Top Tips. What do you think?"

"I – err – "

"Because the finger*tips* are removable. And the gloves are *tops*."

"It's certainly a name worthy of the product."

"That's what I thought. Would you like me to knit you and Jack a pair?"

"I — err —"

"Don't worry. I won't charge you for them. They'll be my little present to you both."

"That's very kind."

"*Top Tips?*" Winky scoffed after she'd left the room. "Here's a top tip. Never drink tea made by someone who thinks those gloves are a good idea. That woman is clearly a teabag short of a brew."

Chapter 8

Rachel Somers had provided me with the names of two of Alison Forrest's close friends. One of those was Susan Shields who had readily agreed to meet me. It was obvious, even over the phone, that she was still distraught over what had happened to her friend.

It turned out that she worked not far from my office, so we arranged to meet in Coffee Games. Fortunately, it turned out to be tiddlywinks day, so the noise was at a manageable level.

Smartly dressed in a red jacket and skirt, Susan worked in the travel agents just off the high street.

"I've never been in here before." She glanced around. "Do they always play games like this?"

"Yeah. A different one every day."

"It's a little distracting, isn't it?"

"You should see it on musical statues day. We can go to another coffee shop or to my office if you'd prefer?"

"No, it's okay."

"How did you know Alison?"

"We were at school together. She was always the really smart one; she used to let me copy her homework sometimes." Susan smiled at the bittersweet memory. "Even when Alison was just a kid, she knew she wanted to be a solicitor. I had no idea what I wanted to do. I kind of fell into this job."

"Did you see her often?"

"We'd sometimes grab lunch together, and we had the odd night out."

"Just the two of you?"

"Sometimes, but usually there was a group of us. Rachel

from her office and—"

"Craig Mann?"

"That's right. The four of us always had a laugh."

"When was the last time you saw Alison?"

"Two days before—" Her words petered out, and she had to take a moment to compose herself. "Sorry. We went for a coffee."

"How did she seem?"

"Okay."

"Just *okay*?"

"A little stressed, maybe."

"About what? Did she say?"

"Not really. I knew she was super busy at work. I assumed it was just that."

"Did she ever talk about her marriage? About Laurence?"

"Sometimes."

I had a feeling that there was more Susan wanted to say, so I gave her a gentle nudge. "Good or bad?"

"We all have problems in our relationships, don't we? I don't want to blow it out of proportion."

"Alison is dead, and Laurence is accused of her murder, so if she said anything, anything that might help to uncover the truth of what actually happened, you have to tell me."

"She and Laurence had been having a few problems. Nothing serious, though, I don't think."

"Didn't she say what?"

"I know she wanted more kids. That might have been part of it."

"Did she ever suggest Laurence might be cheating on her?"

"No, nothing like that."

"What about Alison? Might she have been seeing anyone else?"

"No." Susan hesitated a moment too long before saying, "I'm sure she wasn't, but the truth is Craig definitely had a thing for Alison. He was always flirting with her, and she seemed to enjoy it."

"Might it have gone further than just flirting?"

"No. I'm sure it didn't."

Might there have been more to Alison and Craig's relationship than just friendship? I'd reserve judgement on that until I'd had a chance to speak to him.

***

I'd no sooner left Coffee Games than I received a call from Sheila Forrest.

"Jill. The police have just informed me that they've released Laurence's apartment. You said you wanted to take a look around."

"I do. How soon can that be arranged?"

"How about I meet you there in an hour?"

"Okay. I'll see you there."

Before I went to Laurence's apartment, I had business to attend to in Ghost Town, so I magicked myself over to Cakey C where I found Mad, sitting all alone at a corner table.

"You look like you've just lost a fiver."

"Hi, Jill. I've had an ear-bashing from my mother."

"Sorry if I dropped you in it with Deli."

"It's not your fault. I should have told her I was coming back to Washbridge."

"She must be glad that you're back, though?"

"Yeah, she is. She'll be okay in a few days' time. Right now, she's really angry at your grandmother."

"Over the beauty salon? I don't blame her."

"She said you were going to have a word with your grandmother."

"I did, but it didn't do any good. I warned your mum not to expect anything. Grandma doesn't listen to anyone, and especially not me."

"Mum's scared the new shop will put her out of business."

"There's no reason why it should. Just look at what Kathy has done with her shop. Grandma opened up a bridal shop right next door to her, but Kathy's business is thriving. In fact, she's recently opened a new shop in West Chipping. The key is for Deli to focus on her own business, to make it the best it can be, and not to worry about what my grandmother is doing."

"I'll tell her, but I'm not sure it'll do any good. Your mum and dad have certainly done a great job with this place, haven't they?"

"Yeah. Mainly by ripping off Cuppy C. Even the sign looks the same."

"Where are your mum and dad, anyway? I thought they'd be serving today."

"So did I."

"Who are the young couple behind the counter?"

"I've no idea."

"Did you come over to see your parents?"

"Actually, I've arranged to meet the colonel and

Priscilla. I have a favour to ask of them."

"Looks like they're here now." Mad gestured towards the door. "I have to get going anyway. My feet have barely touched the ground since I got back. We must try and have a night out sometime."

"I'd like that."

Despite the colonel's protestations, I insisted on buying drinks for the three of us. I offered to buy them cake too, but both of them declined, and said they preferred not to snack between meals.

Why was everyone on a crusade to make me feel bad about the *occasional* muffin?

"Thanks for agreeing to meet me, Colonel, Priscilla."

"Our pleasure, as always, Jill." If I wasn't mistaken, the colonel was deliberately wearing his hair a little longer. "You said you needed our help?"

"I need the services of a ghost, and I wondered if you might have someone on the books of Hauntings Unlimited who would fit the bill."

"What exactly did you have in mind, Jill?"

I explained my very specific requirements to the colonel, and to my delight, he confirmed they had someone who was exactly what I was looking for. "Her name is Harriet."

"Do you think she'd be up for the job?"

"I'm sure she would. How long would you need her for?"

"Not long. An hour max. The thing is, though, I'm not sure exactly when I'll need her, but it'll be sometime within the next couple of days."

"How about I speak to Harriet, and ask her to keep

herself on standby for your call?"

"Would she do that?"

"She will if I ask her to. She gets a lot of work through Hauntings Unlimited."

"That would be great. How do I get in touch with her?"

"Just give me a call and I'll despatch Harriet immediately."

"That's fantastic, but what will it cost?"

"Nothing." He waved away my offer. "I've lost track of how many times you've helped Priscilla and myself. This is the least I can do."

"What about Harriet? She'll need to be paid."

"Don't worry your head about that. I'll make sure she isn't out of pocket."

"That's very kind of you."

"Hello, Colonel, Priscilla." My mother appeared at our table. "And you, darling." She gave me a peck on the cheek. "I hope the drinks and service lived up to your expectations?"

"All absolutely exceptional," the colonel said.

"This coffee is excellent." Priscilla nodded her approval.

"What about you, Jill?" My father had joined us now. "What do you think?"

"It's all very nice. I see you have new staff." I gestured towards the young couple behind the counter.

"That's Debs and Stuart. Theirs is a tragic story. Giving them a job was the least we could do."

"What happened to them?"

"They'd just got married and were on their way to the reception in a limousine when it crashed; they were both killed outright."

"I remember now. Mrs V mentioned that to me. So, they

83

do all the hard work, and you two swan around all day. Is that how it works?"

"I'll have you know that your father and I have been in the back, holding a management strategy meeting."

"Will you be taking over behind the counter now that's finished?"

"Later, perhaps. After we've finished our marketing meeting."

***

The Forrests' apartment was located just outside of the city centre. Sheila was waiting for me at the door; she had a small suitcase in her hand.

"Are you okay, Sheila?"

"I'm feeling a little nervous about this."

"If you'd prefer to wait outside, I'll be okay in there by myself."

"No, it's fine. This is something I have to do." She took a key from her handbag and unlocked the door.

I'd thought Mad's new apartment was impressive, but this was even better, and certainly much larger.

"I'm going to Adam's bedroom to get some of his clothes and toys," Sheila said, over her shoulder.

The carpet had been removed from the lounge, but there was still a stain where the blood had soaked through to the floorboards. Other than that, there was nothing to indicate the violence that had taken place there. The room was sparsely but tastefully furnished with a mixture of abstract and landscape paintings on the white walls. Standing on a chrome and glass sideboard were a number of framed photographs. One of them, obviously taken on their wedding day, showed a happy couple, gazing into one another's eyes. All of the other photos were of their son, Adam.

After a few minutes, Sheila joined me in the lounge. In addition to the suitcase, she was also carrying a large bag, crammed full of toys.

"How is Adam?" I asked.

"Confused and upset. He keeps asking when he can go home, and where his mummy and daddy are."

"Doesn't he know his mum is dead?"

"I've told him she's gone to heaven, but he doesn't really understand." Sheila began to well up. "How will he ever understand any of this?"

"Kids can be more resilient than we sometimes give them credit for. By the way, I noticed the door isn't damaged."

"No. It was locked when Laurence came back and found Alison."

"So Alison must have known her killer, or they had a key?"

"I guess so."

"Look, Sheila, you might not like what I have to say, but—"

"Just say it."

"I've spoken to Rachel Somers and to another friend of Alison's, Susan Shields; they both suggested that Laurence and Alison might have been going through a rocky patch."

"I don't believe that. They were perfectly happy."

"Are you sure? Isn't it possible that Laurence went out of his way to give you that impression because he didn't want you to worry?"

85

"No. I know my son. I would have known if he was lying."

"Okay." I wasn't sure if I bought that, but I didn't see the point in upsetting her further. "Do you think you could arrange for me to visit Laurence in prison?"

"I think so. When?"

"As soon as you can organise it."

As I made my way out of the building, I noticed one of the other apartments was vacant. I dreaded to think how much the rent must be—certainly way above my pay grade.

I hadn't learnt a great deal from seeing the apartment, but it was clear that Alison must have let in her killer. That or the murderer had somehow got hold of a key.

***

All in all, it had been a long day, so I called Mrs V to let her know I wouldn't be going back to the office.

"Any messages, Mrs V?"

"Just the one. A woman named Violet Spriggs called. She said your dry cleaning was ready to collect."

"I haven't taken any clothes for dry cleaning."

"She definitely had your name. Might Jack have taken something in for you?"

"I wouldn't have thought so. What's the address?"

"Vi The Dry. It's on Wilbur Street."

"Okay. I'll call in on the way home to see what she's going on about."

Vi The Dry was tucked in between a kebab shop and a

haberdashery.

"Hi, my name is Jill Maxwell. My PA took a message to say that you had some dry cleaning for me to collect, but I don't think that can be right."

"You're the cat lady, aren't you?"

"Am I?"

"Wait there. I'll go and get them for you."

Them?

When she returned to the counter, her arms were full. "I think it's wonderful that you've had these made for your cat." She held up a suit. "I bet he looks handsome in this."

"My memory isn't what it used to be. Remind me, would you, when did I bring these in?"

"A couple of days ago."

"Right. And did we speak at the time?"

"No. We found them on the counter together with a note with your name and number on it."

"Right. And how much does this lot come to?"

"Forty-two pounds and twenty pence, please."

Winky. Was. So. Dead.

Chapter 9

"You paid for the cat's dry cleaning?" Jack almost spat out a mouthful of muesli.

"What choice did I have? My name was on it."

"Didn't the people in the shop think it was a little weird that a cat would have dry cleaning?"

"They seemed to think it was cute."

"I suppose it is. That blue suit of his is very smart."

"It isn't even remotely cute, but that's not the point. The point is that he left it there under my name, told me nothing about it, and expected me to pick up the tab."

"I'm sure he'll pay you back."

"You can bet your life on that. I'll get that money even if I have to blow up that mini-safe of his."

"Anyway, you should try and forget about that. You don't want to be all stressed out for the day ahead, Teach."

"Don't call me that. You know I don't like it."

"I wish my teachers had been as beautiful as you."

"I bet you were a little snot at school."

"I wasn't a snot. I was a swot."

"I'm not really sure what to expect at CASS. Hopefully things will be better now Maligarth has gone."

"What's happening about finding his replacement?"

"I won't know until I've spoken to the headmistress."

"By the way, I assume you're still planning to collect Rhymes' trophy tomorrow night?"

"Unless you've changed your mind and are volunteering to do it."

"No chance."

"That's what I thought. I have no choice because it

would break Rhymes' little heart if I don't get his trophy. I don't plan to hang around any longer than I have to, though. As soon as I have it, I'll be out of there."

***

When I stepped out of the house, I was greeted with a sight that stopped me dead in my tracks. On the pavement, in front of our house, were two giant cats. And I recognised them both: It was Bruiser and Lovely.

Had a wicked witch or wizard used magic to do this to the unsuspecting cats? What would Britt and Kimmy think when they saw them?

If I could work out which spell had been used, I might be able to reverse it, but to do that, I'd need to get closer to the huge felines. I'd have to be careful because Bruiser might still be harbouring a grudge for my trick with the lion.

"Lovely, come here, girl."

"Jill?"

The voice took me by surprise because it wasn't Lovely's; it was our next-door neighbour, Clare's.

"What do you think of the costumes?" said Bruiser, AKA Tony.

This wasn't Lovely and Bruiser; it was my cosplay obsessed neighbours.

"I—err—they're very good. I take it these are for your next con?"

"Yes. It's FelineCon a week on Saturday. We had to get costumes made, so we took photos of two of the neighbours' cats, and we asked the costume maker to copy those. We were just on our way to show Kimmy and

Jimmy, and Britt and Kit."

"I don't think that's a good idea."

"Why not?"

"Haven't you seen the posters?" I pointed to the nearest lamppost. "Both cats have been missing for a few days. Kimmy and Britt are beside themselves with worry."

"We had no idea," Clare said. "Thank goodness we bumped into you. They would have thought we were completely heartless."

As I drove towards the toll bridge, I spotted Britt and Kimmy putting up posters, so I pulled over, and opened the window.

"I take it Lovely and Bruiser have still not turned up?"

Britt shook her head. "I'm beginning to fear the worst."

"Hasn't anyone responded to the posters?"

"Not yet," Kimmy said. "Who would do something like this, Jill?"

"You don't know for sure that someone has taken them."

"What other explanation can there be?"

It was a good question, and one to which I didn't have an answer. At least, not an answer I thought either of them would want to hear.

"On a lighter note." Britt managed a smile. "Jack's friend collects his trophy tomorrow, doesn't he?"

"Is it tomorrow? I had no idea."

"Yes, you haven't forgotten that I'd like to meet him, have you?"

"I'm sure Jack has it in hand, but it wouldn't do any harm for you to remind him the next time you see him."

"I will, thanks."

"I'd better get going. I hope your cats turn up safe and well."

***

"What do you think, Jill?" Mrs V pointed to the two pairs of gloves on her desk.

"Are those the convertible gloves?"

"Yes. Do you prefer the ones where the removable tips are the same colour as the rest of the glove, or where the tips are a different colour?"

"They both have equal merit." Which is to say, none whatsoever.

"That's what I thought. Maybe I should create two separate ranges?"

"Why not?"

"I see you collected your dry cleaning?"

"Err, yeah."

"Your memory is getting worse, Jill. Fancy not remembering that you'd taken it in."

"My head's all over the place. It's what comes of being so busy."

"Ah, good." Winky was on the windowsill. "I was hoping that you'd collect those."

"I don't approve of you leaving your dry cleaning under my name."

"I could hardly leave it under mine, could I?"

"That's not the point. How come you have so much dry cleaning, anyway?"

"I need to get everything ready for my cruise."

"You're still going ahead with that, then?"

91

"Yeah. I'll be on my way in two weeks' time."

"You aren't paying for anything until I get the money I paid out on this lot."

"Chillax. You'll get your money. How much was it? Twenty pounds?"

"Forty-two pounds and twenty pence."

"No problem." He jumped down from the window, scurried under the sofa, and moments later, reappeared clutching a handful of notes. "Here's fifty pounds. Keep the change for your trouble."

"Okay, thanks." This is what it had come to: My cat was now tipping me. "How much is the cruise costing you?"

"Not much. A couple of thousand."

"Two grand? Where do you get that kind of money?"

"It'll be worth every penny."

"Are you sure the cruise company is legit? I still think it looks a little dodgy."

"You know your trouble? You worry too much."

Before I could respond, Harold and Ida appeared in the window.

"The spikes men are back, and they've started work, Jill."

"Don't worry about it. Your ledge will be safe."

"Do you promise?" Ida looked at me with sad eyes.

"Yes, I promise. You'll be perfectly safe."

"Thank you, Jill. That's a great weight off my mind." She took Harold's wing. "Come on. It's time for breakfast."

"I hope you know what you're doing," Winky said. "If you let them down now, they'll be devastated."

"Don't worry. I have it all in hand. In fact, I'm ready to put part one of my elaborate plan into action."

"What is it with you and all these plans? Cunning, ingenious, brilliant, and now elaborate? What's the difference between them?"

"I don't have time to explain that again. You should have been paying attention in the last book."

"You're not making any sense? What book?"

"Never mind. I have to go and see a man about a pigeon."

The Pigeon Purge men were unloading their van.

"If it isn't the pigeon lady." Once again, the man had the stub of a cigarette wedged in the corner of his mouth. "Fancy making us a brew?"

"If I do, will you leave my stretch of window ledge alone?"

"No can do. We've been contracted to spike the whole building."

"I guess you're not worried about Headless Harriet, then?"

"Who?"

"Didn't the landlord mention her?"

"Mention who?" The man's partner in crime had now joined us.

"Headless Harriet. She's a ghost."

They both laughed. "Course she is. And why is she called headless?"

"Take a wild guess."

"Have you seen her, then?" Cig-in-mouth scoffed. "This ghost?"

"I could hardly miss her. She haunts the window ledge outside my office."

"Oh yeah? And why does she hang out there?"

"Because it was from that ledge that she jumped to her death."

"Sure. We believe you, don't we, Joe?"

"Yeah, course we do. What about her head, then?"

"What about it?" I shrugged.

"If all she did was jump off the ledge, how come she lost her head?"

"There was a cart, selling scythes, passing by the building at the precise moment she jumped."

"How do you come up with this stuff?"

"I'm warning you. If you go onto that section of ledge, you can expect a visit from Harriet."

"I'm so scared." He made a show of shaking. "Aren't you, Joe?"

"Terrified."

The two of them were practically in hysterics.

"Don't say I didn't give you fair warning."

***

Before I could deal with the horrible pigeon men, I had a class to teach.

"Come in!" Ms Nightowl shouted.

It was great to have her back. I was pleased to see that all of her old furniture had also returned, and the room had been redecorated from the awful black which Maligarth had favoured.

I nodded my approval. "This room is looking much better than the last time I was here."

"Not only was that man pure evil, but he had absolutely no taste. Take a seat, Jill."

"Thank you, Headmistress."

"The whole school owes you a debt of gratitude. I dread to think what would have happened if you hadn't foiled Maligarth."

"Don't mention it. How long do you expect to be at the helm?"

"As short a time as possible. I've made it quite clear to the governors that I expect them to press ahead with the search for my replacement."

"And you'll be consulted on that appointment?"

"Yes, it's to be a joint decision."

"That's excellent."

"I have even more good news. Philomena Eastwest has agreed to come out of retirement."

"Fantastic. I'm delighted."

"What do you think will happen to Maligarth, Jill?"

"I don't know, and to be honest, I don't much care."

"I heard he did all this just for the money."

"That's what he gave his associates to believe, but personally I don't buy it. The Core may be valuable, but from what you told me, it also has the potential to wreak havoc in the wrong hands. I find it impossible to believe he wasn't aware of that, but the truth is we may never be sure of his motives."

When I walked into the classroom, all of class one-alpha got to their feet and clapped.

"Three cheers for Mrs Maxwell!" Charlie Hedges shouted.

After the hip hips and hurrahs were over, I gestured for them to retake their seats.

"Thank you very much everyone."

"You saved CASS," Ruby Noonday said. "My parents

were threatening to take me out of the school until you got rid of Mr Maligarth."

"I'm delighted you'll be staying with us."

"I'm staying too, Miss," Fleabert Junior shouted.

"Win some, lose some." I grinned.

Everyone, including Fleabert laughed. Although he could still occasionally be a pain in the backside, he'd come on in leaps and bounds since the beginning of term.

Lucinda Blade's hand shot up. "Will you tell us how you got rid of Mr Maligarth, Mrs Maxwell?"

"No, I won't. I know your game. Anything to distract me from the lesson."

"Aww, please, Miss."

"If any of you are genuinely interested, I can always arrange an extra session after school hours. Who'd like to stay for that?" Precisely no hands were raised. "That's what I figured. Okay, so let's carry on with today's lesson."

Ignoring the moans and groans, I took out my notes, and kicked off the discussion I'd prepared about managing one's finances in the human world. I'd chosen that subject because it had occurred to me that, for any sup moving there, the idea of credit cards would come as something of a shock.

"So, you just give them a plastic card, and they give you stuff for free?" Destiny Braden's face lit up.

"No, Destiny, that's not what I said. You still have to pay for the items you purchase, but not straight away."

"What if you don't bother paying for them later?" Fleabert Junior said.

"You'll end up in trouble. That's the whole point I've been trying to make."

As we neared the end of the lesson, I was beginning to regret my choice of subject matter. Instead of taking away the message that credit cards were something they should avoid or at the very least, be very cautious with, most of them seemed to be planning how they would spend what they considered 'free' money. Hopefully, Ms Nightowl wouldn't get wind of this.

I was just about to dismiss the kids when Sally Topps raised her hand.

"Yes, Sally?"

"Now that you've got rid of Mr Maligarth, are you going to get rid of Old Mother Mason too?"

"Yeah!" Charlie Hedges shouted. "Please get rid of her, Miss."

"Who is Old Mother Mason?"

"She's a ghost, Miss. She haunts the dorms at night."

"How come I've never heard of her before?"

"The other teachers reckon she disappeared a hundred years ago, but she's back again."

"And who has actually seen her?" I waited for someone to raise a hand, but no one did. "No one, then?"

"But she's back," Fleabert Junior insisted. "And she's scary ugly."

"How can you know she's ugly if you haven't actually seen her?"

"There are stories about her in the archived journals. You should read them, Miss."

"They gave me nightmares." Destiny Braden shuddered at the memory.

Just then, the bell rang, and the kids quickly forgot about credit cards and ghosts, as they headed for the playground.

Before returning to the human world, I called in at the staffroom where the atmosphere was so much better than on my last visit. Maligarth's departure and Philomena Eastwest's imminent return had lifted everyone's spirits.

Natasha Fastjersey, as usual, was in amongst the cupcakes. "Hi, Jill. Have you heard about Philomena?"

"I have, and it's great news. What do you know about Old Mother Mason, Natasha?"

"There have been a number of rumours that she's back, but I don't know of anyone who has actually seen her. Hopefully, it will stay that way."

Chapter 10

My stint at the school finished, I magicked myself back to the office. The Pigeon Purge guys were working on the ledge outside Clown, and would no doubt be moving onto my section next. It was time to give the colonel a call.

"It's Jill. I'm sorry to give you so little notice, but could you send Harriet over straight away?"

"Of course. She's been on standby waiting for your call. Give me a couple of minutes and she'll be with you."

"Does she know where to find me?"

"Yes, she's been fully briefed."

"Okay, thanks. I look forward to seeing her."

"I should warn you, Jill, the first time you meet her might be a bit of a shock."

While I was waiting for Harriet to appear, I received a phone call from Sheila Forrest.

"Jill, I've managed to arrange for you to visit Laurence on Tuesday."

"Couldn't I get to see him any sooner than that?"

"I'm sorry. That's the earliest date they'd allow it."

"Okay, that'll have to do."

"He's in Longdale Prison. I can give you directions if you like?"

"There's no need. That place is like a second home to me."

"Oh?" She sounded shocked.

"I don't mean I was there as an inmate. I've visited quite a few clients there in the course of my investigations."

"Of course. Sorry, I should have realised. When I spoke to Laurence earlier, he sounded really down. I'm not sure how much more he can take of being locked up."

"I know it's easier said than done, but you have to try not to worry. He's probably a lot tougher than you give him credit for. I've seen lots of people in his position, and they all managed to come through it."

"I hope you're right. I'm really scared right now."

"Are you going to be there on Tuesday too?"

"No, Laurence said he thought it would be best if he spoke to you alone."

"Okay."

I'd just finished on the call when the temperature in the room dropped dramatically, and Winky scooted under the sofa.

That could mean only one thing.

"Jill?" The pretty young woman was not at all what I'd been expecting.

"That's me. Harriet?"

"Pleased to meet you. The colonel speaks very highly of you."

"We go back a long way. I understand he's briefed you on my little problem?"

"He has indeed, and I'm pleased to be able to help. I love animals and birds of all kinds." She glanced over at the window. "I assume it's that window ledge, is it?"

"That's right." I hesitated, wondering how best to put my next question. "There's just one thing, Harriet. I—err—the colonel gave me to believe that you—err—"

"My head?" She laughed.

"Well, yeah."

"The colonel obviously didn't explain how this works, did he?"

"Well, he just said—"

I stopped mid-sentence, stunned by what I saw. As casually as if she was removing a hat, she lifted her head from her shoulders, and tucked it under one arm.

"Is this what you were expecting?"

For a moment, I couldn't speak because I was transfixed by the head which was still continuing the conversation. Eventually, I managed, "Err, yeah. Sorry, that just threw me for a moment."

"Don't worry. That's pretty much the reaction I always get." She walked over to the window. "Shall I make a start?"

"Yes, please. The workmen should be along any minute now. Will you be okay out on the ledge? It's quite narrow. I wouldn't want you to fall."

"To my death, you mean?" She laughed.

"Right, yeah. Sorry, that was a stupid thing to say."

Once Harriet had climbed out of the window, Winky crept slowly out from under the sofa.

"You've had some freaks in this office, but that one takes the biscuit."

"I thought she was very nice."

"Was that before or after she took off her head?"

"That was a bit freaky."

"A *bit*? The woman lifts her head off her shoulders and puts it under her arm, and you call it a *bit* freaky?"

"If everything goes according to plan, Harold and Ida should be able to remain in their home."

"This *elaborate* plan of yours has one minor flaw."

"Oh? What's that?"

"That headless freak will probably scare Harold and Ida to death."

"I hadn't considered that."

"Chances are, one look at Harriet, and they'll move out anyway."

Oh bum!

What Winky had said was true, but it was too late to change the plan now. Harriet was already out on the ledge, and any time now, the workmen would be in for the shock of their lives. I would just have to keep my fingers crossed that it didn't backfire and result in Harold and Ida moving out anyway.

"Are you going to answer that or what?" Winky shouted.

I'd been so busy thinking about Harriet, Harold and Ida that I hadn't realised my phone was ringing.

"Hello?"

"Jill, it's Amber. Is there any chance you could pop over?"

"Now?"

"Yes, please. There's someone here who needs your help."

"Okay. I'm on my way."

"Wow!" Amber still had the phone in her hand. "That was quick."

"What's up?"

"Come and meet Felicity." Amber came out from behind the counter and led the way to a table at the very back of the shop.

The witch seated there was staring at the empty cup on the table in front of her. It was obvious that she'd been crying.

"Felicity, this is my cousin, Jill."

"Hi." Her weak smile didn't reach her eyes. "Amber said you might be able to help me."

"I'll leave you two to talk." Amber turned back to the counter. "Shout me if you need anything."

"I wouldn't say no to a latte." I got in quickly. "And a blueberry muffin wouldn't go amiss."

"Sure. What about you, Felicity?"

"I'm okay, thanks." She grabbed a tissue from her bag and blew her nose. "Did Amber tell you what had happened?"

"No. She just asked me to come straight over. Why don't you talk me through it?"

"My husband, Monty, has disappeared."

"When did he go missing?"

"Yesterday. He didn't come home from work."

"What is it your husband does?"

"He's a postman."

"Has he gone missing before?"

"Never. It's not something he would ever do. He knows how much I worry."

"Did he go to work as normal yesterday?"

"Yes, at the crack of dawn like he always does."

"What time is that?"

"He's usually out of the house by five-thirty."

"I assume you're still in bed when he leaves?"

"No. I always get up and make him coffee and breakfast."

"You do?"

"It seems only fair, doesn't it?"

"Err, yeah, I guess so." I tried to imagine myself doing the same for Jack. "And how was he when he set off for work?"

"Fine."

"It didn't seem like anything was bothering him?"

"No. He just gave me a hug and a kiss as normal."

"When did you realise something was wrong?"

"Not until I got home from work at five o'clock. He always has a cup of tea waiting for me, but there was no sign of him. I thought at first that he must have nipped out somewhere, but then I realised he'd never come home."

"How did you know he hadn't been home and gone out again?"

"His uniform wasn't in the wardrobe; the first thing he always does when he gets home is to take that off. Even then, I wasn't too concerned because he does occasionally go out with some of his friends from work. Normally, though, when he does that, he lets me know. When he still wasn't back by seven, I tried to contact him, but his phone was switched off. By nine o'clock, I was beginning to panic. I rang around everyone I could think of, but no one had seen him."

"What about the police?"

"I tried them, but they won't even file a missing person report for an adult who has been missing for less than seventy-two hours. I tried to explain that Monty isn't the kind of person to do something like this, but they still weren't interested. I came in here for a cup of tea to try and calm my nerves, Amber saw me crying, and asked what was wrong. She seemed to think you might be able to help. Can you?"

"I don't know, but I'll certainly try. Worst case scenario, I don't come up with anything, and you can still go to the

police."

"That's great. What else do you need from me?"

"A photo of your husband and a contact at his place of work would be a good starting point."

Once I had all the information I needed from Felicity, I walked her to the door, and then went back to finish my coffee and muffin.

"Will you be able to help Felicity?" Amber came to join me.

"I'm not sure, but I've said I'll try. How's Bella — err — Jemima doing?"

"Fabulously. The parents all love her. The biggest challenge is trying to make sure we don't call her by the wrong name."

"I hope it works out. She doesn't deserve to be punished for what her mother did."

"You're right. By the way, Pearl and I have come up with our most brilliant plan yet for Cuppy C."

"Please tell me you're joking. This place is doing just fine. Why can't you leave well alone?"

"You see, Jill, that's always been your problem. You're too willing to sit back and rest on your laurels."

"Rubbish! I'm always looking for ways to innovate the business."

"Really? And what was the last thing you did to *innovate* your business?"

"I — err — "

"I'm waiting."

"Don't pressure me."

"That business has barely changed since you took over from your dad."

"Rubbish. Only last month, I purchased a staple remover."

"*Staple remover*?" She laughed.

"It's really difficult to take out staples by hand. That purchase has saved me countless hours."

"Is that the only thing you can come up with?"

"Of course not. I have a full-blown social media presence now."

"And when was the last time you updated any of those?"

"Err, I don't remember the exact date."

"Was it this week?"

"Err —"

"This month?"

"Never mind about my business. What kind of crazy idea have the two of you concocted this time?"

"Cats."

"You're not going to try and stage a musical in here, are you? It's not nearly big enough."

"Not the musical. Just cats."

"I have no idea what you're talking about."

"A cat café of course."

"Are you going to be selling to cats, too? Because if that's your brilliant plan, I have some bad news for you. Cats don't have any disposable income. Winky excepted, obviously."

"That's not what we're doing. There'll be cats here in the tearoom for the customers."

"Why?"

"It's the latest craze in the human world."

"I had no idea. What's the plan, then?"

"To get some cats, of course."

"Is that it? Just bring in a few cats?"

"More or less. That's the great part about it. There's no other expense really."

"Where are you going to get the cats from?"

"We've already got that covered. We've contacted a company called Cat City. They specialise in providing cats to cat cafés. And the best part is that these cats are all trained to be in a café environment from the time they're kittens, so they won't be freaked out by the customers."

"It does at least sound like you've done your research this time."

"We always do our research."

"Hmm. And when does this transformation take place?"

"If everything goes according to plan, it should happen next week."

"As soon as that?"

"Why not? There's no time like the present."

I left Amber and her crazy ideas behind and magicked myself back to the office.

"Hey, Winky, you're a cat."

"I've always said there are no flies on you, haven't I?" He grinned. "Apart from that one time when you forgot about the ham sandwich in your jacket pocket. There were a lot of bluebottles hovering around you that day, I seem to remember."

"Don't remind me. Have you ever heard of cat cafés?"

"Of course I have."

"I don't mean cafés run by cats for cats."

"I'm not stupid. I know what a cat café is. Everyone has heard of them."

"I hadn't."

"Yeah, well, everyone except you, then. They're big business."

"I don't get the appeal of them."

"Of course you don't. That's why you'll never be an entrepreneur."

"Is there a cat café here in Washbridge?"

"One opened a couple of weeks ago, I believe. Why are you so interested in cat cafés all of a sudden? Are you thinking of giving this lot up to do something that might actually make some money?"

"No, I'm not. My cousins are going to convert their tearoom into a cat café."

"Good for them. At least someone in your family has a clue."

***

On my way out of the door, I bumped into the two Pigeon Purge guys, who were packing stuff into their van. Even before they spoke, I could tell Harriet had done her job. Their faces were white, and their eyes were as wide as saucers.

"Have you finished already, guys?"

"We've done as much as we're doing here."

"But I don't think you've done my ledge."

"Why didn't you tell us she was real?"

"Harriet? If I recall correctly, that's exactly what I told you."

"Have you seen her?" He shivered. "She's horrible."

"I've always found Harriet to be a friendly soul."

"But her head! It talks."

"Does Mr Macabre know you haven't finished the job?"

"I don't care if he knows or not. If he wants that last ledge doing, he'll have to find someone else to do it. I'm not going back up there again."

"Fair enough. I assume you guys will be headed home now. *Headed* home? Get it?"

It was obvious they didn't have a sense of humour because neither of them so much as cracked a smile.

Chapter 11

Ever since the inaugural meeting of the community band, Jack had taken to practising the ukulele at every possible opportunity. This morning, as soon as he'd finished his muesli, he was off into the lounge to have yet another strum.

"Do you have to make that awful row at this time of day?" I sighed.

"I think I'm getting better."

"You're not. Trust me on this one. Why don't you try leaning on the lamppost?"

"The George Formby classic?"

"No, I meant why don't you go outside and lean on the lamppost, so that I don't have to listen to that awful noise."

"Your problem is that you don't know good music when you hear it."

"Says you. By the way, I had another really weird dream."

"I've told you why you're having them. It's because you eat custard creams too close to bedtime."

"Don't you want to know what it was about?"

"Not really."

"I'd turned into a muffin, and I was being chased by lots of people who wanted to eat me. It was horrible because no matter how fast I ran, I couldn't get away."

"I reckon there's a message in there somewhere."

"Do you think there's some deep psychological meaning?"

"No, it's because you're obsessed with muffins."

"I don't think you're taking this seriously enough."

"I dreamt about ukuleles."

"Why doesn't that surprise me? Hey, I meant to ask, have you heard of cat cafés?"

"Of course I have. They're all the rage. In fact, one opened in Washbridge a couple of weeks ago."

"That's what Winky said. Where is it?"

"Just around the corner from the police station. I saw it when I was over there last week. They appeared to be doing a roaring trade."

"What's it called? Do you remember?"

"Meow!"

"How very original."

"We should check it out sometime."

"Whatever for? I spend all day with an annoying cat. Why would I want to visit a café full of them?"

"The cats are cute."

"The twins apparently think so too. They're talking about transforming Cuppy C into a cat café."

"That's a brilliant idea."

"I'm just waiting to see what goes wrong."

"They might surprise you."

"They might, but if past experience is anything to go by, I doubt it."

"Incidentally, you haven't forgotten I might be late home tonight, have you?"

"Are you attending a meeting of the ukulele appreciation society?"

"Very funny. There's a joint conference today between the Washbridge and West Chipping forces; it's being held at our station. We're going to discuss ways we can co-operate and share resources. I did tell you about it."

To be fair, he probably had, but it was so boring that I

would have filed it under *don't care*. "Will Sushi be there?"

"More than likely."

"That's interesting."

"Why do you say that?"

"No reason."

"Are you up to something, Jill?"

"Moi? Of course not."

Snigger.

***

"These flowers arrived for you a few minutes ago, Jill." Mrs V handed me the bouquet of tulips.

"Who are they from?"

"I didn't look."

"Mrs V?"

"Well, I did happen to notice the card, but purely by accident. They're from Harold and Ida—no surname. Are they clients?"

"In a manner of speaking. Are there any other messages for me?"

"Just the one: Someone called from Middle Tweaking Theatre. They said you'd enquired about hiring the venue for a day. I assumed they must have got the wrong number, but the lady was quite insistent."

"Actually, I did make an enquiry with them."

"Why do you need a theatre?"

"It's connected to the problems Clown have been having. What did the lady say?"

"That the theatre was free on Tuesday or Wednesday morning next week, and that you should give her a call if you were interested."

"In that case, would you phone her back and book Wednesday morning, please?"

"You shouldn't have," Winky reached for the flowers.

"These are not for you. Harold and Ida sent them to me." I walked over to the open window and popped my head out. "Harold? Ida? Are you there?"

"Hi, Jill." Harold came trotting along the window ledge; Ida was a few steps behind him.

"Thank you for the beautiful flowers, but it really wasn't necessary."

"It's the least we could do," Ida said. "You saved our home."

"I hope the ghost didn't scare you too much."

"Harriet? Not at all. She was lovely."

"The guys from Pigeon Purge probably wouldn't agree."

"Do you think they'll come back and try again?" Ida said.

"I doubt we'll see those particular guys back here, but it's always possible that Macabre might try again using a different firm. You needn't worry, though, because Harriet said that she'd be happy to give a repeat performance if necessary."

Winky was on his phone, and although I could only hear one half of the conversation, something was clearly amiss.

"Where have you looked?" he said. "Try not to worry. I'm sure he'll be okay. Let me know if there's any update."

"What was that all about?" I asked when he'd finished on the call.

113

"Gavin the Grub has gone missing."

"Is he a friend of yours?"

"More of an acquaintance. That was his partner, Gemma the Jems. Apparently, Gavin's been missing for a few days, which isn't like him."

"It's funny you should say that because Lovely and Bruiser have disappeared too."

"That's no loss. No one is going to miss those two losers."

"Their owners do."

"Their *what*?"

"Okay, okay. If you're going to insist on being so pedantic: The people who share their houses with them are worried."

"The mystery thickens. Maybe there's a catnapper hereabouts. You should investigate."

"Why does everyone keep suggesting that? I've got more than enough on my plate at the moment, thank you very much. Why don't *you* investigate it? You're always telling me you'd make a great P.I. This is your chance to prove it."

"I might just do that. Do you have a magnifying glass I can borrow?"

"No, I don't."

"What about a deerstalker?"

"No self-respecting P.I. would wear one of those."

***

I wanted to find out exactly what the police knew about the Forrest case. Somehow, though, I didn't think they'd be particularly receptive to an information request from me. Fortunately, Jack had given me an idea for how I could get inside the building. The only downside to the plan was that for a couple of hours, I'd have to look like Sushi.

After I'd cast the 'doppelganger' spell, I stole a quick look in the mirror, and let me tell you, seeing Sushi staring back at me was not a pleasant experience. Hopefully, though, it would do the job.

"Morning, ma'am." The officer on desk duty nodded. "I thought you were at the conference today?"

"I should be, but something urgent cropped up. Get the door for me, would you?" I gestured to the pile of files I was carrying.

"Of course, ma'am." He used his card to swipe me through.

I quite liked being called ma'am. Maybe I should insist on Mrs V calling me that from now on.

The joint conference meant that there were far fewer people around than on my previous visits to the police station.

I'd just started up the stairs when—

"Susan?"

I turned around to find a plain clothes officer standing there.

"Hi."

"Aren't you supposed to be over at West Chipping?"

"Yes, but something urgent on the Forrest case has cropped up."

"Really? I haven't heard anything about it."

"It only just came through."

I was about to continue up the stairs when he said, "Let me take those for you." Before I could object, he'd grabbed the pile of files. "To your office?"

"Err, yeah."

"After you." He stood to one side to allow me to go first.

Oh bum! Which one was Sushi's office? Hopefully, there would be names on the doors.

There weren't.

As I walked down the corridor, I glanced through the windows on either side, hoping to spot something that would identify Sushi's office. Three doors in, I spotted a pink umbrella in the corner of one of the offices.

With my fingers crossed, I opened the door.

"I thought you wanted to put these files in your office?" My good Samaritan gave me a puzzled look.

"I do, but I just need to leave—err—a note on this desk. Could you drop them on my desk, please?"

"Sure." He carried on down the corridor and went into the office two doors further down.

"Thanks. Just drop them anywhere," I said.

"No problem. Do you need me to take a look at the new Forrest stuff?"

"No, it's okay. I'll let you know if it proves to be anything of interest."

"Okay, I'll catch you later."

"Yeah. Thanks again."

Phew! That was a close call.

I waited until I was sure there was no one around, and then made my way to the incident room. In there, were four large whiteboards: two wall-mounted and two freestanding. The Forrest case was laid out on one of the larger wall-mounted boards, and it made for rather interesting reading. It seemed that the police had one key witness: one of Laurence's neighbours, a Mr Arthur Radford, had reported that he'd seen Laurence return to the apartment almost an hour earlier than he'd claimed to do so. If that was the case, then he would have had ample time to murder his wife before calling the police. The other item of interest related to the murder weapon. It seemed the hammer that had killed Alison had Laurence's fingerprints on it.

Mission accomplished, I made my way out of the incident room, but when I was halfway along the corridor, I heard something that sent a chill down my spine.

"Where did these files on my desk come from, Charlie?" I heard Sushi say.

Oh bum! What was she doing back here?

"You just asked me to put them there." He seemed totally confused by the question.

"I've never seen them before," Sushi insisted. "I think I'd know if they were mine."

"Oh, my mistake. What did you make of the new Forrest intel?"

"What new intel?"

"You just told me that you'd come back because you'd received new info on the case."

"Have you been drinking, Charlie?" Sushi demanded.

"Of course not."

"I came back because they had a power failure over at West Chipping. That useless crowd couldn't organise a booze-up in a brewery."

"So there isn't any new info on the Forrest case?"

"Not that I'm aware of. We don't need it, anyway. That case is cut and dried. Now, if you don't mind, I need to crack on."

"Sure. Catch you later."

Poor old Charlie looked stunned, but that was nothing compared to his expression when he spotted me – still looking like Sushi. Oh bum! What had I been thinking? Why hadn't I cast the 'invisible' spell?

"Susan?" He glanced quickly back and forth between me, in the corridor, and the real Sushi, in her office.

"What now, Charlie?" Sushi snapped. Fortunately, from her position in the office, she couldn't see me.

"You – err – she –" Charlie stuttered.

"You aren't making any sense. Close the door, will you?"

In something of a daze, he did as he was asked, then he turned to me. Before he could say anything, I put a finger to my lips and beckoned him over.

"You're probably wondering what's going on," I said in a whisper.

"You're here – err – and in there. I don't understand."

"Confusing, isn't it?" I cast the 'forget' spell on him, made myself invisible, and then hurried out of the police station as fast as my legs would carry me.

That had been too close for comfort, but at least I'd got what I came for.

***

After that ordeal, I needed a coffee, so I headed for Coffee Games.

"Hi, Jill." Sarah was behind the counter.

"Hi. It's remarkably quiet in here today. What's the game of the day?"

"Chinese whispers. What can I get for you?"

"A blueberry muffin and a —"

I suddenly came over all light-headed, and then everything went black. When I came around, I found myself standing next to a large pane of glass. Through it, I could see the interior of Coffee Games where the customers were all whispering to one another.

But where was I?

I glanced to my left and saw a giant jam donut. To my right was an equally large chocolate brownie. I was just thinking how surreal this was when the realisation dawned on me: I had turned into a muffin.

The next thing I knew, a young man pointed at me through the glass, and then something cold and metallic picked me up.

What was going on?

I glanced up and saw Sarah; she was the one who'd picked me up and placed me on a plate.

"Sarah! It's me!" It was no good; she obviously couldn't hear me.

I had to do something, and I had to do it quickly or I'd be eaten. Fortunately, even though I was now a muffin, I still seemed to have legs, so I jumped off the plate, and then off the table, and sprinted for the door.

"Hey! Come back here!" the young man yelled. "Stop that muffin!"

Soon, half a dozen people were chasing me. My legs were so small that I had no chance of making it to the door before they caught me.

I was done for.

"Jill? Are you okay?" Sarah's voice snapped me back to earth.

"Err, yeah."

"You were miles away. Are you sure you're alright?"

"Yeah, I'm fine. I'd better get going."

"What about your muffin?"

"I've changed my mind."

The sense of relief once I'd made it out of the shop was palpable. That was twice now that I'd experienced a hallucination that had matched one of my dreams. What was happening to me? Was I cracking up?

"What's up with you?" Winky said. "You're as white as a sheet."

"I was a muffin."

"What do you mean, *you were a muffin?*"

"Just now. One minute, I was standing in Coffee Games waiting to be served, and the next, I was a muffin in the cake cabinet. That's exactly the same as the dream I had last night. And I know what you're going to say, but I haven't had a drop to drink."

"I believe you."

"You do?"

"Didn't you have a similar experience earlier in the week?"

"With the squirrel? Yes, I did. What do you think it means?"

"I would have thought that was obvious."

"Not to me."

"That grandmother of yours must be behind it. Have you upset her again?"

"No, I don't think so, but you're right. This is exactly the kind of thing she would do. Thanks, Winky. I need to have an urgent word with that woman."

Chapter 12

Winky was right: Grandma must have been behind the weird dreams thing. I should have realised the first time it happened. That woman was such a piece of work. Not satisfied with dunking me in a tankful of water, she was now intent on invading my dreams.

Enough was enough; it was time I had it out with her once and for all.

Julie wasn't as happy as the last time I'd seen her; in fact, she looked quite glum.

"Is something wrong, Julie?"

"I'm okay."

"Are you sure? You seem a little subdued."

"Wouldn't you be if you had to wear these awful uniforms?"

"When I came in last time, you seemed to be okay with them."

"That's when we could choose which colour we wore. Your grandmother is now insisting we wear only the yellow ones."

"Right."

"Will you have a word with her, Jill? See if you can get her to let us choose the colour we want to wear? She might listen to you."

"I will if I get the chance, but I wouldn't get your hopes up."

Grandma was seated at her desk, and she had a banana on her head.

"It's you." She scowled. "You're like a bad penny."

(2)

"Why do you have a banana on your head?"

"So that's where it is." She picked it up and began to peel it. "I wondered where I'd put that."

Huh? "I have a bone to pick with you."

"Are you still going on about the ducking stool? It's time to let it go and move on."

"No, well yes, I'm still mad about that, but that's not why I'm here."

Through a mouthful of banana, she managed to say, "Why are you here, then?"

"I want you to leave my dreams alone."

"I have no idea what you're talking about."

"I know you're behind it."

"Okay, you got me."

"It was you, then?"

"No, it wasn't. I don't have the first clue what you're going on about."

"I've been having—Yuk, you're not going to eat the peel, are you?"

"Why not? It's the best part."

"Why have you been turning my dreams into reality?"

"Don't you think I have better things to do with my time than mess around with your dreams? I have a new shop launch to plan."

"Well, someone must be doing it!"

"Doing what, exactly? What's happened?"

I told her about the incidents with the squirrel and the muffin. "Who do you think is behind it?"

She finished the last of the banana while she thought about it. "I'm not sure anyone is behind it. Or that it even happened."

"Of course it happened."

"Are you sure it wasn't just a daydream?"

"No. I saw the squirrel. It was as real as you are right now."

"I'm not aware of any spell that will bring a dream to life, so if someone is doing this to you, they must have developed a new spell. There aren't many people who could do that."

"You could."

"Probably, but I repeat, I had nothing to do with it. My money is still on it being a daydream."

"Fair enough." I started for the door. "By the way, the Everettes aren't very happy with those yellow uniforms. Julie asked me to suggest you make every day multi-coloured day."

"Where would be the fun in that?"

"Oh well, I tried. Bye, then."

"Haven't you forgotten something?"

"What?"

"Your apology."

"For what?"

"The false accusation you just levelled at me."

"Okay, I'm sorry. Bye."

"I'll see you tomorrow."

"Why, what's happening tomorrow?"

"Surely you haven't forgotten that it's Witchgiving?"

"Oh yeah, right."

"It's going to be great fun."

Something told me that Grandma's idea of fun and mine were wildly different.

***

I'd made an appointment to see Tiberius Dove who was in charge of Candle Mail, the main postal delivery service that operated in Candlefield.

The headquarters of the postal service was on Candle Island, a man-made island on the River Candle, accessible by bridge. It was an area of Candlefield I'd never had occasion to visit before. The 'island' was home to numerous businesses, the largest of which was Candle Mail.

"Could I have your autograph, please?" the young wizard on reception asked.

I always found such requests a little embarrassing. "Sure."

"I have a poster of you in my bedroom."

That gave rise to three questions: First, who would want a poster of me? Second, who was producing the posters? Third, and most importantly, why wasn't I being paid royalties?

"A poster of me? Really?"

"Yes. It's one of you in the Levels Competition. It took me ages to decide between that one and one of you at the Elite."

"What's your name?"

"Brewster but everyone calls me Brew."

"How many different posters of me were there?"

"I'm not sure. Probably a dozen."

"And where was this?"

"Candlefield Icons. Do you know the cat rescue place?"

"Yeah."

"It's just around the corner from there."

"Thanks, Brew."

Tiberius Dove was a werewolf, and an absolute giant.

"Have a seat, Mrs Maxwell."

"Thanks, and please call me Jill."

"Jill it is, and you must call me Tibs."

"Okay, *Tibs*."

"I believe you're here regarding Monty Featherstone?"

"That's right. His wife, Felicity, came to see me."

"Such a lovely couple. Terrible business this. I had a word with the police on Felicity's behalf, but they don't seem very keen to get involved. Not yet anyway. They seem to think that Monty has 'chosen' to disappear."

"I take it you don't?"

"I might if it was one of my other employees. But Monty? Never. The man is as honest as the day is long. He's punctual to a fault, never misses a shift, and is well thought of by both his colleagues and the customers."

"Do you think it's possible he could be lying badly injured somewhere?"

"He would have been found by now. I've had my people cover every inch of his route. If he was lying injured somewhere, they would have found him."

"Do you have any other theories?" I said.

"The only thing I can come up with is that someone is holding him against his will."

"Why would someone do that?"

"Your guess is as good as mine."

Even though I got the impression that Tibs was keen to help, I was getting nowhere. "Is it possible to at least pinpoint the exact spot where he went missing?"

He thought about it for a minute. "The best we could do would be to try to establish which was the last address he delivered mail to."

"Would you do that?"

"Of course. I'll have one of my people walk the route, and check every house, to see what they come up with."

"And you'll let me know?"

"Of course."

"Just one other thing. Do you have a copy of the route that Monty's round would have taken him on?"

"Yes, I can let you have that right now." It took him only a few clicks of the mouse to print it off. "There you go."

***

I finished work early and called at the Corner Shop on the way home. At first, I didn't think there was anyone behind the counter.

"Jack? Are you back there?"

"I'm down here, Jill."

"Oh?" I leaned over the counter to find Little Jack standing there. "Sorry, I didn't realise you were down there."

"One of my stilts has malfunctioned."

"Oh dear. How are you going to manage?"

"It's okay. I've called Stilt Rescue. They guarantee to attend within the hour, so hopefully I'll be up and running again soon. Well, maybe not running, but definitely walking."

"That's good."

"Did you remember to help yourself to a free drink?"

"No, but I will now." I walked over to the vending machine and made my selection.

"Which one did you choose?" he asked.

"Wild berry."

"My favourite."

Hmm? Once again, it looked and tasted like regular tea. Still, it was free, so I didn't think I should complain.

"Are you still getting backlash from the failure of the shopping app, Jack?"

"No, I seem to have weathered that particular storm. I think the introduction of the new loyalty card has placated most people."

"*Loyalty card?*"

"Don't you know about it? My apologies. I felt sure I'd already given you one."

"No, it's the first I've heard of it. To be honest, I don't usually go in for loyalty cards. If I accepted every time one was offered to me, my purse would be bursting at the seams with them."

"Yes, but do the others offer custard creams as rewards?"

"That's a good point—they don't. Maybe I will take one."

"Excellent. Just wait there." He walked to the other end of the counter and returned clutching a yellow plastic card with the letters TCS printed in red on the front. "There you are, Jill."

"Will I need to activate it?"

"No, it's ready to go. Your purchases today will count towards your points score."

"How can I check how many points I have?"

"Just go to my website—the URL is printed on the back. Enter your card number and it will show your points balance."

"Excellent, thanks."

Since I discovered I was a witch, I've had to do a lot of strange stuff, but collecting a trophy for my tortoise's poetry was certainly right up there. I still thought Jack should have been the one to collect it, but my last-minute appeals for him to go in my place had fallen on deaf ears.

Before I magicked myself down to London, I had to turn myself into a man. Until that moment, I hadn't really given any thought who to base the 'doppelganger' spell on, so for ease, I made myself look like Jack.

The awards ceremony was run by a single publishing house, so it was unlikely that there would be more than a handful of people there. My plan was to grab the trophy, say thanks, and then wing it back home.

What is it they say about the best laid plans?

Alarm bells should have gone off when I saw that the presentation ceremony was being held at a small theatre rather than at the publishers' offices. But they didn't, so when I arrived, I was stunned to see the size of the audience; there must have been at least five hundred people in the theatre.

As if that wasn't bad enough, I discovered that the award ceremony wasn't just for poetry. The publishing company covered the whole gamut of genres, and there was a separate award for each one of them. That explained why there were so many people in attendance.

"Excuse me." I beckoned to one of the people wearing a name badge. "Do you work for the publisher?"

"I do. How can I help?"

"I was just wondering how long the presentation ceremony is likely to last. I only ask because I have to make the last train home."

"No more than three hours I wouldn't have thought."

"*Three* hours?"

"Most people are going to stay overnight. We've laid on drinks at a nearby hotel afterwards."

"Unfortunately, I won't be able to stay for that. Do you know when the poetry award will take place?"

"They're being presented in alphabetical order, so it's going to be towards the end, I'm afraid."

"Right, thanks." That was just dandy. So much for my hopes of making a quick exit.

I had no choice but to take a seat in the audience and wait until it was time for the poetry award to be presented.

Two hours later, and I'd practically lost the will to live. Who knew there were so many different genres? And why did all of the winners feel the need to thank everyone, from their editor through to their third cousin, twice removed? I could barely keep my eyes open. If this went on for much longer there was a danger I'd fall—

"Excuse me!" The man I'd spoken to earlier nudged me awake. "You won the poetry award, didn't you?"

"Yes, why?"

"They're calling your name." He gestured towards the stage.

"Is Mr Robert Hymes with us tonight?" The woman with the microphone was looking around the audience.

"That's me!" I stood up and made my way on stage.

"I was beginning to think you hadn't made it tonight,

Robert." She handed me the tiny trophy. "Congratulations. Would you like to say a few words?"

"Err — okay. Thank you very much for this award."

Having delivered the shortest speech of the night, I made my way back to my seat. There were just three more awards to get through, and then I'd be able to escape.

Fifteen minutes later, and the torture had finally ended. Clutching the trophy, I started for the exit.

"Jack! Over here, Jack!"

I froze as I heard the familiar voice of Britt.

"Oh? Hi, Britt."

"You're a dark horse." Kit came to join us.

"I — err —"

"All this time you pretended the author was a friend of yours." Britt grinned. "Why did you decide to publish under a pen name, Jack?"

"No, you've got it all wrong. I'm collecting this for Robert Hymes."

"Of course." Kit winked at me. "We understand, don't we, Britt?"

"Absolutely. Your secret is safe with us."

Oh bum! "Anyway, I'd better get going."

"You can't leave yet. The publisher has organised a small party at the hotel two doors down."

"But I'll miss my train."

"Don't worry about that, old man." Kit slapped me on the shoulder. "We've got the car. You can come back with us. And don't worry, I'll only be drinking cola."

"Right. Great."

The drinks party went on for another two hours during

which time, Britt grilled me, AKA Jack, AKA Robert Hymes, about my/his poetry. She'd actually gone to the trouble of purchasing a copy of Robert Hymes' book, so she was able to discuss each individual poem in turn.

And the purgatory didn't end there because her interrogation continued on the drive back. By the time we arrived home, I would gladly have taken that book and shoved it—well, you get the picture, I'm sure.

Chapter 13

It was Saturday morning, and Jack wasn't very happy because, just before seven o'clock, he'd received a text telling him he was needed in work.

"There's no orange juice." He slammed the fridge door closed.

"There's a new bottle at the back of the fridge."

"Why did you hide it there?"

"I didn't hide it, and there's no need to get ratty with me just because you have to go into work."

"Sorry, it's just that I was looking forward to us having a lazy day together." He poured himself a glass of juice. "What time did you get in last night? I didn't hear you."

"It was gone midnight."

"How come? I thought you planned to get in and out of the ceremony as quickly as you could."

"I did, but it turned out that there were a million different awards, and poetry was one of the last ones to be given out."

"Were there many people there?"

"More than I expected."

"Where is Rhymes' trophy?"

"It's only a tiny little thing. It's still in my bag in the bedroom."

"I'll have a look at it when I go up to get changed. The little guy will be thrilled."

"He'd better be."

"When are you going to take it to him?"

"It's Witchgiving today. I may as well take it then."

"You get to go to all the cool parties."

"Are you kidding? If it's only half as bad as Aunt Lucy

described it, then it's going to be truly awful. Just having to spend a few hours in Grandma's company is bad enough."

Jack had gone upstairs to change when there was a knock at the door.

It was a banana. A giant one with legs, arms and a face. But that wasn't the weirdest part. On top of its head was a tiny Grandma.

"Why do you have Grandma on your head?"

"So that's where I put her." The banana grabbed Grandma. "I've been looking everywhere for her."

"Don't eat her!" I screamed.

"Jill? Who are you shouting at?" Jack came to see what was going on.

"Err, nothing."

The giant banana and mini-Grandma had disappeared.

"You were talking to someone." He looked out of the door. "Who was it?"

"No-one. Something weird is going on, though. My dreams keep coming to life."

"You've probably just been overdoing it. You should take a few days off work."

"I can't. I have cases I need to work on."

"Come and sit down. Let me make you a cup of sweet tea."

"I don't need a cup of tea," I snapped.

"Now who's being ratty?"

"Sorry, you're right. Come here and give me a kiss."

He didn't need asking twice. "Is that better?"

"Much. Did you take a look at the trophy?"

"Yeah. You weren't kidding when you said it was tiny."

He reached into his pocket and held out a green stone. "And what's this?"

"Where did you find that?" I took it from him.

"It was in your bag. Have you started collecting rocks? What kind of rock is it?"

"I have no idea," I lied, and then I quickly changed the subject. "Did you know that Little Jack has introduced a loyalty card?"

"No, I haven't been in the Corner Shop for a few days. Did you sign us up?"

"You bet I did. Just think of all the free custard creams we can earn."

"How many points do you get per pound spent?"

"I don't know; Jack didn't say. I'll have a look to see what I got for yesterday's shop." I grabbed the laptop, typed the URL for Little Jack's website, and then entered my card number. "Wow! I've got ten thousand points."

"How much is that worth?"

"Hang on, let me check." I scrolled through the on-screen info. "Ten pounds."

"How much did you spend yesterday?"

"About ten pounds."

"That can't be right. You can't possibly have earned ten pounds when you only spent that amount."

"Maybe it's some kind of promotion for new sign-ups to the loyalty card?"

"It could be, but after the shopping app fiasco, my money would be on it being an error."

"I'd better get down there quick to spend the points before he realises."

"You can't do that, Jill. It would be taking advantage of Little Jack."

"I was only joking. Sheesh!"

I waited until Jack had left, and then took out the green stone to have a closer look. How had it ended up in my bag? I intended to find out.

***

I magicked myself over to Candlefield, only to discover that the shop I planned on visiting was closed, even though the sign in the window said it should have opened twenty minutes earlier.

Fortunately, the coffee shop next door, Bean A While, was open for business.

"Morning." The female vampire behind the counter greeted me with a smile full of fangs.

"Good morning."

"What can I get for you?"

"I fancy a cappuccino."

"Small, medium or large?"

"Just a small one, please. You don't happen to know if the shop next door is open today, do you? I tried the door, but it's locked."

"Edward is never on time. He usually gets here by ten."

"Right. In that case, make it a medium cup, and I'll have some toast too, please."

"Coming up. I hope you don't mind me asking, but are you Jill Maxwell?"

"I am, yes."

"I thought I recognised you. I'm Poppy. My flatmate has your poster on the back of the door in his bedroom."

"Really?"

135

"Yeah, he throws darts at it."

"Oh?"

"It's nothing personal. It's just that he had a bet on you to win the Elite Competition, so when you bailed because of that dragon, he wasn't very chuffed."

"Right, I see."

"By the way, I apologise for the fangs." She tapped one of them. "I wouldn't normally have them extended like this; it isn't very polite. It's all down to that new toothpaste. You've probably heard about it?"

"No, I can't say I have."

"It's called Fangbrite, and it's supposed to make your teeth and fangs whiter than white, and to be fair it does. The problem is that it also stops the fangs receding. I didn't know that until I'd used it. It'll be a couple of days before these things start to behave. I hope you didn't think I was being aggressive?"

"No, of course not."

I'd just finished my toast when I spotted the arrival of the owner of the shop next door.

"Thanks, Poppy."

"Call again any time. Hopefully, next time, you won't have to put up with these." She treated me to a final look at her impressive fangs.

Next door, the shop was now open, but there was no sign of life inside.

"Hello? Anyone home?"

"Hold on! I'll be with you in a minute." The man's voice came from behind the door at the rear of the shop.

Moments later, Edward Hedgelog appeared. As soon as he saw me, he froze, and the look of horror on his face confirmed my suspicions.

"Hello again, Edward. Remember me?"

"Jill? This is a pleasant surprise."

"Is it? Is it, though? *Really*?"

"I don't know what you mean?"

"Seriously? Is that the way you want to play this?"

He slumped into the metal framed chair, took a deep breath, and said, "I'm sorry. I didn't know what else to do."

I took out the dream-stone. "What I don't understand is how you got this into my bag."

"Do you remember the other day when you came out of your office and bumped into—"

"The clown! That was *you*!"

"I was sure you'd recognise me. I couldn't believe my luck when I got away with it."

"You must have realised I'd find the stone sooner or later?"

"I didn't expect you to realise what it was."

"I might not have done if it hadn't been for the freaky dream stuff."

"What *stuff*? What's happened?"

"Since you planted the stone in my bag, my dreams have come to life on three separate occasions."

"I'm so sorry. I should have realised that might happen."

"Why did you do it Edward?"

"I've never wanted the stone. I wish I'd never found the thing. It's caused me nothing but problems."

"But why give it to me?"

"I'd come to the end of my tether. I only had three people in the shop all last week, and none of them were interested in getting their bikes repaired. They just wanted me to help with their dreams."

"How did they even know about you?"

"I don't know. It's not like I broadcast the fact that I have the dream-stone. Word just seems to get around, and once they know my name, I'm not that difficult to track down."

"Why don't you just take the stone back to CASS? That's where it came from in the first place."

"Don't you think I've tried? Three times I've returned it, and each time it's found its way back to me."

"How?"

"I have no idea. I half-expected it to do the same thing when I put it in your bag, but it didn't. That has to be significant."

"I'm sorry, Edward, but I don't want it." I held out the stone.

"Will you return it to CASS for me, Jill? It might stay there if you take it back."

"I'm not sure about—"

"Please! I'm at my wits' end."

"Okay, but if it still finds its way back to you after that, you're on your own."

"Thanks. I can't tell you how much I appreciate you doing this."

I couldn't help but feel a little sorry for Edward Hedgelog. The only thing he'd ever wanted to do with his life was to repair bikes. And yet, a chance discovery when he'd been a pupil at CASS had changed his life forever.

Jack finding the dream-stone had come as something of a relief because it explained all the weird dreams that had seemingly come to life. Until then, I was beginning to worry that I was going crazy.

***

After a leisurely walk to Aunt Lucy's house, I took a deep breath, and tried to prepare myself for the day ahead. Surely Witchgiving couldn't be as bad as she'd made it out to be.

Could it?

"You're early, Jill." Aunt Lucy was in the lounge.

"I was in Candlefield, so I thought I might as well come over now. Is that okay? I can come back later if you're in the middle of preparations."

"No, it's fine."

"You look tired."

"I am. I had a broken night's sleep, thanks to Lester."

"He's not ill, is he?"

"No, he's not poorly. The silly man decided to go walkabout at two o'clock this morning."

"Couldn't he sleep?"

"Oh, he was asleep. Fast asleep. He was sleepwalking."

"I didn't realise he did that."

"He doesn't. At least, he never has before. I woke up and realised he'd gone, and by the time I found him, he was out of the house and headed for the gate. Goodness knows where he might have ended up if I hadn't caught up with him."

"Is he alright?"

"He's fine. Once he was back in bed, he went straight off to sleep, but I was wide awake for a couple of hours."

Just then, Lester walked into the room. "My ears are burning."

134

"So they should be," Aunt Lucy said. "I can barely keep my eyes open."

"It's hardly my fault, Lucy. It's not like I chose to sleepwalk. Tell her, Jill."

"I'm keeping out of this."

The twins arrived ten minutes later.

"Aren't Alan, William and the little ones coming?" I said.

"Think about it, Jill." Amber rolled her eyes at me. "What's today called?"

"Witchgiving—oh, right. I guess it's not of much interest to werewolves or vampires."

"You could still have brought the little ones." Aunt Lucy looked disappointed.

"Today is already going to be hard enough without the kids to worry about," Pearl said. "And besides, looking after Lily will take Alan's mind off his teeth."

"Does he have toothache?" I said.

"No. His fangs are stuck."

"Fangbrite?"

"How did you know?"

"Just a wild guess."

"What time is Grandma coming?" Pearl checked her watch.

"She should be here any minute." Aunt Lucy looked out of the window. "She went to collect our outfits."

"Do we have to wear those stupid green costumes?" Amber sighed. "They're awful, and they make me itch."

"You could always try telling your grandmother that you don't want to wear them," Aunt Lucy said.

Like that was ever going to happen.

I suddenly remembered something. "Hey guys, I have to take Rhymes his trophy. Don't start without me, will you?"

"Jill!" Rhymes came rushing over to greet me. Relatively speaking, that is.

"Hi, Rhymes."

"Have you got it?"

"Got what?" I acted dumb.

What do you mean, that wouldn't be difficult?

His little face fell. "I thought you'd brought my trophy."

"I'm just messing with you. It's right here." I took it out of the bag and handed it to him.

What had seemed like a small trophy to me, looked enormous when he held it, and for a moment, I thought he was going to drop it.

"This is fantastic. Just wait until Barry sees it. He's going to be so jealous."

"Where is Barry?"

"He's gone to stay at Dolly's for the day. Tell me all about the presentation ceremony. I want to know everything that happened."

And I told him, but I left out the part where I'd fallen asleep through boredom. When I'd finished, Rhymes put the trophy down, and took a couple of steps back so he could better admire it.

"You know, Jill, I had been thinking of giving up on the poetry, but this has given me the inspiration to carry on."

"That's — err — great."

"And as a thank you for everything you've done for me, I shall dedicate my next collection to you."

"That's very kind, but it isn't necessary."

141

"It's the least I can do because I truly think of you as my muse."

Chapter 14

By the time I got back downstairs, Grandma had arrived. Everyone was in the dining room, and they'd already changed into the green witch's outfits.

"What do you look like?" The words were out of my mouth before I could stop myself.

"It's good of you to join us, Jill." Grandma fixed me with an icy gaze. "Better late than never."

"I was here before you, but I had to deliver a trophy to the tortoise."

"Priorities, Jill. Priorities! Witchgiving is one of the most important dates in the witch community calendar, and it would be nice if you could show it some respect."

"I'm sorry. Can I ask, why *green* costumes?"

"Because it's Witchgiving of course."

"Yes, but—never mind. I guess you don't have a spare costume for me. What a pity."

"Of course I do. I wasn't sure of your size, so I brought you a choice of two. They're on Lucy's bed. Hurry up and get changed because we're about to start."

"Okay."

As I made my way out of the room, the twins were both grinning inanely. Whatever could be amusing them?

It didn't take me long to find out.

The first of the green outfits was at least three sizes too big for me. The second was a perfect fit except for the length; it was practically a mini skirt. I was seriously considering refusing to wear either of them, but then I thought about what Grandma would do to me and decided to make do with the mini skirt.

"Nice knees!" Amber giggled.

143

"Shut it, you!"

"Hurry up and sit down, Jill." Grandma tapped the chair next to her. "You've kept us waiting quite long enough already."

"Sorry. By the way, Grandma, I've solved the mystery of my dreams."

"Do I look like I care?"

"It was a dream-stone."

"Fascinating. Now, onto more important matters. As I'm sure you all know, Witchgiving is a tradition that goes back centuries. On this day, witches all over Candlefield meet as a family to enjoy traditional food, and to discuss potions and spells. Last night, while you lot were no doubt tucked up in bed, I was preparing today's meal."

I raised my hand. "Actually, Grandma, I had a big breakfast, and I'm not very hungry."

"I expect all of you to try each of the dishes. It's the least you can do, given the amount of time I've spent on them. Lucy, would you bring the first course through?"

With none of her usual enthusiasm, Aunt Lucy headed for the kitchen.

"I'll give you a hand." I was on my feet and out of the door before Grandma could object.

"Have you seen the length of this skirt?" I said, once we were in the kitchen.

"You have nice legs, Jill."

"It barely covers my bum. I'm sure she did it on purpose."

"A few hours and it'll all be over."

"What's the first course?"

"Soup." She lifted a huge pan off the hob.

"It's the same colour as these costumes. What's in it?

Peas?"

"Yes. Peas, thistles, toads and rhubarb."

"*Toads?*"

"Just joking." She laughed. "Sorry."

"What does it taste like?"

"Better than it looks, thank goodness." She poured the soup into four bowls, and we each carried two through to the dining room.

"Mmm, yummy!" Grandma was soon slurping it down with gusto.

The rest of us, not so much.

Aunt Lucy was at least making an effort, but the twins were basically just stirring the soup with their spoons. I felt I owed it to Grandma to at least taste it.

Yuk, and double yuk!

"What do you think?" Grandma looked at me, expectantly.

"It's — err — really — err — different."

"Maybe a touch more rhubarb next time? What do you think, Lucy?"

"It's as lovely as it always is, Mother."

"Have you two actually drunk any of it yet?" Grandma glared at the twins. "Even Jill has given it a try."

"Yes, come on, you two." I grinned. "Give it a go."

The twins looked as though they both wanted to strangle me, but I didn't care. That would teach them to mock my knees.

"Right!" Grandma lifted the bowl to her lips to finish the last of her soup. "It's time for the main course, I think." She looked over at the twins who still had full bowls. "You two can clear this lot away while your mother brings in the stew."

Stew? Oh no, it couldn't be, could it?

"It's okay, girls, I'll take these." Before the twins could argue, I'd grabbed the bowls, put them on a tray, and hightailed it through to the kitchen where Aunt Lucy was just taking the pan of stew off the hob.

"What's in that?" I took one look at the brown, lumpy mush, and thought I was going to throw up.

"No one knows. It's Grandma's secret recipe."

"Have you eaten it before?"

"I'm afraid so."

"It can't possibly taste as bad as it looks, can it?"

"It's quite nice, actually."

"Really?"

"No, it's absolutely vile. Just try to eat a couple of mouthfuls. That's all I ever manage."

"Are there any crunchy bits in it?"

"A few, yes."

"Do you know what they are?"

"I've never dared to ask."

Gulp! Surely Grandma had been joking about the toe-nail clippings, hadn't she?

Joking or not, I wasn't taking any chances.

Just as she had with the soup, Grandma eagerly tucked into the main course. Under pressure from her, the twins managed a few mouthfuls, and then turned a shade of green not unlike the colour of their costumes.

"What's Barry doing out there?" I pointed to the window. "I thought he was at Dolly's?"

While everyone followed my gaze, I tipped the mush into the large plant pot behind my chair.

"That's not Barry." Aunt Lucy gave me a puzzled look.

"It's a greyhound."

"Is it? Oh yes. My mistake."

The twins had both spotted my empty bowl and were glaring at me. I wouldn't have put it past them to grass me up, so I got in first. "That was delicious, Grandma."

"It's my own super-secret recipe."

"So I understand."

"Why don't you have seconds, Jill?" Pearl said.

"Yeah." Amber nodded. "I bet there's plenty left."

"I'm very tempted, but I'm too full. You two don't seem to have eaten much yet, though. Come on, girls. Think of all the work Grandma has put into this."

Thankfully, dessert was ice cream, which despite its weird colour (black), was actually very tasty.

After we'd finished, I volunteered to help Aunt Lucy with the washing up.

"What happens next?" I said.

"Prepare yourself to be bored out of your mind for the next three or four hours. We have to spend the whole time discussing spells and potions. It's tedious beyond belief."

Just then, Amber and Pearl came to join us.

"How did you two manage to escape?" Aunt Lucy said.

"Grandma fell asleep, so we sneaked out."

"Maybe if we all stay in here, she'll sleep all afternoon," I said.

"We can always hope." Aunt Lucy grinned.

"By the way, Mum," Pearl said. "That plant of yours is looking rather ill."

"Yeah." Amber gave me a knowing look. "It's almost as though something has poisoned it."

"What's going on in here?" Grandma made her usual

147

quiet entrance. "Come on, you lot, I have a surprise for you."

The four of us exchanged a look, in the certain knowledge that whatever the *surprise* was, it wouldn't be anything good.

As we made our way back into the dining room, I collared the twins. "Why did you have to lie about the plant dying? You were just trying to get me in trouble."

"We weren't lying. See for yourself."

Oh bum! The plant, which an hour ago had looked strong and healthy, was now all brown and withered. Thank goodness I hadn't eaten that stuff.

Grandma waited until we were all seated before saying, "For reasons I'll never understand, it seems that not everyone shares my love for this part of Witchgiving. What better way to spend a few hours than with an in-depth discussion of potions and spells?"

I considered telling her that I'd prefer to have my eyes poked out with a red-hot poker, but then thought better of it.

She continued, "So, in order to keep your interest, I thought we ought to liven things up a little."

"This I have to see," Aunt Lucy said under her breath.

"Pardon, Lucy?"

"Nothing, Mother. I was just clearing my throat."

"Hmm. As I was saying, in order to make things more interesting for those of you with the attention span of a gnat, I've decided to combine our discussion with the game of charades."

"Did you just say *charades*?" Aunt Lucy looked gobsmacked.

"Yes. Whoever is *it* will act out the name of a popular

potion or spell, and once the others have guessed it correctly, we can move onto the discussion. What do you think?"

The stony silence spoke volumes.

Undeterred by the less than effusive response, Grandma kicked off the game.

I feel it would be an act of unnecessary cruelty to describe in detail proceedings from then on. Suffice to say, it took the best part of an hour for the three of us to come up with the correct answer to the first potion. But then, Crabby's Grey Brew would surely have tested the most seasoned charades player.

"At last." Grandma sighed. "So now to the interesting part where we get to discuss this particular potion. As I'm sure you are all already aware, Crabby's Grey Brew is—"

Her riveting monologue was interrupted by the sound of my phone ringing.

I glanced at caller display and could see it was Desdemona Nightowl. "Sorry, I have to take this—it could be urgent. Hello, Headmistress."

"Jill, I'm sorry to call you on Witchgiving. I hope I'm not interrupting anything."

"No, that's okay."

"A few of the children became quite upset overnight because of this Old Mother Mason thing. I know you have some experience of ghosts, so I wondered if I might persuade you to come over sometime to see if you can get to the bottom of it."

"I'd be happy to."

"Thank you. Any time next week will be fine."

"Right now? I suppose I could if it's really urgent."

149

"No, honestly, any time will—"

"Okay then. I'll be straight over." I ended the call.

All eyes were on me now; none more so than Grandma's.

"I'm really sorry." I held up my arms. "There's an emergency at CASS and I have to go straight over there."

"What kind of emergency?" Grandma demanded.

"Yeah, Jill," Amber chipped in. "What kind of emergency is it?"

"Err, two children have gone missing." I stood up. "But don't let me spoil the rest of your day." I turned to Amber. "Weren't you going to tell everyone about Crabby's Grey Brew?"

Snigger.

***

"You really didn't need to come straight over here." Ms Nightowl still had the phone in her hand.

"I really did, trust me."

"Are you sure you have the time to spare?"

"Absolutely, you've actually done me a huge favour."

"Green suits you, Jill."

Oh bum! I was still wearing the awful green mini skirt.

"Just hold on a second, Headmistress." I quickly magicked myself back to Aunt Lucy's bedroom, got changed, and magicked myself back to CASS. "That's better. Now, what was it you were saying about this ghost?"

"There have been rumours for some time now that Old Mother Mason has returned. To be honest, I dismissed those rumours at first. Children have been known to imagine things before, but this time, two members of staff have also confirmed seeing the ghost."

"Why would she return after all this time?"

"That's what I'm hoping you'll be able to find out. Although several people have now seen the ghost, none of us are able to communicate with her. I believe that's something you can do. And, am I right in thinking that you're also able to travel to—err—what's it called? Grande Tramagne, is that it?"

"Yes, but no one calls it that. Everyone calls it Ghost Town or G.T. for short. And, yes, I am able to go there. I'll be glad to help. How do you suggest we proceed?"

"Could you come over one day after the children have retired for the night? The ghost seems to haunt the corridors outside the dormitories."

"Okay, but I do have quite a lot of work on at the moment. Would it be alright if I gave you a call during the week to arrange something?"

"Of course. That would be most helpful. Anyway, I mustn't keep you any longer. You'll want to get back to your Witchgiving celebrations."

"What? Yes, of course. I'll be in touch in the next few days." I was just about to magic myself away when I remembered something. "Headmistress, while I'm here, can I give you something?" I took the green stone from my pocket.

"Is this what I think it is?"

"A dream-stone? Yes."

"Wherever did you get this?"

"An alumnus of yours had it, but to be honest, it's brought him nothing but trouble. He asked if I'd return it to CASS."

"I don't really know what to do with it."

"I'm sure you'll think of something. Anyway, I'd better get going."

***

Tempted as I was to return to Aunt Lucy's, and another few hours of potions and spells charades, I opted to head straight home.

Or at least, straight to the Corner Shop. I figured I would cash in my loyalty points to buy custard creams, chocolate and ginger beer, which I planned to enjoy while binge watching a TV boxset.

It seemed that I would be in for a long wait because the queue was out of the door.

"What's going on?" I asked the woman in front of me.

"I've no idea. I only came here to redeem my loyalty points."

"Me too." The man in front of her joined the conversation. "So has everyone else, apparently."

"I only spent five pounds," the woman said. "For that, I have five pounds in loyalty points."

"So do I." The man nodded.

I was beginning to think Jack was right. It looked as though Little Jack had yet another PR disaster on his hands. A few moments later, my suspicions were confirmed. Although I couldn't see Little Jack, it appeared he was speaking through some kind of megaphone.

"Ladies and gentlemen. Please accept my sincere apologies for this unfortunate mishap. It appears that the loyalty points earned yesterday were added at one hundred times their actual value. This has now been adjusted accordingly. Once again, my sincere apologies."

"One hundred times too much?" I tried but failed to do the maths. "What does that mean?" I asked the man standing close to me.

"That your ten pounds of loyalty points are now worth only ten pence, love."

Great!

Chapter 15

It was Monday morning, and Jack had just nipped out to the Corner Shop.

Sunday had been a lovely day. We'd done nothing in particular, just chilled out and enjoyed one another's company. It was nice that we'd both been able to put our work to one side, and to focus our attention on one another for a change. It was on days like that that I realised just how much I loved that guy and how much he loved me.

"Where are you Jill?" It sounded like my darling hubby was back. "I'm going to kill you!"

"What have I done now?"

"Guess who I ran into on the way back?"

"It wasn't Don Nutt, was it? Has he been rubbing it in again about beating you at magnetic fishing?"

"No, it wasn't Don. I bumped into Britt and Kit."

"What did they say to get you so riled up?"

"As if you don't know."

"I don't have a—oh wait, was it about the presentation?"

"Why did you make yourself look like me when you collected the trophy?"

"You should be flattered."

"Well, I'm not. They think I'm Robert Hymes now."

"It never occurred to me that Britt and Kit would be at the presentation."

"Why didn't you tell me that you'd bumped into them?"

"It totally slipped my mind. Anyway, it's done now."

"Not for Britt it isn't. She wants 'Robert' to do a reading at the poetry society she's just joined."

I laughed, but immediately regretted it. "Sorry."

"You will be sorry because you're the one who's going to give the reading."

"But they're expecting you?"

"So? You'll just have to do what you did at the presentation. You'll have to make yourself look like me again."

"But, Jack—"

"Britt is going to let me know where and when the reading will be held."

Oh bum!

What did I say about loving that guy? Scrub that. He was so mean.

I was on my way out of the house when my phone rang.

"Kathy?"

"Jill, are you busy?"

"I was just setting off for work."

"Could you pop over on your way in?"

"You aren't on my way into work."

"I know, but it'll only take a minute."

"I've heard that before."

"It's not for me, it's for Mikey."

"Is he okay?"

"Yeah, he's fine. Will you call in?"

"Okay, but I won't be able to stay long."

"I'll have a cup of coffee waiting for you."

***

155

"Thanks for coming over, Jill." Kathy, Mikey and Lizzie all met me at the door.

"Shouldn't you two be at school?"

"It's an insect day." Lizzie beamed.

Huh? "Is the school infested?"

"She means *inset* day," Kathy said. "There seems to be more of them every year."

"Come and see Colin." Mikey grabbed my arm and pulled me into the lounge.

"See who?" That's when I spotted the cage. "Whoa, you have a parrot."

"He's not a parrot, Auntie Jill. He's a canary." Lizzie corrected me.

"When did you get Colin?"

"On Saturday." Kathy rolled her eyes. "It was Pete's idea."

"Come and have a closer look at him." Mikey dragged me over to the cage.

"Do you like him, Auntie Jill?" Lizzie said.

"He's very — err — yellow. Does he do anything?"

"What do you expect him to do?" Kathy gave me a look. "Handstands? Recite poetry?"

That wasn't nearly as far-fetched as she might think.

"Of course not, but he doesn't seem to be doing anything. He's just sitting there. Shouldn't he be flying from perch to perch or chirping or something?"

"Morning, Jill." Peter walked into the room.

"Morning. Aren't you at work today either?"

"I thought I'd take a day off, seeing as how the kids are at home."

"How come everyone is off work today except me?"

"When you and Jack get around to having kids, you'll

be able to take inset days off too," Kathy said.

"I wouldn't hold your breath."

"Come on kids." Peter held up a sports bag. "We want to get to the swimming baths before they get busy."

I gave Lizzie a kiss, but when I tried to kiss Mikey, he pulled away.

"Bye, then. Have a nice swim both of you."

"Don't be offended." Kathy grinned. "Mikey doesn't even like Pete and me to kiss him now. He says he's too big."

"That must be hard for you."

"Not really. I kiss him anyway. I'll go and make that coffee."

She'd no sooner stepped out of the room when—

"Oi, you!" It was the canary.

"Are you talking to me?"

"I don't see anyone else in here, do you?"

"What's up?"

"You may well ask. Where do I even begin? For starters my name is Bob. What self-respecting canary would call himself Colin?"

"Right, but to be fair, they had no way of knowing that."

"I was kidnapped."

"What do you mean, *kidnapped*?"

"I used to live in a cushy apartment. Granted, the people there were all a bit weird, but they sometimes left the cage door and window open, so I could sneak out to visit my lady friends."

"Lady *friends*? How many do you have?"

"Who's counting? It's only fair to share myself around,

don't you think?"

Wow! "So if you had it so good, why didn't you stay there?"

"Come on! Pay attention. Didn't I just say I was kidnapped?"

"By who?"

"I don't know. They didn't give me their business card. They sold me to a shop, and then this crowd of no-hopers bought me."

"That's my relatives you're insulting."

"How can they be relatives of yours? None of them understands a word I'm saying."

"It's complicated."

"Are you going to help me or not?"

"Help you how?"

"Get me back to my apartment, or at the very least, organise it so that I can still visit my lady friends?"

"I'm not sure about that."

"Come on. Please, I'm begging you."

"Okay. I'll see what I can do."

"Jill?" Kathy was standing in the doorway with two cups of coffee in her hands. "Why are you talking to the canary?"

"I'm not."

"I heard you say something about seeing what you could do."

"I—err—I just thought maybe he was a little bored. He looks like he needs a toy."

"I suppose you could be right." She handed me the cup. "I'll give Pete a call later and ask him to drop by the pet shop to see what they have. Maybe that'll cheer Colin up."

I seriously doubted it.

I could still feel the canary's eyes burning into me as Kathy and I drank coffee and chatted.

"Did you hear about the incident at school last Friday, Jill?"

"What incident?"

"I thought Jack might have mentioned it."

"No, but then he doesn't have much to do with Washbridge these days. What happened?"

"One of the other mums, Adriana, was walking to school with her daughter, Sherie, when a horrible monster of a man jumped out in front of them and snatched her handbag."

"Were they hurt?"

"No, thank goodness. She had the good sense not to resist, so he just took the bag and did a runner. Sort of."

"What do you mean, *sort of*?"

"Adriana reckons he was walking weirdly as though he'd hurt his leg."

"What did the police have to say?"

"They're taking it very seriously because a similar thing happened at another school a couple of weeks ago. The woman tried to resist the man, fell and banged her head on a wall. She died later from her injuries. The police have promised to put extra patrols at all schools in the area until he's caught."

***

"Did you have a good weekend, Jill?" Mrs V was busy working on her range of Top Tips gloves.

"Yesterday was nice enough." Saturday and

Witchgiving, not so much.

"I have some very big news."

"Does it involve Top Tips gloves?"

"No, much more exciting than that. Armi and I are looking for a new house."

"Really? What prompted that?"

"We thought it would be nice to live somewhere we'd chosen together."

"Does that mean you'll be moving away from Washbridge?"

"No. We both like it around here, so we're only looking at properties in a fifteen-mile radius. In fact, Armi has come up with a list of houses for us to view this week."

Winky was shooting the breeze with Harold.

"Morning, you two."

"Morning, Jill." Harold gave me a little wave of his wing. "Tell her, Winky."

"Tell me what?"

"It's happened again." Winky jumped down from the windowsill and onto my desk. "Bobby the Brew has gone missing."

"He's a cat, I take it?"

"Yeah. A good friend of mine too. What are you going to do about it?"

"*Me*? I thought you were supposed to be investigating?"

"It's horses for courses. I'm the entrepreneur, and you're the private investigator. Allegedly."

"They've probably just gone walkabout."

"All of them? I don't think so. That's four now that we know about. How many more might have been taken by this evil catnapper? It could be dozens. Hundreds even."

"Look, and I'm not trying to be dismissive or uncaring, but who would want to nick a load of moggies?"

"A load of —" He took a deep breath. "*Moggies*? Did you really just say that?"

"You know what I mean."

"No, I don't. You're going to have to explain it to me."

"Okay, I apologise, but my question still stands, who would want to steal a load of — err — cats?"

"Instead of swanning around in here, that's precisely what you should be trying to find out. Here." He handed me a photograph. "That's Gavin on the left, and that's Bobby, second from the right; it was taken last year."

"I'm sorry, but I don't have the time. I have urgent cases to work on."

"You'd better have time to take me to my quiz. You promised you would."

"I'd forgotten about that. When is it?"

"This afternoon, and I can't afford to miss it."

"I said I would, and I will."

"Make sure you're back in plenty of time. I've not forgotten what happened with the boxing match. We were almost late for that because of your dilly dallying."

"It's a pity for you we weren't. It would have saved you from a good hiding."

"How many more times do I have to tell you? I had it all under control. Another couple of rounds, and I —"

"Would have been in hospital."

"There's no talking to you. Just make sure you're not late this afternoon."

***

Sheila Forrest had arranged for me to visit her son, Laurence, in prison on Tuesday. Before that, though, I wanted to speak to Craig Mann, another one of Alison's friends.

"Come in." He met me at the door to his flat. Unshaven, he looked as though he'd been sleeping in his trousers and t-shirt. "I'm sorry for the mess. I haven't been able to think straight since I heard about—" His words trailed away. "Would you like a drink? I could make coffee?"

"No thanks. I'd rather get straight down to business."

He slumped onto the sofa. "I can't believe she's gone," he said as much to himself as to me.

"I believe you and Alison were close?"

"She was such a lovely person. She didn't deserve this. I hope they lock him up and throw away the key."

"Laurence?"

"Who else? She should have left that loser years ago."

"Did she ever say anything to you to suggest that Laurence was capable of violence?"

"Not as such, no."

"How would you describe your relationship with Alison?"

"We were friends. Close friends."

"Nothing more than that?"

"What do you mean?"

"Were you having an affair with her?"

"No! Alison would never have cheated on him."

"But you had feelings for her?"

"Yes. I loved her." He stood up and walked over to the window. "And she had feelings for me, but she would never have acted upon them because of Adam. She didn't want him to suffer."

"When did you last see her?"

"On the afternoon of the day she —" He turned to face me. "On the day *he* murdered her. I don't know why I'm even talking to you. Why are you trying to help that worthless scumbag?"

"I'm just trying to get to the truth."

"The truth is that he killed her in cold blood, and I hope he rots in hell. I'd like you to leave now, please."

I could have argued, but there seemed to be little point. Two things were clear: Craig had been in love with Alison, and he was convinced that Laurence had murdered her. I had no way of knowing if Alison had felt the same way about Craig. What if she hadn't? What if she'd rebuffed his advances? Might he have reacted badly? Should I be treating him as a potential suspect?

***

My visit to the police station had turned up one vital piece of information. Laurence's alibi: that he'd been in the park when Alison was murdered, had been severely undermined by the testimony of his neighbour, a Mr Arthur Radford. In his statement, Mr Radford had claimed to see Laurence return home an hour earlier than Laurence said he had.

A fussy little man, Arthur Radford lived alone in the flat immediately above the Forrests.

"I don't believe in those teabag things." He was spooning loose tea from the packet into the teapot. "It just doesn't taste the same. Would you care for a biscuit? I have jaffa cakes."

"No thanks. Just the tea will be fine."

"Pardon?"

His hearing aid was either switched off or needed a new battery, so I was forced to shout, "I said just the tea will be fine."

I'm no expert on the finer points of brewing tea, but I was always under the impression that when using loose tea, one should pour it through a strainer. If so, no one had told Mr Radford.

I didn't so much drink the tea as chew it.

"Mr Radford, I believe you told the police that you saw your neighbour come home on the night of the murder?"

"I thought you *were* the police?"

"Like I said on the phone. I'm a private investigator. I work alongside the police."

"You help them, you mean?"

"Yeah, something like that. So, if you could just tell me what you saw."

"I always keep the curtains open of an evening. I like to watch the buses go past. I used to work on them, you see. I was a bus driver for almost forty years. Mind you, I don't like these modern —"

"Your neighbour? Mr Forrest?"

"Oh yes. I'd just seen the eight-fifteen go by. That's how come I knew the time."

"Is it possible you could have got the time mixed up? Could it have been the nine-fifteen you saw?"

"I might be getting on a bit, but I can still tell the time. It was definitely the eight-fifteen. Forrest came home a couple of minutes later."

I was still picking bits of tea leaf from my teeth after I'd left Mr Radford's flat.

"Excuse me, Miss!" An old lady appeared at the door of the adjoining flat.

"Hi."

"I couldn't help but overhear you talking to Arthur."

"Sorry about that. I had to shout."

"He's deaf as a post that one, and too tight-fisted to buy new batteries for that hearing aid of his. You were asking about Laurence, weren't you?"

"Yes, I've been hired by his mother."

"Such a lovely young man. Lovely couple. He would never have done what they say he did."

"That's what I'm hoping to prove, but your neighbour's testimony isn't helping. He says he saw Laurence come home earlier than Laurence claims he did."

"I wouldn't set much store by anything Arthur tells you. He spends most evenings watching soaps on TV. I should know; I can hear every word."

"He says he likes watching the buses."

"Maybe, but not if it interferes with one of his soaps. He watches them all."

"Right, well I'd better be making tracks."

"If you see Laurence give him my best, would you?"

"Will do. Bye."

165

Chapter 16

Why on earth had I done it? Why did I keep agreeing to act as Winky's unpaid chauffeur?

But then, I was quite intrigued by the quiz he was going to take part in. I'd always fancied myself as a bit of a general knowledge buff. Whenever I'd taken part in pub quizzes, people always wanted me on their team.

What do you mean you find that hard to believe? It's true.

Fortunately, the studio where the quiz show was to be recorded was only a few miles outside of Washbridge.

"Are you sure this is it?" I pulled up in the car park of Washbridge Crown Studios.

"Yes, but it's around the back, in the basement. It's okay. I can find my way from here."

"Are you sure?"

"Positive." He jumped through the open window and shot across the car park.

I was about to drive away when curiosity got the better of me. It might be interesting to watch the quiz show being recorded, and it wasn't like I had anything else arranged for the rest of the afternoon.

To make sure I didn't lose sight of Winky, I cast the 'faster' spell to catch up with him.

"Ticket, please?" One of the two cats on the door blocked Winky's way.

"I'm one of the contestants."

"Name?"

"Winky."

The doorcat checked his clipboard. "Okay, in you go."

"How many contestants is that?" the second doorcat asked his colleague.

"We're just missing one: Trixie Lace."

"She'd better look sharp or they'll have to get a volunteer from the audience again."

Trixie Lace, eh? That gave me an idea. I quickly turned myself into a cat, and then sashayed over to the door.

"Ticket, please."

"I'm one of the contestants."

"Name?"

"Trixie Lace."

"You've only just made it. Hurry up."

"Thank you."

Once inside, I was ushered to the green room where all the other contestants were gathered. I wasn't too surprised to find Winky trying to chat up a pretty little Persian cat, but she seemed distinctly unimpressed.

"Everyone! Can I have silence, please?" A bored-looking cat holding a clipboard had appeared at the door. "We'll be recording all four heats and the final today. Your names will be called at random to take part in one of the four heats." He read from the list in his hand. "The contestants for the first heat are: Lucky, Winky, Scoots and Trixie Lace. Will the four of you please follow me through to the studio? The rest of you will be able to watch the recording on these monitors. Help yourselves to refreshments, and please try to keep the noise to a minimum."

In the studio, the feline audience greeted us with polite applause. I had hoped that I'd be seated away from Winky, but we ended up next to one another.

"Hello, gorgeous," he whispered. "What's your name?"

167

"Trixie Lace."

"What are you doing afterwards?"

"Meeting my boyfriend."

"Oh."

Thankfully, that was enough for him to lose all interest in me.

A few minutes later, the quiz was under way. I was looking forward to beating Winky, and to seeing the shock on his face when we got back to the office, and I revealed that I was the victorious Trixie Lace.

Things didn't exactly work out the way I'd envisaged them, though.

How was I supposed to know that the questions would all be based upon the feline world?

"Who discovered America?" the quizmaster asked.

I hit the buzzer.

"Yes, Trixie Lace?"

"Most people think it was Columbus, but there's a school of thought that it may in fact have been Eriksson." That answer should definitely have been worth double points in my opinion.

"Incorrect. Anyone else?"

I was about to object when Winky buzzed.

"Yes, Winky?"

"America was discovered by Eddie the Explorer."

"Correct. Eddie was of course aboard the Santa Maria. If you look on your screens, you'll see a painting of the intrepid explorer."

This was ridiculous. Eddie didn't discover America. He was just a cat who had stowed away aboard Columbus' ship.

And things went downhill from there.

Who invented the printing press? Gutenberg, I hear you say. But no. Apparently the genius behind that was in fact Peter the Print.

Who developed the theory of relativity? You may well think it was Einstein, but in fact that particular honour goes to Philip the Physics.

Who knew?

Not me, that's who.

When the final buzzer sounded, Winky was way ahead on one-hundred and twenty points. Meanwhile, I was on minus twenty-five.

"Bad luck, Trixie Lace," Winky said as we made our way back to the green room. "There were some tough questions today."

"Well done on getting through to the final," I managed to say through gritted teeth.

"Will you stay to watch me?"

"I'd love to, but I have —err—stuff to do."

***

I was still grumbling to myself when I arrived home. What kind of quiz contest only asked questions related to felines?

Yes, yes, I do realise the answer to that question is a quiz for cats, but that doesn't make it any less ridiculous.

I'd no sooner stepped out of the car than Britt came hurrying over to see me.

"Jill, do you have a minute?"

"Actually, I—err—"

169

"I won't take up much of your time, I promise."

"Sure. Have you found Lovely yet?"

"No. Kit says she'll turn up soon, but I'm beginning to fear the worst."

I considered telling her about Winky's two friends who had also disappeared, but I figured that would only make her worry even more. "I'm sure Kit's right. She'll be back soon."

"I do hope so. Anyway, I wanted to talk to you about Jack's poetry recital. Or should I say, *Robert*?" She winked at me. "Jack has probably told you that he's agreed to do a reading for my poetry society."

"He did mention something about it."

"Well, the thing is, the guest who was scheduled to attend this month's meeting has cried off at the last minute. Something about a verruca, I believe. That leaves us without a guest reader for the meeting on Thursday evening."

"This Thursday?"

"Yes, I was just wondering if Jack might be able to step into the breach, so to speak. I realise it's very short notice, but it would be doing us a massive favour."

For once the fates had looked kindly on me. This had given me a golden opportunity to get out of the stupid poetry reading.

"I'm sure he would have loved to help you out, but I happen to know he has a longstanding engagement on Thursday night. A police federation thing, I believe."

"Oh well, it can't be helped. It's a little disappointing because the next meeting won't be for another three months."

"He'll be gutted, I'm sure."

My short chat with Britt had certainly lifted my mood. Three months from now, she would most likely have grown bored with the whole poetry thing, which would mean I was off the hook.

Result!

I was so pleased about the cancellation of the poetry reading that I decided to make dinner, even though, strictly speaking, it wasn't my turn.

"I'm home." Jack breezed into the kitchen looking very pleased with himself. "That smells good, but isn't it my day to make dinner?"

"It should be, but I thought it would be nice to give you a little surprise."

"Thank you, darling." He gave me a peck on the cheek. "You're so good to me."

"That's true, and if you play your cards right, I'll have an even nicer surprise for you later this evening."

His face lit up. "That sounds like fun."

"It will be, trust me."

"This is delicious." He nodded his approval. "You've surpassed yourself today."

"Thank you."

"By the way, I bumped into Britt on the way in. She seemed a little down in the dumps."

"She's worried about Lovely."

"That's true, but it wasn't only that. She was disappointed that I wouldn't be able to attend their poetry society meeting on Thursday."

"Yeah, about that. I—err—"

"She seemed to be under the impression that I had to attend a police federation thing."

"I might have—err—"

"Anyway, I told her that I didn't have anything on this Thursday, and that I'd be happy to do the reading."

"You did *what*?"

"I told her that you must have made a mistake." He was grinning from ear to ear. "That is what happened, isn't it, Jill?"

"I'd talked my way out of doing that stupid reading, but now, thanks to you, it's back on again. What were you thinking?"

"That this is all of your own making. You shouldn't have used my identity when you collected the trophy."

"What if I call your bluff and refuse to do the reading? You'll have to do it then."

"No, I won't. Rhymes is your tortoise, so this is your responsibility." Jack put his knife and fork on the empty plate. "That was delicious. I can't wait until later for my other surprise."

"Dream on, buddy. You've got no chance."

***

Later that evening, Jack and I were in the lounge. I still hadn't completely forgiven him for the poetry reading incident, but we had at least called a truce.

He cuddled closer to me on the sofa. "Now that we're friends again, how about that little surprise you promised me?"

"You don't deserve it."

"Come on. You know you want to."

He was right, and I could feel my resistance melting. "Okay, but—" Just then, there was a knock at the door. "Who's that?"

"I'll go and see." Jack was up on his feet.

"If it's one of the neighbours, get rid of them. Don't invite them in whatever you do."

Moments later, he called from the hallway, "Jill, it's Mrs V and Armi."

Mrs V? She'd never called at our house before. It must be something urgent, so I hurried out into the hall.

"Mrs V? Is something wrong?"

"Of course not, dear. I hope you don't mind us dropping by like this, but we've just viewed a house a couple of miles from here. I suggested to Armi that we pop in so he could see his cuckoo clock. He's dying to see it on your wall."

Jack glanced at me and mouthed the words, "*Cuckoo clock?*"

Ignoring him, I did the only thing I could.

Lie, big time.

"That's such a shame. Any other time, and it would have been fine. It's just that we—err—we have the carpet fitter in the lounge at the moment."

I daren't look at Jack; I could only imagine what he was thinking.

"I didn't see their van," Mrs V said. That woman was way too observant.

"No, that's because—err—his partner dropped him and the carpet off, and then went to do another job. He'll be picking him up later."

173

"I can't hear anything in there." Mrs V leaned closer to the lounge door.

"That's one of their selling points, isn't it, Jack? In fact, they call themselves Silent Carpets."

"Never mind," Armi said. "I told you we should have called ahead, Annabel."

"Maybe we could come back another day?" Mrs V suggested.

"Err, yeah. No problem."

"Would you like a drink while you're here?" Jack said.

"No, thanks. We should be getting back. It's almost our bedtime, isn't it, Armi?"

"Yes, dear, but thanks for the offer."

After seeing them out, Jack turned his gaze on me.

"What?" I shrugged.

"What did you do with it?"

"With *what*?"

"You know what. The cuckoo clock that Armi made specially for you?"

"I—err, you know, I honestly can't remember."

"Jill!"

"Okay. It's in the spare bedroom."

"What's it doing in there?"

"Have you ever spent any time in the same room as a cuckoo clock?"

"No, but I've always liked them."

"That's only because you've never had to put up with one cuckooing all day. I have, and it's enough to drive you insane."

"Why did you accept it in the first place, then?"

"I didn't like to hurt Armi's feelings by turning it

down."

"You do realise that we're going to have to put it up in the lounge before they come back."

"I know."

"And what was all that rubbish about carpet fitters?"

"It was the best I could come up with."

"Why didn't you use magic?"

"Silly me. Why didn't I think of that? I could have used the *move the cuckoo clock out of the spare bedroom and mount it in the lounge* spell. Anyway, they believed me, didn't they? So it's all good."

"Not really."

"What do you mean?"

"The carpet in the lounge has seen better days. When Mrs V and Armi come back, they're going to realise you were lying about the carpet fitters."

"What are you saying?"

"I'm saying we're going to have to get a new carpet fitted before they return."

Oh bum!

Chapter 17

The next morning, over breakfast, Jack seemed somewhat distracted.

"Penny for them?" I nudged him.

"Sorry?"

"You were miles away."

"I was thinking about the lottery."

"That thing? I wouldn't get your hopes up. We've no chance of winning."

"We'll soon know. The winners are going to be announced on the local news any minute now."

"Have you always been such an optimist?"

"It's better than being an eternal pessimist like you."

"At least I'm never disappointed."

"Come and watch with me." He jumped up and headed to the lounge.

"No thanks. It's a waste of time. I'll stay here and finish my coffee."

Less than a minute later, there was an almighty cheer. "Yes! Get in there!"

Just how gullible did he think I was? If he expected me to go charging in there, just so he could say *gotcha*, he had another think coming.

"We won!" He came rushing into the kitchen.

"Sure we did."

"It's true, honestly, we did. Or at least, you did."

"What do you mean, *I did*?"

"I made a note of the ticket numbers, and yours just won first prize."

"Is this some kind of wind-up?"

"No, I swear. You can double-check it on the website."

"What is first prize?"

"No one knows. It's the only prize they haven't announced in advance. It must be something really spectacular."

"When do I get to find out what I've won?"

"Not until you go to collect it from the council offices on Saturday. It sounds like they're going to make a really big deal of it. The local radio and TV are bound to be there. Where is your ticket, anyway?"

That was a good question. In fact, it was a *very* good question.

"It's in my handbag."

"Are you sure?"

"Of course I am."

But it wasn't.

Not in my handbag or in the pockets of any of the clothes I'd worn in the last two weeks. What had I done with it?

"Did you find it?" Jack shouted when I came back downstairs.

"Yeah. Got it."

"Put it somewhere safe. That ticket is very valuable."

"Don't worry, I will." I gave him a quick kiss. "See you tonight."

***

"I'm really sorry about last night, Mrs V."

"That's alright, dear. We should have called ahead instead of just dropping by unannounced like that. How does your new carpet look?"

177

"It's — err — very nice."

"What colour is it?"

"It's — err — green."

"Lovely. I look forward to seeing it when we pop over again. By the way, did you know the winning lottery numbers have been announced?"

"Yeah. I won first prize, apparently."

"You don't look very pleased about it."

"I would be if I hadn't lost the ticket."

"You haven't, have you?"

"It looks that way."

"What did Jack say?"

"He doesn't know yet. I was hoping I might find it, but I've looked everywhere and there's no trace."

"Oh dear."

"Who's your favourite cat?" Winky was looking remarkably pleased with himself.

"Not you."

"Really? In that case, you won't be wanting this." He held up a slip of paper.

"I don't have time for your — wait a minute — is that — ?"

"Your winning lottery ticket? Yes, I believe it is."

"Where did you find it?"

"It was under your desk. Now, tell me again, who's your favourite cat?"

"You are!" I picked him up and gave him a big hug.

"Put me down, woman."

"Sorry." I grabbed the ticket. "Thank you. You've saved my skin."

"My pleasure."

"Is that it? You must want something in return."

"For simply doing the right thing? Of course not. Your happiness is reward enough."

"Aren't you feeling well?"

"I'm feeling great, and very pleased with life. And do you know why?"

"Why?"

He reached under the sofa and produced a trophy. "Guess who won the quiz last night?"

"I'm not surprised. You were the best contestant by far."

"How can you possibly know that?"

That was a very good question. "I—err—I just figured you would be. You're one smart cat."

"That's very true. It was a walk in the park. I won the final by thirty clear points."

"Well done you."

"Thanks. Mind you, the standard of competition was pretty poor. Even worse than I expected it to be."

"Oh?"

"Yeah. One contestant in particular: A proper little cutie called Trixie Lace. She was quite a looker, but honestly, she was as thick as two short planks."

The cheek of the cat. Still, he had found my winning lottery ticket, so I would let him off this once. And besides, I was never going to let on that I'd been Trixie Lace. If I had, I would never have heard the end of it.

***

I'd promised to pay a visit to Cuppy C for the grand opening of the cat café. I couldn't help but think that the twins had rather rushed into this particular endeavour, but fingers-crossed things would go swimmingly.

179

Who was I trying to kid?

"Where are the cats?" I glanced around the tearoom, but there wasn't a single feline to be seen.

"Amber's in the back with them." Pearl looked and sounded harassed.

"How come you're both here today?"

"Mum agreed to have Lil and Lily so we could focus on the big launch, but everything's already gone pear-shaped."

"Why? What's wrong?"

"The milkman hasn't turned up. He would normally have made his delivery a couple of hours ago. We're down to our last couple of pints."

"Where is he?"

"We don't know. Amber is ringing the depot now."

As if on cue, Amber came through from the back, and it was obvious from the look on her face that all was not well. "They don't know where he is."

"What do you mean, *they don't know*?" Pearl said.

"That's what they told me. Apparently, they've found his van, but there's no sign of him."

"Well that's just great! What are they going to do?"

"They're sending a reserve driver over there now to continue with the round. They reckon we should have our delivery in about an hour."

"What are we supposed to do until then?"

"Tell everyone they'll have to take their drinks black?" I suggested.

The twins both glared at me. "You're not being helpful, Jill!"

"Sorry. How about nipping out to a local shop to pick up a few pints until the main delivery arrives?"

"That would be great, Jill, thanks." Amber reached into the till and grabbed twenty pounds. "You'll have to hurry, though."

"I—err—I didn't mean—"

She thrust the cash into my hand. "Go on. Get going. There's no time to lose."

"Yeah, hurry up." Pearl ushered me to the door. "And bring a mix of whole milk, semi-skimmed and skimmed."

"Right. Okay. Where is the closest shop, by the way?"

It turned out to be a ten-minute walk away. And who knew milk could be so heavy?

Breathless and with my legs about to collapse under me, I arrived back at Cuppy C just over twenty minutes later.

"I'm back! Where do you want these?"

"Just put them anywhere," Pearl said. "We'll put them in the fridge in a minute."

"I thought you'd have a queue of people waiting for this?"

"The reserve milkman got here quicker than expected. He arrived not long after you'd left."

"Do you mean I carried all this lot for nothing?"

"Don't worry, it'll all get used. At least you're back in time for the cats' debut."

I slumped into one of the seats. "I need a coffee."

Thirty minutes later, and the tearoom was considerably busier, as people arrived in time for the launch of the new cat café.

"Ladies and gentlemen." Pearl tapped on a cup with a teaspoon. "Thank you for coming here this morning. Amber and I are both very excited about our new venture.

But enough from me, I know you're keen to meet the feline stars of this show." She gave Amber the signal to open the door to the back room where the cats had been waiting patiently.

The small crowd applauded as the cats, of all shapes and sizes, made their way into the tearoom. Some of them weaved between the legs of the customers. Others jumped onto vacant chairs. And a few of the braver ones leapt onto people's laps.

"What do you think, Jill?" Amber came and joined me at my table.

"I'm impressed. I didn't think there would be so many of them."

Pearl came to join us. "I think we're onto a winner this time."

It certainly seemed that way. At least it did until an elderly couple came through the door. Then everything happened so quickly it took me a moment to figure out what was going on.

As soon as the door had opened, all the cats had headed for the exit.

"Go after them!" Amber cried out.

Pearl charged out of the door, and by the time Amber and I caught up with her, two streets away, she was doubled over, panting for breath.

"Where are they?" Amber looked up and down the road.

"I don't know. When I came around this corner, they'd disappeared."

"Twenty cats can't just disappear into thin air," I said.

"They just did."

By the time we got back to Cuppy C, the customers

were already starting to leave, clearly disappointed by the feline exodus.

"What are we going to do now?" Amber turned to her sister.

"We'll have to get some more cats. I'll give Cat City a call."

I couldn't help but feel sorry for the twins. For a few minutes there, I'd really thought they were onto something. Now, it was going to cost them a small fortune to replace the runaway cats.

***

The people I'd interviewed on my previous visits to Longdale Prison had rarely been happy, but Laurence Forrest looked and sounded suicidal.

"It's bad enough that I've lost Alison." He sobbed. "But for them to think I could do something like that, it's—it's just—" His words trailed away.

"I'm going to be brutally honest, Laurence. Right now, things aren't looking good for you."

"But I didn't do it. I would never have hurt her. You have to believe me."

"It doesn't matter what I believe. It's what the jury believe that's important, and right now the police have the murder weapon with your fingerprints on it. And then there's the witness who has testified that you came home an hour earlier than you claimed to have done."

"I've explained to the police about the hammer."

"Tell me about it."

"It does belong to me, so it's hardly surprising that it

183

has my fingerprints on it. But the thing is, it went missing a few weeks ago."

"Missing? What do you mean?"

"It disappeared. I needed it to hang a picture, and I couldn't find it anywhere."

"And yet it was used to kill your wife. How do you explain that?"

"I can't."

"And what about your neighbour who says you came home an hour earlier than you say you did? Is he mistaken?"

"No, he's lying. Old man Radford and I have never got along."

"Why is that?"

"He's a busybody who's always sticking his nose in."

"Is that all?"

"I reported that he was keeping a dog. They aren't allowed under the terms of the lease. That's why he's doing this. Ask him!"

"I will. Can we talk about Alison and your relationship now?"

"I loved her. She loved me. That's all there is to it."

"I heard you were having a few problems."

"Who told you that?"

"That's not important. Is it true?"

"All couples have bad patches, don't they?"

"Did she ever threaten to leave you?"

"No, neither of us would have done that to Adam."

"Did you mind Alison going out with her friends?"

"Of course not. We both needed to have time away from one another occasionally."

"Can you think of anyone who would want to do this?

To kill Alison and frame you?"

"No. I've been racking my brain to try to make sense of this, but it makes none. We didn't have any enemies. We didn't owe money. There's no reason for anyone to have done this."

I came away from the prison even more pessimistic than when I'd arrived. I had hoped that Laurence would give me something new to work with, but there had been precious little in what he'd told me that might help.

His claim that the hammer had 'disappeared' a month before the murder was barely credible. And he'd dismissed out of hand the idea that the marriage was in trouble. Was he simply in denial or had things not been as bad as some of Alison's friends had suggested?

The one tiny glimmer of hope had been what Laurence had told me about the neighbour, Arthur Radford. Was it possible that Radford had lied to the police just to get back at Laurence for having reported his dog? It seemed a bit of a stretch, but then I had nothing else to work with. Another visit to our friend, Mr Radford, was definitely called for. If he was lying and I put enough pressure on him, maybe he'd withdraw his original statement.

185

Chapter 18

I'd heard back from Tiberius Dove at Candle Mail. He'd had his people walk Monty Featherstone's route to try and establish where the postman had gone missing. Although he couldn't pinpoint the precise address where Monty had disappeared, he knew it was on one of two streets. One of those was the road where Aunt Lucy lived. Maybe she would remember seeing the postman that day? It was a long shot, but I had nothing else to go on, so I magicked myself over to her house.

"Jill? How lovely to see you." She had Lil in one arm and Lily in the other.

"It looks like you have your hands full there."

"I agreed to have both of them today because the twins are launching this cat café thing. Have you heard about it?"

"I was actually in Cuppy C this morning for the launch."

"Please tell me it went okay."

"It didn't begin well."

"Oh?"

"But then it got better."

"That's good."

"But then it got much worse."

"Oh dear. You'd better tell me what happened."

"When I got there, their milk delivery hadn't arrived. Apparently, the milkman had gone AWOL."

"That explains it."

"Explains what?"

"There was a milk van parked outside next door's

house for ages this morning. I was beginning to wonder what was going on, when another milkman turned up and drove it away. What happened next at Cuppy C? You said things got better."

"Yeah, the cats went down a treat."

"I sense a *but* coming."

"The customers seemed to really like the cats."

"I'm still waiting for that *but*."

"*But* then the cats all ran away."

"What do you mean, *ran away*?"

"As soon as someone came through the door, they bolted."

"All of them?"

"Yeah."

"Where are they now?"

"That's anyone's guess. Pearl chased after them, but they'd disappeared."

"Oh dear, those poor girls. How did they take it?"

"They weren't thrilled, as you might imagine. When I left, they were trying to get some more cats."

"Let me put these two down, and we'll have a cup of tea."

"How's Lester?" I asked once Aunt Lucy had put the little ones down for a nap, and we were seated at the kitchen table.

"He's driving me mad with his sleepwalking."

"Has he done it again?"

"Yes, and by the time I caught up with him last night, he was in next door's garden. I told him I thought he should see a doctor, but he refuses. You know what men are like."

187

"I certainly do. Anyway, the reason I came over was to ask you about your postman."

"The man who went missing?"

"Yeah. Do you know him?"

"By sight, but not by name."

"I'm trying to pinpoint where he disappeared. His employer has narrowed it down to this street or the next one. I don't suppose you can remember if he made a delivery to you last Wednesday, can you?"

"I know for sure that he didn't."

"How can you be so certain?"

"Because I was waiting for the new recipe book I'd ordered. I saw the postman through the window. He was next door at your grandmother's house, but when I went out to meet him, he was nowhere to be seen. I assumed he hadn't got any post for me, and that he must have carried on down the road. I was rather disappointed because I was really looking forward to getting that book."

"Has it arrived now?"

"No, there's still no sign of it. I contacted the supplier and they swear that it was posted at the beginning of last week."

***

Curiosity had got the better of me. I'd never won anything of any significance before, so I was dying to know what my lottery prize would be. I figured that if I called in at the council offices, they might be prepared to let me in on the secret if I promised not to tell anyone else.

Their offices were located in Washbridge Town Hall, a huge building, which must have cost an arm and a leg to maintain. In the centre of the large entrance hall was a semi-circular desk, above which was a sign which read: I'm here to help you.

The young man behind the desk looked as though he wanted to be anywhere but there. He certainly didn't look very keen to help anyone.

"Hi, I'm here about the lottery."

"If you're after a ticket, I'm afraid you're too late. There'll be another draw next year, though."

"I have the winning ticket."

"Has it been validated?"

"Err, no."

"Do you have it with you?"

"I do." I handed it to him.

"You're correct. You've won first prize. Congratulations."

"Thanks. I was hoping you might be able to tell me what I'd won."

"I can't do that, I'm afraid. First prize is being kept under wraps until the day of the presentation."

"I understand that, but I thought you might be able to tell me, provided I agreed to keep it a secret."

"I'm very sorry, but I couldn't tell you even if I wanted to."

"Why not?"

"I don't know what it is."

"Who does?"

"As far as I'm aware, only the council leader, Raymond Hall."

"Could I have a word with him?"

"He's abroad on council business."

"When will he be back?"

184

"Late on Friday evening. Just in time for the presentation ceremony on Saturday."

"Right. Thanks, anyway."

What a bummer. I hated surprises, but it looked as though I would just have to wait to find out what I'd won.

As I came out, I saw a car transporter pull up at the barrier beside the council offices. On the back of it was a brand-new Jag.

Maybe that was my prize. If so, then wow!

The barrier lifted and the transporter disappeared into the underground car park, so I hurried over to the small cabin where the security guard was stationed.

"Excuse me."

"Yes, love?"

"The car that just came through?"

"You mean the Jag?"

"Yeah. Who's it for?"

"I could tell you." He grinned. "But then I'd be forced to kill you."

"Does it happen to have anything to do with this Saturday?"

"It might do. Might not." He winked.

Message received and understood. "Okay, thanks."

That confirmed it. I'd won a brand-new Jag! I always knew I would get lucky one day.

Result!

***

If it hadn't been for Winky finding my lost lottery ticket, I wouldn't be getting my new car on Saturday. I figured I owed him one.

"Would you like some salmon, Winky?"

He looked up from his brochure and gave me a quizzical look. "I've already had some."

"Would you like some more?"

"What are you after?"

"Nothing, I'm just being nice."

"Well don't. It's freaking me out."

"You're not still thinking of going on that cruise, are you?"

"I'm going to book it this weekend. I can't wait: The lovely blue ocean and lots of sunshine. To say nothing of all the hotties that are bound to be on board."

"I still think it sounds dodgy."

"You worry too much."

Despite Winky's confidence, I still harboured some doubts about the cruise. I wasn't sure why, but it had triggered my *something doesn't smell right* alarm. Any other time, I might have shrugged it off, and let him risk his money, but I felt like I owed him one, so I decided I'd check it out—just to put my mind at ease.

Feline Cruises were based on a small industrial estate on the outskirts of Nottingham. I had assumed the enterprise would be run by felines, and that I'd have to transform myself into a cat in order to get inside their offices.

When I arrived at the address on the brochure, there was no sign of Feline Cruises. Instead, what I found was an operation called Cruise Time, which from the outside, at least, looked like a regular travel agent. That confused me a little, but I decided to check it out anyway. First, though, I had to cast the 'block' spell, so if there were any sups inside, they wouldn't realise I was a witch.

"Good afternoon, madam." The eager young witch was at my side as soon as I walked through the door. "Are you looking for anything in particular?"

"Not really. Just somewhere hot."

"What kind of budget do you have?"

"I thought maybe a couple of thousand."

"And will madam be travelling alone?"

"Yes, it's just me. Unless of course, I can bring my cat with me?"

I'd hoped she might take the bait, but she just smiled and said, "It's always hard to leave them behind isn't it?"

"None of your cruises allow pets, I don't suppose?"

"I'm afraid not."

"That's a pity." I started flicking through one of the brochures. "Someone could probably make a killing if they catered for pets, particularly cats, don't you think?"

Her smile had now disappeared, and she looked distinctly uncomfortable. "I'll leave you to browse."

"Okay, thanks."

Whilst pretending to study the brochures, I watched her walk over to the wizard who was seated at a desk at the back of the room. With her hand cupped over her mouth, she began to whisper to him.

Little did they know that I'd cast the 'listen' spell and could hear every word.

"She can't possibly know."

"But she keeps asking about taking her cat on a cruise."

"That doesn't mean anything. She's just a cat lover."

"She said someone could make a killing if they offered cruises for cats."

"I don't think it's anything to worry about, but you'd better keep an eye on her."

"What if she comes back tomorrow night?"
"Don't panic. She won't."

Oh yes, she will.

***

"What happens if Mrs V and Armi come around here while you're gone?" Jack was putting up the cuckoo clock. "How am I supposed to explain that the carpet isn't new?"

"They won't come tonight. And besides, I'm going to CASS so it'll only seem like a matter of seconds to you before I'm back."

"How does that even work?"

"We've had this conversation before, and the answer is still the same: I don't know. I have to get going because the headmistress is expecting me."

"This always feels weird. I no sooner say goodbye to you than you're back."

"Bye."

***

"Thanks for doing this, Jill." Desdemona Nightowl was behind her desk. "I'm still not one-hundred percent convinced we have a ghost, but several children and a couple of teachers insist they've seen it—err—her, so now panic has set in."

"In that case, the sooner I get to the bottom of this the better."

"The children were told they had to be in their beds half-an-hour ago so that you don't have them to contend

143

with."

"Where shall I station myself?"

"The reports all place the ghost in the corridors outside the dorms."

"Any particular one?"

"Most of the sightings have been in and around Wrongacre dormitory."

"Okay. I'll start there."

"Excellent. I'll tell Miss Goodbody to keep you supplied with coffee, to help you stay awake."

"Thanks."

"And I believe you're partial to custard creams?"

"That's just a wicked rumour." I grinned.

"I hope not because I had some brought in specially for you."

"In that case, it would be rude not to eat at least a couple."

Two hours later, and I was still sitting outside the Wrongacre dormitory. For the first hour or so, I'd heard kids' voices from inside the dorm, but it was now deathly quiet.

I'd finished my second cup of coffee and was beginning to think the reports about Old Mother Mason might be true because someone had eaten almost half a packet of custard creams.

Or maybe that was down to me.

It was kind of creepy sitting there all alone. Yes, I do realise how ridiculous that must sound, coming from someone who routinely interacts with ghosts and all manner of supernatural creatures, but it was true, nonetheless. It was the anticipation that got to me. The waiting for something to happen, for something to make me jump.

"What the?" I almost fell off my chair when someone ran a bony finger across my scalp.

Yuk! And double yuk!

I looked up to see the ghostly shape of an old woman who appeared to be standing on the ceiling. Her face, which was even more wrinkled than Grandma's, was only inches from mine.

"What are you doing down there?" she asked in a croaky voice.

"More to the point, why are you standing on the ceiling?"

"I find it helps me to think."

"This is giving me a crick in my neck. Do you think you could come down here, please?"

"If I must." She did a weird kind of somersault and landed at my side.

"Thanks. I assume you're Old Mother Mason?"

"Less of the *old*, cheeky madam."

"Sorry, but you are Mrs Mason, aren't you?"

"Molly Mason at your service. And who would you be? You're too old to be one of the pupils. Are you a teacher?"

"No, well yeah, but only part-time."

"How come you can see me, anyway? I didn't attach myself to you."

"It's just something I'm able to do. I'm able to travel to Ghost Town, too."

"I won't have any truck with that place. Went there once, and I didn't think much of it."

"Where do you live?"

"Right here of course."

145

"But I was told you hadn't been seen for years until recently."

"That's because I normally keep myself to myself down in the cellar. There are too many noisy children up here for my liking."

"What made you change your mind and come up here again?"

"I'm looking for my dog, Rocky."

"Where is he?"

"You're not very bright, are you? If I knew where he was, I wouldn't be looking for him, would I? I left the cellar door open, and when I woke up the next morning, he'd gone. I've been trying to find him ever since."

"This dog of yours, is he — err — ?" I hesitated.

"Is he what?"

"You know. Dead? A ghost?"

"I would jolly well hope so. He's been by my side for a couple of centuries now."

"The problem is that you've been scaring some of the children."

"Why would they be scared of Molly Mason?"

I resisted the urge to ask if she'd looked in a mirror recently. "You know what kids are like."

"I can't help that. I have to find Rocky."

"How about I try to find him for you?"

"Why would you do that? I don't have any money."

"You wouldn't have to pay me, but I would need you to stay in the cellar until I find him."

"How long will that take?"

"I don't know. Is he wearing a nametag?"

"He is."

"That ought to make things a little easier. I'll look for

him, but you have to promise to stay out of sight until I find him."

"Can't I help you to look?"

"No, just stay in the cellar."

***

Jack hadn't moved from the spot where I'd left him.

"I'm back."

"That never gets any less weird. How did you get on?"

"Okay, but now I have to try and find a ghost dog named Rocky."

"I'm going to make a cup of tea. Would you like one?"

"Yes, please."

"And custard creams, I suppose?"

"Err—"

I can hear you lot tutting. Okay, okay, you've guilt-tripped me out of it.

"Err, no thanks. Just the tea."

"What are you doing, Jill?" Jack said, after we'd taken our tea through to the lounge.

"Nothing."

"Yes, you were. You were pretending to drive a car."

"I wasn't."

"You were definitely pretending to steer a car. What was that all about?"

"I was just thinking it would be nice to have a new car."

"We've discussed that. We can't afford it just yet."

"We'll see." I went back to 'steering' my Jag. I couldn't wait to see Jack's face when he found out what I'd won.

147

Chapter 19

The next morning when I arrived at work, I heard the most awful noise. It appeared to be coming from my offices, and it sounded as though someone was being strangled. My first thought was that a disgruntled client might be attacking Mrs V, so I took the stairs two at a time and burst into the outer office.

"Jill, you scared me to death." Mrs V was standing behind her desk.

"Where are they?" I glanced around the office.

"Where's who?"

"I thought I heard—never mind."

"Last night was magnificent, Jill."

"What was?"

"The concert of course. Don't you remember I told you I was going?"

"Oh yeah. Brian—err—Tiger?"

"Brian Lion. It was the best concert I've ever seen. He sang all the old favourites: The Carrots Are Lonely Now, My Caravan Knows Secrets and for his encore, he sang his new release called Only My Gnome Knows. It brought tears to my eyes."

"I can imagine. Were you by any chance singing one of his hits just now?"

"I was, yes, until you came bursting through the door and scared me to death. Why were you in such a hurry?"

"No reason. Just part of my new keep-fit regime."

Winky was lying on a blue exercise mat, stretching his legs in the air.

"What are you doing?"

"What does it look like?"

"It looks a bit like you're doing yoga."

"To the untrained eye, maybe, but this is Pilates."

"Since when did you do Pilates?"

"Since forever. You don't get to have a body like this without plenty of exercise."

"How come I've never seen you do it before?"

"I've normally finished before you're even out of bed, but I'm running late this morning." He jumped to his feet. "I'm done now. You should give it a try."

"No thanks. I get all the exercise I need."

"Lifting muffins?"

"I'll have you know I just ran up the stairs."

"I can tell. You're as red as a beetroot."

"Rubbish."

"Now you're here, I wish to register a complaint."

"What is it now?"

"The old bag lady. She's been singing ever since she arrived. Of course, I use the term *singing* in the loosest sense of the word. Something about a caravan and a gnome."

"Those are the greatest hits of Brian Lion."

"Who?"

"Apparently, he's very big with the yarnies. Mrs V went to see him in concert last night."

"That's no reason to subject me to her warbling. Can't you have a word with her?"

"I think she's got it out of her system now. Anyway, how come you were running late this morning? Heavy night?"

"I was helping to look for Gavin the Grub and Bobby the Brew until the early hours."

199

"Any joy?"

"None. They seem to have disappeared into thin air. Any word on Bruiser and Lovely?"

"As far as I know, they're still missing too."

"Something's definitely afoot in my opinion, but you don't seem to be doing much about it."

"I've already told you. I don't have time to look for a few missing cats."

"Typical. It's just me, me, me, with you, isn't it?"

"That's not fair. I'm just crazy busy."

"Hmm. Have you found out what you've won on the lottery?"

"Not for sure, but I have an idea of what it might be."

"Go on, then. I'm all ears."

"I'll give you a clue." I began to steer my imaginary car.

"A year's supply of wool?"

"How on earth did you get wool from that?"

"That's what the old bag lady does with her hands when she's winding her wool."

"No, it's not wool. Something much better."

"A divining rod?"

"What?"

"It looked as though you were searching for water."

"I was steering a car!"

"Really? I'd never have guessed. So, what have you won? A rally driving weekend?"

"No. I've won a car."

"In your dreams." He scoffed.

"I'm telling you. I was at the council offices when it was delivered: A brand-new Jag."

"Are you sure?"

"Positive. I saw it with my own eyes, and when I asked

the security guard about it, he said it was related to Saturday, which is the day the prizes are presented."

"Wow! You owe me big time. If I hadn't found that ticket, you'd have been stuffed. What do I get?"

"You said you didn't want anything, but I think it's only fair I show my gratitude, so I'm going to double your salmon allowance for the next month."

"Three months. That's only fair."

"Okay, three months it is."

***

I wanted to have another word with Laurence Forrest's neighbour, Arthur Radford. If I could get him to admit that he'd lied about seeing Laurence returning early, maybe that would be enough to get the police to look for other possible suspects.

I'd just stepped out of the office when I got a phone call from Peter.

"Jill, are you in Washbridge?"

"Yeah. I've just left the office."

"Could you pop into the shop, to check that Kathy is okay?"

"Why, what's wrong?"

"There was an incident when she took the kids to school this morning. Someone tried to snatch her handbag."

"Is she okay?"

"She says so, but I'd feel a lot better if you made sure. I'd go over there myself, but I'm out of town and it would take me an hour to get back."

"I'll go straight down there now."

"Will you call me to let me know if she's alright or if I

201

need to come over?"

"Of course. Don't worry, I'm sure she'll be fine."

Although I'd done my best to reassure Peter, I was still apprehensive about what I might find when I got to the shop. I knew my sister—she would have said she was okay whether she was or not.

"Jill?" Kathy was tinkering with the window display. "Are you alright? You look like you're about to collapse."

"I ran all the way down here."

"Why?"

"Peter called me. He told me about the incident at school."

"I told him I was okay. He shouldn't have bothered you with it."

"Are you sure you're alright?"

"Better than you by the look of it. Do you want a cup of tea?"

"Please."

While Kathy was in the back, making the drinks, I gave Peter a quick call to put his mind at rest.

"Thanks." I took a sip of tea. "What happened at school?"

"It must have been the same man who snatched Adriana's bag."

"I thought the police had put on extra patrols?"

"They were supposed to, but there was no sign of them this morning."

"Did he hurt you?"

"No, but I reckon I hurt him. I clobbered him around the head with my handbag, and you know how much stuff I have in there. He turned tail and took off."

"Did it upset the kids?"

"Luckily, they'd already gone inside so they didn't see anything. I was just walking back to the car when he jumped out at me."

"Did you get a good look at him?"

"Not really. It all happened so quickly, and he was wearing a hat pulled down over his face. I do have a video, though."

"I'm surprised you had the presence of mind to do that."

"I didn't. One of the other mothers saw what was happening and recorded it on her phone. She sent copies to me and the police."

"Can I see it?"

"Sure. It's a bit shaky and you only get to see him from the back as he hobbles away."

"*Hobbles*? Just how hard did you hit him?"

"Not hard enough to cause that. I reckon he must have a gammy leg." She took out her phone. "Watch."

Just as Kathy had said, the video was very short and jumped all over the place. Whoever had taken it had clearly had a shaky hand. The man was already halfway down the road before the video started, and the last sighting of him was when he took a right down a side street.

"How long did it take for the police to arrive?"

"They didn't. At least not while I was still there. I'm expecting them to get in touch sometime today."

"Can I see the video again?"

"Here." She handed me the phone. "I need to get this window finished."

I played the short clip several times more.

203

"Do you see what I mean about the hobbling?" Kathy said while she adjusted the hem on a dress.

"Yeah, I do." Although I didn't say anything to Kathy, it was the man's gait that I was studying. If I wasn't mistaken, he wasn't so much hobbling away as hopping. "Is it okay if I send a copy of this to my phone?"

"Be my guest."

"I should get going. Oh, by the way, Kathy. How's that new car of yours?"

"Fantastic. I love her."

"Don't you find it a little on the small side?"

"Not really. It's perfectly big enough."

"Haven't you ever fancied something a bit bigger? Something a bit more upmarket? A Jag for example?"

"We can't afford a Jag. What's this all about, Jill?"

"Nothing."

"You're up to something. I can tell. What is it?"

"I'd like to tell you, but I'm sworn to secrecy. You'll find out on Saturday."

"Isn't that when you find out what you've won in the lottery? Is it a car? Have you won a Jag?"

"I couldn't possibly comment."

***

I'd been knocking on Arthur Radford's door for the best part of five minutes, but either he wasn't in, or his hearing aid was on the blink. Either way, the trip had been a bust.

I was just about to set off down the stairs when someone called to me.

"Excuse me, young lady." It was the elderly woman who I'd spoken to on my last visit. "Are you looking for

Arthur again?"

"I am, yes." I walked over to her. "You don't happen to know where he is, do you?"

"I saw him go out about half-an-hour ago. He's probably gone down the bookies. He goes there most mornings."

"Is he a bit of a gambler?"

"I don't think so. He just goes there for the free drinks. Plus, it saves him money on heating. Talking of drinks, I was just going to make a cup of tea. Would you care to join me?"

"Sure, why not?"

"I don't get many visitors." She handed me the cup. "Here, help yourself to a biscuit."

I took one look inside the biscuit barrel, but then gracefully declined. When would people realise that mixing biscuits together like that was simply wrong?

"Do you have family, err—Sorry, I've forgotten your name."

"Louise Roach. Call me Lou, everyone does."

"I'm Jill. Do you have family, Lou?"

"I have a daughter and a couple of grandkids, but they live down south, so I only get to see them a few times a year. How's young Laurence doing? Have you heard?"

"I visited him yesterday. He's having a tough time of it."

"Poor man. It's not right what they've done to him."

"That's why I was hoping to talk to your neighbour again. His testimony is one of the main reasons that Laurence has been charged with murder. I wanted to ask him if he was sure of what he'd seen." Despite the hot tea,

205

I was beginning to feel quite chilly. "Aren't you cold in here, Vi?" Lou

"Frozen to the marrow, love."

"Can't you claim any allowances for the heating?"

"It's not the money. I can pay my way. It's the boiler — the thing has been on the blink for ages."

"Have you called the landlord?"

"I spoke to the maintenance man who came to Laurence's flat a few weeks ago, but he wasn't interested. In fact, he was really offhanded with me. He seemed really angry about something — I think Laurence or Alison must have upset him."

"Couldn't you give the landlord a ring?"

"I'm not very good on the phone. In the old days you could speak to a real person. Nowadays, it's all *press one for this*, and *two for that*. It's beyond me."

"Would you like me to give them a call for you?"

"Would you, love? That'd be really kind."

"If you give me your landlord's number, I'll call them for you now."

She went over to the sideboard, rummaged through the drawers, and came back with a sheet of paper. "All the information is on there."

I used my own phone to make the call, and just as Lou had predicted, I had to battle my way through an automated menu system. Even when I'd succeeded in doing that, I still didn't get to speak to a human being. Instead, I was forced to record a message. I figured I'd have more chance of getting a return call if I said I was interested in renting the vacant flat I'd seen on my previous visit.

"That was very crafty of you." Lou grinned.

"When they call back, I won't let them go until they promise to sort out your boiler."

"Thanks, Jill. Are you sure you won't have a biscuit? I have lots to choose from."

***

I'd spent longer at the flats than I'd intended, and now had no chance of making it to Middle Tweaking Theatre on time by car. That left me with no option other than to magic myself over there. Unfortunately, I didn't know where the theatre was, so I decided to aim for Myrtle Turtle's back garden, which I knew from my previous visit, was secluded.

"Jill?" Myrtle, who was watering her plants, gave me a puzzled look. "Where did you come from?"

"I—err—came through the house. I hope you don't mind. I did knock, but there was no answer."

"I didn't hear you. How did you get into the house?"

"Err, the door was ajar."

"Really? I must be getting careless in my old age. To what do I owe this unexpected pleasure?"

"Actually, I'm looking for the theatre. I didn't notice it on any of my previous visits."

"I'm not surprised. It's actually located just outside the village. It's an old church hall that has been converted. What's your interest in it?"

"It's a long story."

"Why don't I walk you down there, and you can tell me on the way?"

"Thanks, that would be great."

As we made our way through the village, I gave Myrtle

207

the Cliff Notes version of clown wars.

"You get involved in some very peculiar cases, Jill."

"Isn't that the truth?" I glanced over at the church, which was covered in scaffolding. "What's going on over there?"

"The bells needed replacing; they were too dangerous to leave in place any longer. It's proving to be a very long job, though."

"What's the delay?"

"Money, as always. We managed to raise enough to get the old bells removed, but we're a long way short of being able to buy the replacements."

About ten minutes after Myrtle had left me at the doors of the theatre, PomPom and his clowns arrived in his minibus.

"Did you find it okay?" I (AKA Trudy Lewchuse) said.

"I got lost a couple of times, but I'm here now."

"How many clowns have you brought with you?" I glanced into the back of the minibus.

"Seven. I had hoped to get a couple more, but it was rather short notice."

"No problem. If you could ask them to make their way to the dressing room, then you and I can go through to the auditorium."

"I'm confident you're going to enjoy today's performance, Trudy."

So was I, but probably not for the reason that PomPom expected.

A few minutes later, PomPom and I had taken our seats in the theatre.

"Are you ready, Trudy?"

"I was born ready."

"Great." PomPom took out his phone and made a call. "Ding Dong? We're ready for you now." With the call ended, he turned to me. "I think you'll like Ding Dong. He's one of our most popular clowns."

"I'm looking forward to it."

I couldn't fault Ding Dong's entrance; he did a series of backflips onto the stage. Once there, he went into his main act. Behind him there were a number of handbells, which he began to play—very badly. One deliberate 'mishap' followed another. First, one of the handles fell off. Next, he dropped one of the bells onto his foot.

"What do you think so far?" PomPom whispered.

"Not bad."

"Just wait until you see the big finale."

That finale required Ding Dong to attach a bell to each foot and hand, and another to the top of his head.

"What's he doing?"

"He plays the wedding march. It took him years to master it."

With all five bells attached, he began to gyrate.

The forlorn look on poor Ding Dong's face when the bells refused to ring, was a picture.

"I can't hear anything," I said to PomPom, all innocent-like.

"I don't understand it." PomPom looked mightily confused. "I've seen him do this act a dozen times, and he's always nailed it."

"It's a bit of an anti-climax, isn't it?"

"Thank you, Ding Dong." PomPom waved the despondent clown off the stage.

Little did either of them know that I'd used magic to silence the bells.

Snigger.

And so it continued. The second act was Bubbles whose bubble machine refused to produce a single bubble. Then came String Bean who was billed as the world's tallest clown. Unfortunately for him, one of his stilts broke halfway through the act. Rhubarb and custard were a double act who threw custard pies at one another. That fell flat because neither of them could land one on the other's face no matter how many times they tried.

By now, PomPom was clearly embarrassed, but he tried to put on a brave face.

"I saved the best until last. You'll love Spins."

"I hope so."

Spins' act involved plates and poles. His failed attempts to keep the plates spinning on the poles were designed to have the audience in stitches. And for the first few minutes, all seemed to be going well.

"Didn't I tell you?" PomPom said. "Audiences love him."

But then something strange happened: The plates stopped falling. Spins was obviously thrown by this unexpected turn of events. He watched, and he watched, and he continued to watch while the plates seemingly defied gravity.

"Thank you, Spins." PomPom signalled for him to call it quits.

As soon as the clown was off the stage, I reversed the spell, and all of the plates crashed to the floor.

By now, PomPom looked more than a little defeated.

"I'm sorry about that, Trudy. I don't know what happened today."

"I do."

"Sorry?"

"I know what happened today. Someone sabotaged your acts."

"Do you really think so?"

"I *know* so because I was the one who did it."

He stared at me, clearly unsure if he should take me seriously. "You? Why?"

"Because I could. And because you did the same to your competitor, Clown."

"Did Jimmy and Kimmy put you up to this?"

"I am working for them, yes."

"This is outrageous. I have a good mind to — err — "

"To what? Report it to the police? I don't think that will work out very well for you, considering that you're guilty of doing the exact same thing."

"Why bother with all of this charade today?"

"I wanted to make sure I had your attention, and that you could see what I am capable of doing to your business."

"How did you do it? You were sitting next to me all the time."

"That would be telling. Suffice to say, I've done it once and I can do it again. And I will unless you promise not to sabotage Clown again."

"Okay, okay. I promise."

"You'd better keep your word because if I hear there's been any more funny business, there'll be much worse to come. *Funny business*? Get it?" I laughed.

211

Unsurprisingly, he didn't seem to appreciate the joke. "I'll leave them alone. You have my word."

Chapter 20

I wasn't expecting this to be an easy meeting, but it had to be done.

I'd magicked myself to Candlefield and tracked down Circus Fantastico who were about to embark on a week of performances on Candlefield Green. The crew were still busy erecting the big top ahead of the first show, which was scheduled for the following day.

"Excuse me," I said to one of the wizards who was having a rest from the back-breaking work.

"If you're after free tickets, you're out of luck, lady."

"No, that's not why I'm here."

"Sorry, I just assumed. As soon as people see us putting up the big top, they start to hover around like bees, trying to scrounge free tickets."

"I'm actually looking for the clowns."

"If you're looking for a job with them, you're out of luck." He looked me up and down. "You have one too many eyes, and legs."

"No, I just need a word with them."

"They're over there." He pointed beyond the big top. "At the far side of the site."

"You wouldn't happen to know the name of the head clown, would you?"

"The guy in charge is called Ned. He's a miserable so and so. For a clown, that is."

"Thanks."

I made my way over to the far side of the site where I found the familiar circle of caravans. At first glance, there didn't appear to be any cycloppers around, but then I spotted two youngsters: a boy and a girl.

"Excuse me, I wonder if you can tell me where I can find Ned?"

"Who are you?" The girl eyed me suspiciously. Her single eye might have freaked some people out but having spent so much time with Winky I was used to it.

"My name is Jill Maxwell."

"What do you want Ned for?" It was the boy's turn to interrogate me.

"It's a private matter. If you could just point me to his caravan, I'd be most grateful."

"He doesn't like visitors," the girl said.

"I'll take my chances."

"That's his caravan over there."

"The green one?"

"Yeah, but don't say we didn't warn you."

"Okay, thanks."

Standing outside the green caravan, I braced myself for what would surely be a difficult conversation.

I'd just raised my hand to knock on the door when it flew open.

"It's you!" The tall cyclopper glared at me.

"Hello again." Just as I'd feared, it was the same guy I'd had the run-in with on my previous visit to the circus.

"How's life at the CCIA?"

"Oh? It's—err—"

"Remind me again what that stands for."

"Err—it—err—"

"Let me help you. I believe it's the Candlefield Circus Inspection Authority, isn't it?"

"Yeah, about that, I—err—"

"Except of course that there's no such thing, is there?"

"Look, I think we may have got off on the wrong foot last time."

Oh bum! *Wrong foot*? What was I thinking?

"What did you just say?"

"What I meant was that there may have been a slight misunderstanding the last time I was here."

"When you say *misunderstanding*, what you really mean is that you lied. There is no such thing as the CCIA, is there?"

"Well, no."

"So, you did lie."

"Yes, and I'm sorry. Very sorry."

"You accused us of stealing clown shoes."

"That was my bad."

"What brings you back here today?"

"I wanted to ask you a favour."

"You've got some nerve. I'll give you that." He laughed. "You lie to us, accuse us of being thieves, and now you want us to do you a favour."

"It sounds bad when you put it like that."

"What exactly is this favour?"

"I need your help to identify one of your people who has been robbing women in the human world. One of the women who tried to resist him, fell and banged her head, and died from her injuries."

"How dare you come here and throw around more of your unfounded accusations?" He'd turned a deep shade of red. "I think you'd better leave, or I won't be responsible for my actions."

"Wait. Take a look at this, please." I held out my phone.

"What is it?"

"Watch." I played the video for him.

"Give that to me." He snatched the phone from my hand, and for a moment, I thought he was going to smash it. Instead, he replayed the video several times. "Where was this taken?"

"I'm right, aren't I? That is one of your people, isn't it?"

"I can't be sure." He hesitated. "But, yes, it does appear to be. Where was it taken?"

"Outside a school in Washbridge. He'd just tried to snatch my sister's handbag."

Clearly dazed, Ned shook his head. "I don't know what to say."

"That is a cyclopper, right?"

"I believe so."

"I need your help to find him and bring him to justice."

"No!" He suddenly became very animated. "This is my responsibility and I'll deal with it."

"But I—err—"

"I said I'll deal with it."

"How do I know that I can trust you?"

"Because you have my word. I'll find out who this is, and they will be dealt with."

"*Dealt with*, how?"

"They'll be handed over to the authorities."

"The Candlefield police?"

"No, to the rogue retrievers. This relates to crimes committed in the human world, so they should be the ones to deal with it."

"Okay."

"I'd like to thank you for bringing this to my attention. The cycloppers are a proud people, and whoever has done this has brought shame upon us."

"Does that mean you and I are good now?"

"Provided you don't start accusing us of stealing clown shoes again."

"I won't. I promise."

That had actually gone much better than I could have hoped for. I only had Ned's word that he'd put an end to the rogue cyclopper's activities, but judging by his reaction, I was confident he would make good on his promise.

***

While I was in Candlefield I decided to call in at Cuppy C, to find out how the twins were coping after the cat café debacle.

Pearl and Jemima were behind the counter.

"Have they got you working in the tearoom now, Jemima?"

"Goodness no." She smiled. "I'd be hopeless at it."

"You couldn't be any worse than Jill," Pearl quipped.

"Thanks." I shot her a look. "Who's watching the kids?"

"Mindy is upstairs with them. Jemima is on her break."

"How are things going? Has there been any feedback from the parents?"

"They all seem to be happy with our new employee." Pearl patted Jemima on the shoulder. "It's like Belladonna never left."

"That's good. Can I get a caramel latte, please?"

"And — ?" Pearl said.

"Just the coffee, thanks."

"Aren't you feeling well?"

217

"Anyone would think I always had cake with my coffee."

"And they'd be right."

"What's the latest with the cats?"

"Cat City are bringing a new batch over tonight, ready for the relaunch tomorrow morning."

"Let's hope this lot hang around a little longer than the others did."

"They better had. It's costing us a small fortune."

It was only when I had my drink that I spotted Daze and Blaze seated near the window.

"Hey, you two. Can I join you?"

"Sure." Daze pulled out the chair next to her.

"You both look very serious. Is something wrong?"

"We have a code red," Blaze said.

"I'm guessing that's serious."

"It's our highest-level alert." Daze took a bite of her toasted sandwich. "It's only issued when one of the sups on the Most Wanted list is thought to be in the vicinity."

"Most Wanted list? I didn't realise there was such a thing."

"It's not something we publicise to the general population, but every rogue retriever has a copy."

"When you say, *in the vicinity*, what do you mean, exactly?"

"The sups on the list are wanted for all manner of heinous crimes committed in the human world. The alert means that one of them has been sighted back here in Candlefield."

"Which one of them has triggered the alert?"

Before she could answer, the pager in her pocket

beeped. "Sorry, Jill, we have to go."

"Okay, good luck."

I'd been nursing my coffee for some time when an elderly wizard walked over to my table.

"Are you Jill Maxwell?"

"Yes, I am."

"I thought so. Would you mind signing my handkerchief?"

"Sorry?" Just the thought of it turned my stomach.

"It's okay." He laughed. "It's not one I've ever used." He fished it out of his pocket and laid it on the table. "I couldn't decide between the mouse mat and this, but I figured I could carry this with me. I never dreamt I'd actually bump into you."

"That's my photo on there. Where did you get this from?"

"Candlefield Icons. They have all sorts of your memorabilia." He handed me a pen. "I really do appreciate this."

"No problem." I scribbled my signature on his handkerchief.

"Thanks. I can't wait to show it to the lads down the Donkey."

"*The Donkey*?"

"The Dandelion and Donkey. That's my local. You're welcome to join us for a drink if you like?"

"That's very kind, but I'm a bit pushed for time at the moment."

That was twice now that someone had mentioned buying 'my' memorabilia from Candlefield Icons. I found it quite flattering that people would lay out money to buy something with my picture on it.

What do you mean you'd pay good money *not* to have my picture on it? Cheek!

The question now was, who was getting all the money, and where was my share?

It was time that I checked out Candlefield Icons, so I used the 'doppelganger' spell to ensure I wouldn't be recognised. Kathy's face would do nicely.

Located just around the corner from the cat rescue centre, it was a much larger shop than I expected.

"Hi!" The female vampire came skipping across the shop floor. Young and very pretty, she had a very distinctive dress sense, and yet somehow, she managed to pull it off. Who knew that a blue tutu, pink tights and black DMs could work so well?

"Hi, there. I didn't even realise this shop was here."

"It's not the best of locations, is it? The owner is hoping to move nearer to the marketplace later this year. Were you looking for anything in particular?"

"Do you have anything with Jill Maxwell on it?"

"Who?" She laughed. "Only joking. Of course we do. You'll find all of it over in that corner, along with all the other famous witch stuff. Did you have anything particular in mind?"

"Not really. I'll have a browse if that's okay?"

"Sure. I'm Vannie, give me a shout if you need any help."

Wow! Let me tell you, it's quite weird to see your face plastered on t-shirts and posters, but even weirder to see it on egg cups and bum-bags. My picture was everywhere.

The only other witch to get more of a look-in was Magna Mondale.

"Do you see anything you like?" Vannie had come over to join me.

"I'm spoiled for choice. Do you sell much of this stuff?"

"Jill Maxwell, you mean? Not compared to our bestselling stuff, but she certainly has a following. More so since she quit the Elite Competition to rescue that dragon. That seems to have struck a chord with a lot of people."

"I imagine she gets a cut from everything sold, doesn't she?"

"I wouldn't know about that." Vannie shrugged. "I suppose so. You'd have to ask the owner."

"Who is that?"

"Sylvester. Sylvester Songspinner."

"Is he in today?"

"No. We rarely see him in here."

"You wouldn't happen to know where he lives, would you?"

"No, sorry. Can I give him a message for you?"

"That's okay." I started for the door.

"Don't you want to buy any of this Jill Maxwell stuff?"

"No, thanks. She's vastly overrated in my opinion."

***

I'd no sooner magicked myself back to the human world than I received a call from Edward Tucker, landlord of the building where Laurence Forrest lived.

"Jill Maxwell? You left a message that you were interested in one of my properties."

"Yeah, sorry, I lied about that."

221

"I don't understand?"

"I apologise for the subterfuge, but I thought by saying that I'd have a better chance of getting you to return my call."

"If you aren't interested in renting, what do you want?"

"I'm ringing on behalf of one of your residents, a Mrs Louise Roach."

"Of Bluebell Court? Is she alright?"

"She'd be much better if her boiler wasn't on the blink. It's been like that for weeks."

"Why didn't she call me before now? I pride myself in making prompt repairs, especially when it involves the heating or water. And particularly when it's one of my vulnerable tenants."

"She asked one of your maintenance men to report it when he visited her neighbour's flat. That was a few weeks ago now."

"Hold on while I just double-check." I could hear him clicking away with a mouse. "I don't have any reports related to Mrs Roach's flat. The last time one of my men was at that building was a few weeks ago now."

"Were they visiting the Forrests' flat?"

"Yes, that's right. I'm really sorry, but it doesn't appear a report was ever filed. I can only apologise. The employee in question had always been very reliable, but then — err — never mind. It's not important."

"Did something happen?"

"It was all very strange. The guy's name was Paul Hattersley. He'd been one of my best men — no hint of a problem until that day."

"The day he was at Bluebell Court?"

"Yeah. He'd gone there to repair a sticking window,

and when he got back, he said he was quitting. Just like that."

"I told him he couldn't just walk out, that he'd have to work his notice, but he said he couldn't. Some sort of personal emergency, but he wouldn't say what. That was the last I saw of him."

"I don't suppose you could let me have Hattersley's contact details, could you?"

"Sorry, but I can't do that. Data protection and all that."

"No problem. Please make sure you get someone to look at Mrs Roach's boiler."

"There'll be someone over there later today."

As soon as I'd finished my call to the landlord, I called Sheila Forrest.

"It's Jill Maxwell."

"Any news, Jill?"

"Nothing yet. I was wondering if you could get Laurence to give me a call? He is allowed phone calls, isn't he?"

"Some, yes. I got him to add your number to his list when I hired you, so there shouldn't be any problem. What's it about?"

"Nothing in particular, just a few things I forgot to ask when I visited him."

"Okay, I'll ask him to call you, but I'm not sure when it will be."

"The sooner the better."

Chapter 21

I'd called Mad to ask if she could spare me a few minutes sometime. As it turned out, it was her day off, and she said I was welcome to go straight over there. On the way into the building, I bumped into two of her neighbours, Dorothy and Neil, who were going at it hammer and tongs on the stairs.

"Hi, you two."

"Hey, Jill." Dorothy's face was red with rage. "Sorry, this idiot has got me so riled up that I didn't see you there."

"Take no notice of her, Jill," Neil said. "She's overreacting as usual."

"How am I overreacting? My mother is going to have a fit when she comes over next week." Dorothy turned to me. "This fool left the window open and my canary has escaped."

"You were the one who opened his cage door," Neil protested.

"Only because I didn't think anyone would be stupid enough to leave a window open overnight."

"I've explained the reason for that. It was sweltering the evening before."

"You could have closed the window when you went to bed."

"When did the bird go missing?" I asked.

"It's a couple of weeks ago now," Neil said. "I don't know why she's still banging on about it."

"You know very well why I'm *banging on about it*. My mother gave me the canary, and she's not going to be very impressed when she finds out he's gone."

"Couldn't you just buy another one?" I suggested.

"That's what I told her," Neil said.

"I might have to do that." Dorothy sighed. "But Bob was a bit of a character. I reckon Mum will know if we get a substitute."

"Did you say Bob?" This was starting to ring a familiar bell.

"Stupid name, I know," Dorothy said. "I didn't choose it. He came with it."

"He wasn't by any chance a bit of a ladies' man, was he?"

"Yeah, how did you know?"

"Err, just an educated guess. I used to keep canaries myself when I was a kid."

"We'd better get going," Neil said. "I'm doing a show later."

"I heard you were a part-time magician now."

"Yeah, it's fun. I mainly do kids' parties."

"Are you his assistant, Dorothy?"

"Work with this idiot? Not likely."

"I hope your canary turns up."

"Come in, Jill." Mad had a towel wrapped around her head.

"That's quite the look you've got going there."

"My mum's having a dinner party tonight, so I thought I'd better make an effort."

"Deli? A dinner party?"

"I thought she was joking when she told me, but apparently, she's got new neighbours and she's trying to impress them."

"I'm surprised you agreed to go."

225

"She didn't give me much choice. She's still guilt-tripping me because I didn't let her know I was moving back here. I can probably still wangle you an invitation if you like?"

"Thanks, but I think I'll pass."

"I don't blame you. You said you needed some advice."

"Yeah, I could have picked your brain over the phone, but then I wouldn't have got a drink, would I?"

"Is that your idea of a subtle hint?" She grinned. "Tea or coffee?"

"Tea would be lovely."

Once we had our drinks, I told Mad about Old Mother Mason, and her recent reappearance at CASS.

"And now I'm supposed to find her dog, Rocky, but I don't have a clue where to start. I thought you might be able to give me some advice."

"If this was a dog lost in the human world, what would you do?"

"Probably start by checking with the dog rescue centres."

"There you go, then. You've answered your own question."

"I'm not sure I understand. Are you saying there are dog rescue centres in the ghost world?"

"Why wouldn't there be?"

"No reason, I guess. It just hadn't occurred to me. But the dog has been living in CASS with Old Mother Mason for centuries."

"So what? He probably just wandered off and got lost."

"It's worth a try. Do you happen to know where the dog rescue centres are?"

"The main one is Pooch Pound. It's near GT Gardens. I'd start there and if you draw a blank, ask them to point you in the direction of the others."

"Sounds like a plan."

The search for Rocky would have to wait until tomorrow because I was starving, and I wanted to grab dinner before my visit to Feline Cruises AKA Cruise Time.

**

"Just talk me through it again." Jack was loading the dishwasher. We'd just finished the meal he'd lovingly prepared.

"It's quite simple. I'm going to investigate this cruise operation because I think there's something dodgy going on."

"Really? Cruises for cats? What could possibly be dodgy about that?"

"Winky is all set to hand over his money this weekend."

"What do you think is going on?"

"That's what I intend to find out. When I was there yesterday, I overheard them say that something would be happening tonight, something they didn't want me to know about. I intend to find out what that is."

"Will this entail you turning yourself into a cat?"

"Maybe. I won't know until I get there."

"What kind of cat will you be?"

"Why does that matter?"

"I'm just trying to picture you as a cat. I see you as a Persian."

"You're getting all weird again."

227

"Or maybe a Birman."

"Enough with the cats. Let's change the subject."

"Okay. You haven't forgotten it's the poetry recital tomorrow have you?"

"I've been trying very hard to."

"I wish I could be there to see you."

"And how would you explain that there were two versions of you?"

"I could say we were twins."

"Or you could just do the recital yourself instead of making me do it."

"He's your tortoise. I'm not reading that rubbish."

"If you really loved me, you'd do it."

"Haven't you learned by now that kind of emotional blackmail doesn't work?"

Before I could respond, there was a knock at the door.

"Who's that?"

"It might be Bertie."

"Who's Bertie?"

"He's the local reporter for TenPin Monthly. I told you about him yesterday."

"Oh yeah, I remember." Actually, I didn't. As soon as Jack mentioned anything bowling related, I tuned out. "Just remind me why he's coming?"

"To interview me, of course."

But, as it turned out, it wasn't Bertie.

"Good evening." The man at the door was wearing a white coat and hat. "I hope I'm not disturbing your dinner. My name is Billy Bass. I'm a mobile fishmonger." He pointed to the white van parked on the road in front of our house. "I wondered if I can interest you in having fresh fish delivered to your door?"

Before I could tell him to sling his hook, Jack got in first.

"We already have someone who delivers fish to us. Terry Salmon, do you know him?"

"Of course. I'd be the last person to criticise Terry, but the quality of his fish is poor, and his prices are ridiculous." He handed Jack a leaflet. "I'll leave you this to study, and if you decide you'd like top quality fish at rock-bottom prices, just give me a call."

"Okay, thanks," Jack said, and then closed the door.

"He was a piece of work, wasn't he?" I led the way back to the kitchen. "For someone who didn't want to criticise his competitor, he did a pretty good hatchet job on Terry."

"I guess all's fair in love and fishmongering." Jack laughed at his own joke. "I might as well at least take a look at what he has to offer."

"I should be making tracks."

"Have you decided what kind of cat you're going to be?"

"No, I haven't, and even if I had, I wouldn't tell you. Enjoy your interview with Bertie."

***

When I arrived at the offices of Cruise Time, I was rather surprised to find that they were closed. Perhaps my visit the previous day had spooked them? I was just about to magic myself back home when I heard meowing—a lot of meowing. It seemed to be coming from behind the neighbouring unit, which had no sign on the front, and from the outside at least, appeared to be empty. Gingerly, I edged around the building, and peeked around the back.

There was a line of some twenty or so cats, queuing to

board a coach. Seeing them aboard, were the witch and wizard who I'd encountered the previous day.

"All aboard," the wizard said. "It's only a couple of hours now until the ship sets sail."

The cats all looked excited to be embarking on the holiday of a lifetime. It appeared that the coach was about to ferry them to the coast where they'd board their cruise liner. Perhaps I'd been worrying over nothing.

And yet, I still had a niggling doubt in my mind. I had originally planned to turn myself into a cat, but instead, I went with invisibility. As soon as the last cat was on the coach, I sneaked on board.

A few minutes later, the wizard climbed onto the coach and closed the door behind him. "Everyone ready?" The cats nodded enthusiastically. "Okay, off we go." He gave the driver the thumbs up, and the coach pulled away.

No sooner had we started to move than I sensed the wizard was casting a spell. Although I couldn't make out what it was, the effect was plain to see: All of the cats fell silent and stared ahead through glazed eyes.

The coach didn't even leave the industrial estate. Instead, it took a circular route around it, and then returned to the unit from which it had left only a few minutes earlier.

The wizard opened the door, and the cats filed off the coach. Waiting there to greet them was the witch. "Welcome to the cruise ship Whiskers. Please come on board." She opened the back door to the unit, and the cats filed inside. Still invisible, I hurried off the coach and followed them.

The cats, who were still out of it, were seated on rows of benches, facing a huge screen.

"Welcome passengers, one and all." The wizard had taken up a position facing the rows of seats. "I'm Captain White. On behalf of Feline Cruises it is my pleasure to welcome you aboard this luxurious ship. We will be setting sail shortly."

Moments later, the large screen came to life with images of a blue ocean. As the cats stared silently at the screen, the wizard and witch made their way to the door.

I followed them.

"That's the best one yet," the wizard said.

"And no sign of that nosey parker from yesterday."

"I told you there was nothing to worry about. Just make sure you keep them supplied with food and drink every day."

"Okay. How long is this one?"

"Just five days."

"We took a record number of bookings yesterday."

"I know. At this rate, we're going to need another unit."

I'd seen all I needed to see.

Once I was some distance from the unit, I reversed the 'invisible' spell, and gave Daze a call. She'd finished work for the day, but said I was welcome to nip over to her place.

***

"Come in, Jill. I was just going to have a beer—non-alcoholic, obviously—do you want one?"

"Not for me, thanks."

"Come through to the living room. I need to sit down; my feet haven't touched the ground all day. What was it you wanted to talk to me about?"

"I may have some customers for you." I told her about the cruise scam and how the wizard and witch were fleecing unsuspecting cats out of their cash.

"I've seen something like this before."

"Really?"

"It was a few years ago. A wizard who went by the name of—err—what was it now? Oh yes, Fabian, Fabian Frostmore. Hold on a minute, let me just check something." She took out her phone and made a call. Moments later, she'd confirmed her hunch. "He was released from prison two months ago. It didn't take him long to get started again."

"Was he doing the same thing last time? Cats and cruises?"

"No, it was dogs then. Canine Cruises, if memory serves. How did you happen to stumble across this lowlife?"

"Winky was on the point of booking a cruise."

"That's your cat, isn't it? How can he afford to go on a cruise?"

"That cat is loaded. If there's a money-making scheme to be had, he's all over it."

"I hope he appreciates what you've done."

"He doesn't know yet."

"Blaze and I will pay Mr Frostmore and his assistant a visit in the morning."

"What about the cats he's got there now? They'll still be under his spell."

"We'll be able to sort that out."

"Okay, thanks. I'd better get back to Jack."

"Before you go, I have something to tell you. I was

going to give you a call in the morning. We had a cyclopper brought in earlier today. He'd been stealing handbags in Washbridge, and tragically his actions have resulted in a woman's death. I believe you already know all about this."

"Who brought him in?"

"The head cyclopper."

"Ned?"

"That's him. He told me that it was you who'd brought the thief to his attention."

"He tried to snatch Kathy's bag. A big mistake that earned him a smack around the head."

"No more than he deserved. He won't be seeing the outside of a prison cell for a very long time."

"By the way, Daze, I meant to ask, who on the Most Wanted list triggered the red alert you've been working on?"

"It's a really nasty one. Two sirens who have been on our Most Wanted list for ages have apparently sneaked back into Candlefield. We have to catch them before they hurt someone."

Sirens? Oh bum!

Chapter 22

"What's wrong, Jill?" Daze took my arm. "You look like you've just seen a ghost."

"You did say sirens, didn't you?"

"Yes, why?"

"My Greek mythology isn't the best, but aren't they supposed to lure sailors to their deaths?"

"That's right, but of course the reality is slightly different. It isn't just sailors — it's any man who happens to cross their paths."

"And they do it by singing?"

"Yes, but I still don't understand why you've turned so pale."

"I hope I'm wrong about this, but I have a horrible feeling that I know where your sirens are. And if I'm right, Lester could be in a whole lot of trouble."

"Lester? Your Aunt Lucy's husband?"

"Yeah. He started sleepwalking recently, and every time it's happened Aunt Lucy has found him headed towards the house next door."

"I still don't understand what that has to do with the sirens?"

"New neighbours moved into that house a few days ago: Two sisters, Aunt Lucy said. And get this, they're always singing."

"It's still a bit of a stretch."

"No, it isn't. Over the last few days, the postman and the milkman have both gone missing, and as far as we can make out, they disappeared somewhere close to Aunt Lucy's house."

"We'd better get over there."

"I'm right behind you."

***

This was no time to stand on ceremony, so I charged into Aunt Lucy's house, with Daze a few steps behind me.

"Jill? Daisy?" Aunt Lucy was alone on the sofa, watching TV. "Whatever is the matter?"

"Where's Lester?" I screamed at her.

"He's visiting a friend."

"Are you sure? Did you see him go?"

"You're scaring me, Jill. Please tell me what's going on."

"There's no time. Stay here."

I was headed for the door when Daze called me back. "Jill! Wait!"

"We have to get around there. They might have Lester."

"Who might have him?" Aunt Lucy was understandably frantic now.

"We need something to put in our ears." Daze turned to Aunt Lucy. "Do you have any cotton wool?"

"Yes, but I'm not doing anything until one of you tells me what's going on."

Reluctantly, because I was conscious that every second counted, I told Aunt Lucy of my suspicions: That I thought her neighbours were in fact sirens.

"Oh my goodness." Clearly shaken, she leaned against the wall for support.

"The cotton wool, Aunt Lucy."

"Sorry. I'll go and get it."

"Listen, Jill." Daze took my arm. "This isn't going to be easy. The sirens are extremely dangerous."

"We'll be alright once we have the cotton wool in our

235

ears, won't we?"

"I'm not sure if it will be enough. Their voices are an extremely powerful weapon."

"What's the plan, then?"

"I need you to go in first and try to distract them. Once you've done that, I'll sneak up and throw the net over them."

"Will that work? I thought you used the net to bring people back from the human world?"

"It sends them straight to prison here in Candlefield regardless of where they happen to be."

"Okay, that sounds like a plan."

"I want to come with you." Aunt Lucy came hurrying down the stairs, cotton wool in hand.

"It's far too dangerous." Daze took a card out of her pocket. "We need you to stay here, and if we're not back in fifteen minutes, call Blaze on this number and tell him what's happened. He'll know what to do."

"Okay." She tore the cotton wool in half and handed us both a piece.

I was about to put the cotton wool in my ears when Daze said, "I'll use hand signals from now on."

"Okay. Let's do this."

Once we were next-door, she made a number of hand gestures, which I interpreted to mean I should take the front door, and she'd go around the back. I gave her a thumbs up, and then waited for thirty seconds until I was sure she'd be in position.

How to get into the house? I could have used invisibility, but the whole point was to cause a distraction while Daze sneaked up on them.

Meanwhile, time was ticking by, so I knocked on the door.

What? Of course I had a plan. Of sorts.

Moments later, the door opened, and I came face to face with the two sisters.

One of them seemed to be mouthing something, and I was just about to ask her to speak up when I remembered the cotton wool in my ears.

"Pardon?" I pretended to scratch my ear while discreetly removing the cotton wool.

The woman had a face like thunder. "I said, can we help you?"

"Actually, I'm here to help you. Do you ever suffer from dry skin?"

"Sorry?"

"Dry skin? Is it a problem for you?"

"We don't have time for any of this, and we never buy at the door."

She was going to close the door in my face when her sister grabbed her by the arm. "Pea, wait. You know I've been having problems with my skin lately."

"We don't know who this woman is."

"I represent—err—Candlefield Cosmetics. We sell a wide range of products suitable for all skin types."

"Let her in, Pea. It can't do any harm to take a look."

"You're always the same, Aggy. It'll be rubbish like all the other stuff you've wasted money on."

"Please."

"Okay." She stood to one side. "You'd better come in."

As Aggy led the way across the hall, I took a good look around. I'm not sure what I expected to see, but the house

237

was remarkable only for how ordinary it was.

"Hurry up!" Pea ushered me into the lounge. "We don't have all day."

"Sorry."

"Okay, let's see this wonder cream," Aggy said.

"The cream?" Oh bum! "I don't actually have it with me but look." I held out my hands. "See? They used to be incredibly dry, but just look at them now."

"What's going on?" Pea demanded. "Who are you really?"

"I told you. I'm from Candlefield Cosmetics."

"You're a liar!" Pea turned to her sister. "She must be a retriever."

"No, I'm not. I'm—"

Both sisters began to advance towards me, and as they did, they began to sing.

The sound that came from their mouths was like nothing I'd ever experienced. I reached into my pocket for the cotton wool and stuffed it in my ears, but it made very little difference; the noise was unbearable. I backed slowly into the corner of the room and dropped onto my knees. The only thing that could save me now was magic, but my head was so scrambled by their singing that I couldn't think straight. I was growing weaker by the second, and I wasn't sure how much more I could stand. Consciousness slowly began to slip away.

The next thing I knew, someone was shaking me. It was Daze, and she appeared to be pointing to her ears.

"What?" I managed to get to my feet.

She gestured again to her ears, and this time I realised she was telling me to remove the cotton wool.

"Are you okay, Jill?"

"I think so. Did you get them?"

"Yeah, they should be behind bars by now. Dry skin cream? What were you thinking?"

"I honestly have no idea."

"Are you sure you're okay?"

"I am now. We should take a look around. You look down here; I'll look upstairs."

Once Daze had silenced the sirens, my head had quickly cleared, and I was now firing on all cylinders again. I checked all three bedrooms, but there was no sign of the postman or milkman. Same with the bathroom—nothing.

Daze was standing at the bottom of the stairs. "Anything up there?"

"No."

I started down the stairs, but before I was halfway, a noise stopped me dead in my tracks.

"Did you hear that?"

Daze nodded. "I think it came from the loft."

We both hurried back upstairs, and I pulled down the loft ladder.

"Be careful up there, Jill."

I felt around in the dark until my hand brushed against the light cord.

"Have they gone?" said the mousy little man in a postman's uniform, who was cowering at the far side of the loft space.

"Yes, it's safe now."

"Are you sure?" A second man appeared from behind a dusty set of drawers.

"I'm positive. Come on, I'll help you to get down."

239

Out on the street, the two men didn't appear to be any the worse for their ordeal.

"You must be Monty." I approached the mousy man. "I've met your wife, Felicity."

"She must be worried sick. Do you have a phone that I can borrow to call her?"

"Of course." I handed it to him, and then turned to the other man. "I'm sorry, but I don't know your name."

"It's Sid. I can't thank you enough for rescuing us. Another day or two and I reckon we'd have been goners."

"I'm surprised they left you alive this long," Daze said.

"From what we overheard, I think they intended to take us to their other sister who they'd left behind in the human world. I dread to think what they had planned for us once we got there. Could I borrow your phone?"

"Sure." Daze handed it to him, and he called his wife to let her know he was safe.

Aunt Lucy came hurrying over to join us. "Was Lester in there?"

"No, there's no sign of him," I said. "We checked everywhere. I'm sure he's okay. Why don't you try calling him?"

"I have. A dozen times already, but it keeps going to voicemail. If anything has happened to—" She was interrupted by her phone ringing. "Lester? Why didn't you pick up?" She was on the verge of tears. "I've been worried that's why. Where are you? And you're sure you're alright? Okay. Yes, I'll explain everything when I see you later."

***

When I magicked myself back to the house, Jack was lying on the sofa watching TenPin TV.

"Did you find out if the cruises are legit?" he said.

"They weren't. It's a scam."

I explained to him how the wizard had been using magic to make the punters think they were on a cruise ship when in fact they were locked away in an industrial unit in Nottingham.

"You have to hand it to the guy," Jack said. "It was an ingenious plan."

"It's not the first time he's done it either. According to Daze, he did the same thing a few years ago with dogs."

"Winky definitely owes you one for saving his money."

"That's not the only thing I've done since I left you. I've also rescued a postman and a milkman."

"How come?"

"Why don't you pour me a nice glass of wine, and I'll tell you all about it?"

And that's what I did, over a glass of red and a box of chocolates.

No, I didn't eat the whole box. Sheesh! Jack had at least two.

"Sirens?" He took a sip of wine. "I thought they were a Greek myth."

"So did I, but I can assure you they're very real. When they started to sing, I thought my head was going to explode."

"From what you've said, it sounds as if Lester had a lucky escape."

"He did. If Aunt Lucy wasn't such a light sleeper, he could easily have ended up in their clutches."

241

"What do you think they would have done to the two men you rescued?"

"Nothing good, that's for sure. Their third sister is still somewhere in the human world. They'd planned to take their captives back to her."

"Where do you reckon she is?"

"No idea. In a cave somewhere, probably. Then again, she could be living around the corner from us."

"I won't dare go to sleep now in case I sleepwalk."

"Don't worry. If you do, I'll come to your rescue."

"You? Don't make me laugh. You'd sleep through an avalanche."

Chapter 23

The next morning, I was on my way out to the car when Britt called me over.

"Morning, Jill. Tonight's the big night. I'm so excited."

"Right?"

"You haven't forgotten, have you? Jack—err—sorry, I mean Robert Hymes is giving a reading for my poetry society."

"Oh yeah. Of course."

"You should join us too. Guests are always welcome, and there's no pressure to become a member. Unless you want to of course."

"I'd love to come, but wouldn't you just know it, I already have a prior engagement. Is there any news on Lovely?"

Britt's face fell, and I knew the answer even before she spoke. "Nothing. Kit says I should resign myself to the fact that I may never see her again."

"I'm so sorry." I considered asking if she'd like to adopt Winky, but that would have meant I'd have to live next-door to him, so I thought better of it.

***

Mrs V was busy knitting. "Morning, Jill."

"Morning. I haven't heard you mention Armi's magician's act for a day or two. Has he given up on it?"

"I wish. I long for the days when all he thought about was cuckoo clocks."

"Is he still practising, then?"

"Every night, but I've refused point blank to take part.

243

Once sawn, twice shy."

"Someone I know has started doing magician shows for kids. He must be doing okay because he's gone from working full-time to part-time in his other job."

"I think Armi's hoping to do shows for kids eventually, but from what I've seen of his act up to now, that's not likely to happen for a long time."

"How's the house hunting going?"

"No luck so far, but we do have another property lined up to view. We're going to see it tomorrow evening. While we're out, I thought we might drop in on you to see the cuckoo clock, if that's convenient."

"Of course. We'll be pleased to see you. The clock is looking really good."

"Armi always gets a kick out of seeing his clocks in-situ."

Winky was on the sofa; he was wearing a Hawaiian shirt, shorts and sunglasses.

"What on earth do you look like?" I laughed.

"I'm in holiday mood. It's not long now until I set sail on the high seas."

"About that, I have some bad news, I'm afraid."

"I don't want to hear it, Negative Nancy."

"I'm afraid that you have to. It's about the company behind Feline Cruises."

"What about them?"

"They're running a scam. There are no cruises; it's all just an illusion."

"How would you know?"

"I was concerned for you, so I went to check them out. They cast a spell on the unsuspecting feline passengers, and then lock them away in an industrial unit for the duration of the 'cruise'."

"I don't believe you. You're just saying that because you're jealous because I'm going on a cruise and you can't afford a weekend in Skegness."

"I'm not jealous. I'm looking out for you."

"Prove that it's a scam."

"Can't you just take my word for it?"

"I want to see it with my own eyes."

"Shouldn't that be *eye*?"

"That's a low blow, even for you."

"Sorry, I didn't mean that. Give me your paw, and I'll take you there, so you can see for yourself."

Moments later, we landed outside Cruise Time, and it seemed we'd timed it just right.

"Jill?" Daze was clearly surprised to see me. "What are you doing here?"

"I wasn't expecting to be here, but this one—" I gestured to Winky who was still recovering from the journey. "He doesn't believe me about the scam."

"You'd better take him over to the unit. Blaze is helping those cats on the current 'cruise'."

"What happened to Frostmore?"

"He and his assistant are behind bars in Candlefield."

"Okay, thanks. Come on, Winky." I led the way over to the unit where Blaze was ushering the feline 'cruise passengers' out into the daylight. They all looked disorientated and confused.

"Morning, Jill," Blaze gave me a little wave. "This was a good catch you made. Frostmore is a slippery character."

"Is it okay if we take a quick look inside?"

245

"Be my guest."

Winky followed me into the unit where the large screen was now playing to an empty room.

"See?" I spread my arms. "This would have been your cruise."

"The cheating lowlifes! They almost had my money."

"This is the point where you thank me."

"Thanks," he said, in almost a whisper.

"Sorry? Did you say something?"

"Thank you."

"You're very welcome. Come on, we'd better get back. And for heaven's sake, get changed out of that ridiculous outfit."

***

Today was the relaunch of Cuppy C's cat café. The place was full; there wasn't a spare seat to be had.

"I didn't think you were coming, Jill." Amber was clearly stressed out.

"Sorry, I had a cat thing of my own to attend to. I haven't missed anything, have I?"

"No. Pearl's in the back. When I knock on the door, she's going to let the cats come through."

"It looks like you have another good turnout."

"People are really looking forward to this."

"Let's hope the cats hang around a little longer than they did the last time." I grinned.

"It's no laughing matter, Jill. That setback cost us a lot of money."

"Sorry."

"Anyway, this time we've posted Mindy at the door.

She's going to make sure that none of the cats make a run for it." Amber turned to Mindy. "Are you ready?"

After Mindy had given her the thumbs up, Amber knocked on the door to signal to Pearl to release the cats.

And in they marched. Now I'm no expert on cats, but I could have sworn that at least two of them looked rather familiar. They seemed to bear an uncanny resemblance to two of the cats who had appeared at the first launch. The customers neither knew nor cared about that. They were too busy cooing all over the felines who were strutting between the tables.

Every time more customers arrived, Mindy made sure to open the door only wide enough and long enough to allow them inside. All seemed to be going swimmingly.

Until—

"I have a delivery for you out the back." The delivery driver appeared at the door that led out into the alleyway at the back of the shop.

"The door! Shut the door!" Pearl yelled at him, but it was too late because the cats were already headed past him.

"No!" Amber screamed, but it was to no avail. The cat café was once again minus its cats.

As the disappointed customers began to leave, Amber and Pearl took a seat at one of the many now vacant tables.

"What are we going to do?" Amber said.

"We can't keep spending money on more cats." Pearl sighed. "We'll go bankrupt at this rate."

"Something about this just doesn't pass my sniff test," I said.

"What do you mean?"

247

"I can understand one or two cats making a break for it, but for all of them to do it? And for it to happen twice? That just doesn't make sense."

"What are you saying, Jill?" Pearl said.

"I'm saying something weird is going on. Didn't you notice that two of the cats looked like those that were here on the first launch day?"

"Actually, I did notice that." Amber nodded. "But I assumed that was just a coincidence."

"I think this warrants further investigation. Would you like me to check into it?" I offered.

"Yes, please. We can't carry on like this."

"Okay. You'd better give me the contact details for Cat City, and I'll see what I can find out."

I waited until I had left Cuppy C before giving Cat City a call.

"Cat City, Felix speaking."

"Hi. I'll be opening a cat café in a few months' time, and I'm looking for someone who can supply a number of cats suitable for living in that environment. Is that something you can help with?"

"Absolutely. How many cats were you thinking of?"

"I'm not sure. I'd like to pop over and discuss it with you if that's possible?"

"Sure. We're rather busy today, but we'll certainly be able to spare you some time tomorrow morning at ten if that works for you?"

"That sounds great."

"What's your name, please?"

"Kitty Sears."

"What a fabulous name. I look forward to seeing you

tomorrow."

"Me too. Oh, and Felix, would it be possible to see some of your cats while I'm there?"

"No problem."

***

I'd no sooner finished speaking to Cat City than I received a phone call from Longdale prison, asking if I'd accept a reverse-charge call from Laurence Forrest.

"Jill? My mother said you wanted me to call you. Do you have any good news for me?"

"Not yet, I'm afraid. I wanted to ask you about a visit you had at your flat recently from a maintenance man."

"What does that have to do with anything?"

"Maybe nothing, but I'd still like you to tell me about it."

"There's nothing much to tell. I'd called the landlord because we were having a problem with one of the window locks."

"Did you have to wait long for them to come out?"

"No, they've always been pretty good at sorting out problems when they arise."

"Do you remember the man who came to do the job?"

"Not really. I saw him in, showed him the window that was causing the problem, and then left him to it."

"You didn't have any kind of falling out with him?"

"No. Why would you ask that?"

"I spoke to your neighbour, Louise Roache. She approached the man after he'd been at your flat, and she thought he seemed worked up about something."

"I don't understand that because nothing happened. In

249

fact, when I went to check how he was getting on, he'd already left."

"Wasn't that a bit strange? For him to leave without saying anything?"

"I seem to recall that Alison and I were having a blazing row about something at the time, so he probably didn't like to walk in on us. He'd sorted out the window lock, and that's all I was concerned about. I still don't know what this has to do with anything."

"Probably nothing. Thanks for calling me, Laurence."

"You'll let me know if there are any developments?"

"Of course."

One of the things I'd learned from my dad was that you should trust your instincts, and this was definitely one of those times. There was something about the maintenance man's visit that bothered me. Specifically, I was curious about what had got him so riled when he left the Forrests' flat. And why had he resigned immediately after that visit? I could well be headed up a blind alley; it wouldn't be the first time, but I wouldn't rest until I knew more about him. Edward Tucker, the landlord, wasn't going to allow me to see his ex-employee's record, but that wasn't really an obstacle because this girl got skillz.

What? Didn't you know I'm down with the kidz?

Edward Tucker worked out of an office just down the road from Kathy's first shop. As I was walking past, she spotted me and beckoned me inside.

"Where are you off to?"

"I'm working on a case. I'm on my way to steal some personnel records."

"Very funny. What are you really doing?"

"Nothing particularly interesting. How's the wedding business?"

"Thriving. I should have done this years ago instead of wasting my time working for other people."

"Are Peter and the kids okay?"

"Fine, thanks. Mikey's a bit disillusioned with his canary, though."

"How come?"

"It doesn't seem very happy. We've bought a load of toys for it, but they haven't made any difference."

"He's probably lonely. He needs a lady friend."

"When did you become the canary whisperer?"

"It's just a hunch. What are you going to do about it?"

"There's not much we can do. Mikey's beginning to wish he'd gone for his second choice of pet."

"What was that?"

"A rabbit, but he can't have one now that he has the canary."

"What if I could find a good home for the bird?"

"Do *you* want it?"

"Me? Not likely, but I might know someone who does."

"Really? Well, if you do, go for it. If we can rehome the canary, then we'll buy Mikey his rabbit."

"Okay. I'll check with my friend and let you know."

"Great."

Once I was out of the shop, I gave Dorothy a call.

"It's Jill. Did your canary ever turn up?"

"No. I'm a dead woman walking. When Mum finds out, she'll kill me."

"I think I know where he is."

251

"Really?"

"Yes. Unless there are two lovelorn canaries called Bob in Washbridge, he's currently living at my sister's house."

"Where did she get him from?"

"I'm not sure. A pet shop, I think, but that's not the point. He's supposed to be a pet for their boy, Mikey, but it isn't working out. The lad would prefer to have a rabbit. I've just spoken to my sister, and she'd be happy to give the canary to a good home. I told her I might know someone who would take it."

"That's great, Jill. When would I be able to collect him?"

"I'll give you Kathy's phone number and you can arrange it between you."

"Brilliant."

"Just one thing. I wouldn't mention that he used to belong to you. I just told her you were a canary fancier."

"No problem, and thanks again. I owe you one."

Chapter 24

Edward Tucker's offices were on the ground floor of the building, so this was going to be easy peasy. I'd make myself invisible, sail inside, find the file I needed, and then I'd be on my way. What could be easier?

Or so I thought.

Seriously, who keeps a dog in their office? Yes, I know I have a cat, but that's an entirely different proposition.

"Buster! Settle down!" Tucker shouted at the Westie. "What's wrong with you today?"

The dog was taking not a blind bit of notice because he had sensed that there was someone else in the room. As soon as I'd slipped through the door, the dog had started barking, growling and running back and forth, trying to locate the source of the scent.

I had planned to wait until Tucker had slipped out of the office for a few minutes, and then to rifle through his files, but that wasn't going to work now that Buster was on my case.

It was time for plan B. Or, to be more accurate, it was time for me to come up with a plan B.

I was still trying to decide what to do when Tucker solved the problem for me.

"Come on." He grabbed a lead from out of the top drawer of his desk. "Let's see if we can't walk this off." The Westie ignored him and continued to bark in my direction. "Buster!" He clipped the lead to the dog's collar, and dragged him, still barking, out of the office.

Phew! That was too close for comfort.

It didn't take long to find the personnel file for Paul

Hattersley. Rather than trying to make notes and risk the return of Buster, I simply pocketed it and made my exit.

***

"You're it!" A young man tapped me on the shoulder, and then scooted away.

It was clearly 'tag' day in Coffee Games, but I wasn't in the mood for such silliness.

"Could I get a caramel latte, please, Sarah?"

"Sure, but you do realise you're *it*, don't you?"

"I don't have time to play games today."

"You can tag me if you like."

"Okay." I reached over and tapped her on the shoulder. "You're *it* now."

And then, much to my surprise, she leapt over the counter and began to chase the other customers. Only when she'd managed to tag someone else did she return to make my coffee.

To ensure that I wasn't disturbed again, I found a table at the back of the shop. I then scribbled a message on a sheet of A4 paper, which I placed on the table. It read:

No tagging allowed – I'm too busy!

Much to my relief, and if I'm honest, my surprise, the other customers respected the notice, and I was left in peace to study Hattersley's file.

When I'd spoken to Tucker on the phone, he'd indicated that Hattersley had been a model employee, and the file certainly bore that out. It also included the names and contact details for his two previous employers, but most important of all, it listed Hattersley's address.

It was time to pay our Mr Hattersley a visit.

"Are you looking for Paul, love?" A woman, with a long-haired cat in her arms, appeared in the doorway of the next-door flat.

"Paul Hattersley, yeah."

"He moved out a couple of weeks ago."

"You wouldn't know where I could find him, would you?"

"No, I haven't seen hide nor hair of him since he left."

"Did you know him well?"

"No. He was a bit of a quiet one. I never saw him speak to anyone."

"Okay, thanks."

Curiouser and curiouser.

***

One of Hattersley's previous employers was based in Newcastle. I gave them a call.

"Rhodine Estates, Ted Rhodine speaking."

"My name is Jill Maxwell. I'm a private investigator working in Washbridge."

"Moving to Newcastle, are you? You've come to the right place. I have a few properties—"

"Actually, no. I was hoping to speak to you about an ex-employee of yours, Paul Hattersley."

"What about him? What's this about?"

"It's rather complicated, but it relates to a case I'm working on. I can't go into detail, I'm afraid, but I believe Hattersley may be able to help with my enquiries. He's just left his current job and moved out without a forwarding address. Until I can locate him, I thought I

255

might get a better idea of the kind of man he is by speaking to his previous employers."

"He was one of the best workers I've ever had. Very quiet, though. Always kept himself to himself."

"Why did he leave?"

"Your guess is as good as mine. He just rang up one day, and said he wasn't coming back. I wasn't very happy about that, as you might imagine. He said it was a personal matter and that he was sorry, and then he hung up."

"You gave him a reference, though?"

"Yeah, well I figured he'd done a good job while he was here, and if he really had suffered some kind of personal tragedy, I didn't want to make matters worse by refusing him a reference. He hasn't gone and done anything bad, has he?"

"Thank you for your help, Mr Rhodine. I'm most grateful."

Before moving to Rhodine Estates, Hattersley had worked at Carmichael Properties in Liverpool. Freddy Tranter, the proprietor there, told me a story not dissimilar to the one I'd heard from Ted Rhodine. Hattersley had been a model employee who had kept his head down, and never caused any problems. But just as with his other two employers, he had simply quit on the spot one day. Another personal tragedy apparently.

That was way too much of a coincidence for my liking, but not much help if I couldn't actually track down Hattersley. I did still have one slim hope: The personnel file I'd taken from Edward Tucker included a contact mobile phone number for his next of kin who was listed as his brother, James.

I gave the number a call and it rang out before going to voicemail. With little or no expectation, I left my name and number, and a message asking him to give me a call back.

*****

It was time to pay a visit to Pooch Pound in GT. It turned out to be much like any dog rescue centre in the human world, except of course, there were one hundred percent more ghosts.

"You're not a ghost?" The young man was sporting a yellow and white striped blazer, matched with white trousers; he looked like he should have been handing out deckchairs at the seaside.

"That's correct. I'm not a ghost."

"How can you be in GT, then? I don't understand."

I spent the next few minutes explaining to him who I was and how come I was able to visit GT.

"Just wait until I tell my Mum about you. She'll never believe it. Would you mind if I took a selfie with you?"

"Err, okay."

"Thanks." He took out his phone and took a quick snap of the two of us. "I'm Timz, by the way. That's T-I-M-Z, but the 'Z' is silent."

"Right."

"How can I help you today?"

"I'm looking for a dog."

"You're definitely in the right place, then. What breed did you have in mind?"

"Actually, I'm looking for a specific dog: One that went

missing recently. His name is Rocky."

"I see. And what breed is Rocky?"

"That was an awfully good question, but one I hadn't had the sense to ask Old Mother Mason.

"I don't actually know. I do know he was wearing a nametag, though. Maybe you could check your records to see if you've had a dog called Rocky handed in recently?"

"I'll take a look." He tapped away on his computer. "Oh?"

"What?"

"I have good news and bad news."

"What's the good news?"

"I do have a dog named Rocky."

"And the bad news?"

"Rocky! Leave Rocky alone. Rocky, stop pulling on that lead! Don't do that, Rocky!"

You would be forgiven for thinking that I'd found myself one extremely overactive pooch, but you'd be wrong. In fact, I had five dogs: a rottweiler, a pointer, a border collie, a springer spaniel and a dachshund. All of whom were named Rocky. Who knew it was such a popular name?

When Timz—with the silent 'Z', had shown me his computer records, I'd been stunned. So stunned, in fact, that I'd stupidly agreed to his suggestion that I should take all of them for Old Mother Mason to see. If I'd been thinking more clearly, I might have had the good sense to take a photo of them instead.

"Rocky, don't do that just there—" Too late. It was just as well Tim—with the silent 'Z', had had the foresight to furnish me with a number of doggy-poo bags. I would just have to hope that I had enough.

Once I'd finished with my poop-scooping duties, I gathered the dogs together as best I could, and then magicked myself over to the headmistress' office at CASS.

"Jill?" Ms Nightowl looked somewhat surprised to see me and my canine companions. "You didn't tell me that you'd swapped jobs?"

"Sorry?"

"I assume you're working as a dogwalker now?"

"These? No, they belong to Old Mother Mason. Or at least, one of them does. I just don't know which one. Stop that, Rocky!"

"I see. I think."

"This is the reason she's been haunting the dorms. Her dog has gone missing, and she's been searching for him."

"Right? But why do you have five of them?"

"I forgot to ask what breed her dog was. The only thing I know is that he's called Rocky."

"And all of these —?"

"Are called Rocky, yes. I just wanted to let you know I was here in case you started to receive reports of a strange woman walking around the school with a pack of dogs."

"Right, thanks. As it happens, there haven't been any sightings of the ghost for the last couple of nights. At least none that have been reported to me."

"I'll get down to the dorms and see if I can find her."

"Okay. Good luck."

I'd just started for the door when the headmistress called me back. "Err, Jill." She pointed at the carpet. "You've left something behind."

"Which one of you did that? Sorry, Headmistress. I'll

see to it."

I spent the next hour wandering up and down the corridors outside the dorms, in search of Old Mother Mason, but there was no sign of her.

The dogs were becoming more and more restless, and I suspected it was well past their dinner time. I had no choice but to go down to the cellar and hope I'd find Mason down there.

Wouldn't you just know it, all of the dogs were okay with the semi-darkness of the cellar except for the rottweiler.

"Come on, you big lump, there's nothing to be afraid of."

The cellar covered a vast area, and it would have taken hours to search it all.

"Hello! Mrs Mason! Are you down here?"

The only thing I could hear was my own words echoing back to me.

Another hour later, my feet were aching, and I was beginning to think I was going to have to take the dogs home with me, but then I heard footsteps.

"Mrs Mason!"

"Who's that?" Her voice came from somewhere in the shadows.

"It's Jill Maxwell. We met the other day."

Moments later, she came floating through an arch to my right. "What brings you down here? And why do you have so many dogs with you?"

"I've been searching for your Rocky."

She put two fingers in her mouth and whistled. A few seconds later, a pug came trotting into the room, and began to growl at the other dogs.

"This is my Rocky." She scooped him into her arms. "Don't be rude to our visitors," she scolded him.

"But, I—err—when did he come back?"

"A couple of days ago. He'd been out in the forest, chasing baby dragons, I reckon."

"That's why you haven't been up to the dorms?"

"Yes. Like I said the last time you were here, I prefer it down here. Those children are far too noisy."

"Right. What am I supposed to do with this lot?"

Luckily for me, Old Mother Mason was a dog-lover through and through, and she wouldn't hear of me taking the other dogs back to Pooch Pound. Instead, she decided to adopt all five of them.

Result!

***

After Saturday, I would no longer need my old banger because I would be the proud owner of a brand-new Jag. Much as I loved my old car, it was time to bid her farewell, so I thought I'd see what I could get for her.

Not much as it turned out.

Three of the car dealers I called at laughed in my face. Another, Lance, offered to take it off my hands at no cost, as a favour to *a pretty, young thing*. Needless to say, I told him where he could shove his offer, how far and how hard.

In the end, though, I had to accept the inevitable.

"Is that Washbridge Breakers Yard?"

"Yep. Wally Bridge speaking. What can I do you for?"

"I wondered if you'd be interested in my car?" I gave

261

him all the relevant details: make, model, mileage etc.

"Tenner."

"Ten pounds? Is that all you'd give me for it?"

"Nah, love, you've got it the wrong way around. You have to give me a tenner to take it away."

That was outrageous. It was an even worse offer than the one I'd had earlier, but it was too late to go back to Lance because I'd already told him where to shove it.

Oh well, what did it matter? After Saturday, I'd be driving around in my spanking new car.

"Okay. Ten pounds it is."

"Where and when can we collect it?"

I gave him the address. "Do you work weekends?"

"We never close, love."

"In that case, can you collect it on Saturday afternoon?"

"No problem. Consider it done."

Chapter 25

"Go on," Jack pleaded. "Pretty please."

"I'm not doing it while you're here. Go upstairs."

"But I want to see you turn yourself into me."

"No, it's freaky enough having to do it at all, but I'm definitely not going to do it while you're watching."

"Go on, *Robert*, please."

"Get upstairs!"

"Spoilsport. I can still watch you leave through the bedroom window."

"Not if I use magic to tie you to the bed."

"That sounds like it could be fun."

"You're impossible. Just go away!"

But before he could, something somewhere beeped.

"What was that?" Jack glanced all around.

I checked my pocket, and just as I suspected, the Z-Call button was glowing orange. "I need to make a phone call."

"What's going on, Jill?"

"Hold on." I called Z-Watch.

"Z-Watch. Ike Cann speaking."

"Ike, it's Jill Maxwell."

"Passphrase, please?"

"Crazy just got crazier."

"Hi, Jill. What can I do for you?"

"My Z-Call button just went off."

"Did it? Hold on a minute while I check."

"Okay."

"What's going on?" Jack mouthed.

"Zombies, I think."

"Jill?" Ike was back on the line. "The monitor shows

263

there's a single rogue Z in your vicinity. I can have someone over there in a couple of minutes."

"It's okay, I'll see to it."

"Are you sure?"

"Absolutely. Thanks, Ike."

"What's happening?" Jack demanded.

"It looks like you're going to have to do the poetry recital after all."

"Why?"

"Because there's a herd of zombies headed this way. I have to stay here and deal with them."

"Oh no you don't. This is just a hoax, isn't it? It's your way of getting out of the recital."

"I wouldn't lie about something like this."

"I don't believe you."

"Come and see for yourself." I led the way into the kitchen, and just as I'd hoped, there in the field, in the distance, was the zombie Ike had told me about.

"I can't see anything." Jack was staring out of the window.

"Over there!" I pointed.

"Oh yeah. I can only see one, though."

"Up to now, but the others won't be far behind. If I don't stop them, the street will be overrun by the time I get back from the recital. And to be honest, I don't fancy being married to a zombie."

"What? Do you think they might—err—turn me into one?"

"That's kind of what they do."

"I'll do the recital. You stay here and get rid of the zombies."

"Are you sure? I'm happy to do the reading."

"No, I'll do it. Where is Rhymes' book?"

"On the hall table."

"Okay." He gave me a quick peck on the lips. "Will you be alright here?"

"I'll be fine. I'll see you later."

I waited until I'd seen Jack leave, and then made my way out into the back garden. By now, the solitary Z was much closer.

"Thanks, buddy," I shouted to him. "I almost feel bad about having to do this."

But I did it anyway, and the lightning bolt soon despatched him.

I never thought the day would come when I was pleased to see a zombie, but this one had done me a real solid. I'd been dreading the poetry recital, but thanks to the Z, I now had the evening to myself.

Snigger.

***

I had my feet up on the sofa, and a box of chocolates and a glass of wine on the coffee table next to me; life was sweet. The only thing that would have been better was if I could have seen Jack, reciting Rhymes' poetry. I had considered making myself invisible and sneaking into the recital, but I couldn't trust myself not to laugh.

I should have spent the evening watching mindless TV, but I couldn't get the Forrest case out of my mind. In particular, I was intrigued by what I'd discovered about Paul Hattersley. On three separate occasions, he'd walked out of jobs where, until that point, he'd been considered a

265

model employee. On each occasion, he'd claimed a personal tragedy had left him with no choice but to quit. Either the guy was the unluckiest man in the world or something more sinister was behind his sudden exits.

I fired up my laptop and searched the local newspaper headlines, in Newcastle and Liverpool, for the dates around the time that Mr Hattersley had done his disappearing act. What I found was very interesting indeed.

In Newcastle, one week after Hattersley had walked out of Rhodine Estates, the headline in the Newcastle Chronicle read: Husband arrested for brutal murder of wife.

I traced the story through the following months up to the point where the man, Harry Douglas, was convicted of his wife's murder. He was sentenced to life imprisonment. As if the story wasn't already tragic enough, the couple's only child was reported as having been taken into care.

And there was more.

A couple of weeks after Hattersley had walked out of his job in Liverpool, the Liverpool Times ran a headline that read: Husband arrested for wife's murder.

Ron Ploughright was eventually convicted of beating his wife, Carol, to death. After the trial, the article quoted his sister, Irene Sutherland, as saying that an innocent man had been jailed, and that she would continue to fight to prove his innocence. The article also mentioned that the couple's only child, a girl named Chelsea, was going to be cared for by the sister.

There were too many coincidences now to ignore.

On a whim, I searched the Liverpool phone directory

for anyone called Sutherland. There were five in total, but none with the initial 'I'. Still, it was worth a punt.

I drew a blank on the first three, but then—

"Hello?" The man barked into the phone.

"I'm sorry to trouble you. I'm looking for Irene—"

"Irene, it's for you." He dropped the receiver.

Moments later, someone else picked it up. "Hello?"

"Is that Irene Sutherland?"

"Speaking. Who is this?"

"You don't know me, but my name is Jill Maxwell. I believe your brother was jailed for—"

"Are you the press? If you are, you can do one. I've got nothing to say to you."

"I'm not the press. I'm a private investigator, based in Washbridge. I'm currently working on a case that has similarities to your brother's. A woman has been murdered, and her husband, my client's son, has been charged with her murder."

"I don't see what that has to do with Ron."

"Maybe nothing, but there's a chance, and it's only a slim chance I must emphasise, that the same person could be responsible for both murders."

"Who is he? Who did it?"

"I can't say anything else until I know more about your brother's case."

"What do you need? I know everything there is to know about it. I should do, I've lived and breathed it ever since it happened."

"This is going to seem like a really weird question, but did your brother own his own property or did he rent?"

"They rented. He and Carol had a flat near the city centre."

267

"Do you know who the landlord was?"

"I have no idea. What does that have to do with anything?"

"Is there any way you could find out?"

"Ron is due to call me in the morning. He calls me first thing every Friday. I suppose I could ask him."

"While you're speaking to him, ask him if he recalls a maintenance man visiting the flat just before the murder, would you?"

"Okay, but I still don't understand how any of this is relevant."

"Call me tomorrow after you've spoken to your brother, and I'll explain everything then."

***

I'd just settled down to watch TV when the door opened, and in walked Jack.

"You're back early. Did you get cold feet?"

"No, I gave the reading, and then made my excuses and left. I told them it was police business, so no one asked any questions."

"How did the recital go?"

"How do you think it went? That tortoise is the worst poet ever."

"What did the audience make of it?"

"That's the weirdest part: They all seemed to lap it up; they couldn't get enough of it. I'd only intended reading one poem, but they insisted I read another four. I'd still be at it now if I hadn't told them that duty called."

"You're a star." I gave him a kiss.

"Never mind the soft soap. If you ever drop me in it like

this again, Jill, I will be forced to kill you. Speaking of which, how did you get on with the walking dead?"

"It was touch and go for a while. I've never seen so many zombies, but I managed to come through it unscathed."

"I'm ready for a nice sit down and a glass of wine."

"You deserve one. I'll pour you a glass."

But before I could, there was a knock at the door.

"It must be a zombie." The colour drained from Jack's face.

"Don't be daft. Of course it isn't."

"How can you be so sure?"

"Because a zombie wouldn't knock."

Despite my reassurances, Jack tucked in behind me as I went to answer the door.

"Mrs V? Armi? What a pleasant surprise."

"I know I said we'd come around tomorrow night, but we've just been to look at another house a few miles away. Is it okay for us to take a quick look at the cuckoo clock now?"

"Of course, come on in."

"I was just about to have a glass of wine," Jack said. "Would you care to join me?"

"I'll have one, please," Mrs V said. "But not for Armi, he's driving, aren't you, my little gingerbread man?"

"I am, dewdrop. A glass of water would be nice, though."

"I'll see to those," Jack offered. "Jill, you can show our guests the clock."

"And your new carpet," Mrs V chipped in. "I'm looking forward to seeing that."

Oh bum! What colour had I said it was? Red? No.

Brown? No. Blue? Yes, that was it. I quickly cast a spell, so that when our guests walked through to the lounge, they would see the 'new' carpet.

"I thought you said it was green, Jill?" Mrs V looked puzzled.

"Did I? I meant greeny blue."

"It's navy, though, isn't it?"

"Err, yeah. I suppose it is. Do you like it?"

"It's lovely, and so is the clock. Doesn't it look handsome on the wall?"

"It's fantastic," I said, summoning up as much enthusiasm as I could.

"I think it's amazing how you're able to make something so intricate and beautiful, Armi." Jack was back with the drinks. "I wish I could do something like that."

"Don't be so modest, Jack," I said. "You have your own special talents."

"Like my bowling, you mean?"

"Actually, I was thinking more about your poetry."

He glared at me, and if I wasn't mistaken, he was planning how to kill me and then dispose of the body.

"I didn't know you wrote poetry, Jack," Mrs V said.

"I don't. Jill is pulling your—"

"He's actually just got back from a recital of his work, haven't you, darling?"

"I—err—"

"Why don't you read some of your poetry for Mrs V and Armi?" I grabbed the book that Jack had dropped onto the coffee table and handed it to him.

"They don't want to hear that," he protested.

"Of course we do, don't we, Armi?" Mrs V took a seat

on the sofa.

"Definitely." Armi sat next to her.

"Okay then, but just the one."

"Who is Robert Hymes?" Mrs V had noticed the name on the book.

"That's Jack's pen name, isn't it, darling? He's too modest to publish under his own name. Off you go, Jack."

Resigned to his fate, he began to recite one of Rhymes' masterpieces. The only thing more painful than the poem was the expression on our visitors' faces.

When he'd finished, Jack said, sheepishly, "It isn't very good, I'm afraid."

"Nonsense." I clapped. "That was excellent. Why don't you read another?"

"Actually." Mrs V got to her feet. "We should be going."

"Already? But you've only just arrived. Why don't you listen to Jack read some more?"

"We'd love to, but I left the oven on, didn't I, Armi?"

"I thought we were going to pick up a—"

"It's been lovely seeing you both." Mrs V grabbed Armi by the hand and dragged him to the door. "But we really must be going."

Once they'd left, I dissolved into laughter. It was only when I'd managed to wipe the tears from my eyes that I realised Jack wasn't sharing in the hilarity. He was staring at me stony-faced.

"I imagine you think that was funny?"

"Come on, Jack. Surely you can see the funny side."

Chapter 26

"Morning, Mrs V."

"Morning, dear. I hope you didn't mind us barging in on you like that last night?"

"Of course not. Armi seemed very pleased to see the cuckoo clock."

"He was. He enjoys seeing people getting pleasure out of his creations."

"And you both seemed to enjoy Jack's poetry reading." As witnessed by their speedy departure.

"Err, yes, it was — err — very — err —"

"*Enjoyable?*"

"That's right. Very enjoyable indeed."

"He's so very talented that husband of mine. I'm sure I could persuade him to read you some more of his work if you'd both like to drop by again sometime."

"We are very busy at the moment. What with the house hunting and everything. Maybe later in the year."

"Of course. He's quite a slow writer, but he may have some new work for you to hear by then."

Winky was unwrapping a long, narrow parcel.

"What have you got there?"

"My telescope of course."

"I'd forgotten you'd ordered that. How did it get here? I didn't see the postman."

"By FelEx."

"Don't you mean FedEx?"

"I know what I mean. FelEx stands for Feline Express." He lifted the telescope out of the box. "Isn't she a beauty?"

"It's very nice. What are you going to use it for?"

"I thought I might bake a cake with it." He rolled his eye. "What do you think I'm going to use it for?"

"I know what a telescope does. I was asking what you'll be looking at with it?"

"The sky of course."

"Nothing else, I hope?"

"I'm not some kind of Peeping Tom if that's what you're insinuating."

"Can I take a look through it?"

"Sure. Knock yourself out."

"I can't see anything. It isn't working."

"It might help if you removed the lens cover."

"Oh yeah. I knew that. That's better. It's very powerful, isn't it? I can see those flats across the road really clearly."

"I told you it was good."

"What are those two up to over there?"

"Oi! You were the one who said no spying on people."

"I'm not spying on anyone. I just noticed those two cats on top of that building."

"Here, let me see." Winky nudged me to one side. "That's Sid the Soot and Simon the Sweep."

"Let me guess, they're chimney sweeps?"

"Of course they're not. Why would you think that?"

"I just—err, never mind. Why are they up on the roof?"

"They're just drifters. They're always moving around."

"Isn't it dangerous?"

"Only if they fall off."

Thankfully, my phone rang and rescued me from that inane conversation.

"Is that Jill Maxwell?"

"Speaking."

"This is Irene Sutherland. I promised to ring you today

273

after I'd spoken to my brother."

"Did you ask him who he'd rented the flat from?"

"Yes. His landlord was a company called Carmichael Properties. I asked him about the maintenance man too. Ron said that one called a couple of weeks before Carol was murdered. He remembers because he and Carol were having a shouting match at the time."

"About what?"

"Nothing important. Just a silly squabble. Why did you want to know all of this stuff, anyway?"

"I wouldn't want to raise your hopes, but your brother's conviction and his wife's murder follow a pattern that I've identified. My client's case is very similar."

"Does that mean you'll be able to get Ron out of prison?"

"It's way too early to be making promises. I'm not even sure I'm right about any of this."

"Why don't you take what you know to the police?"

"Because they wouldn't be interested. Not without proof."

"Ron can't take much more of being locked up for something he didn't do."

"Please don't go raising his hopes. Not yet, at least. It would do more harm than good."

"When will you know if you'll be able to help?"

"I can't say for sure, but as soon as I do, I promise I'll be in touch."

This had all started out as a wild hunch on my part, but it was now looking as though there might actually be some mileage in it. The problem was, unless I could track down the itinerant Paul Hattersley, there was nothing I could do about it.

***

It was time to pay a visit to Cat City.

"Hi, I'm looking for Felix."

"That's me. Felix Le Chat at your service."

"Le Chat? Isn't that French for *the cat*?"

"Is it? I had no idea." He laughed. "I'm just messing with you. Yes, it is but my real name is Felix Mouser."

"Really?"

"No. I'm still messing with you. It's actually Homer Schloemer."

"I'm Kitty Sears. I rang yesterday."

"I remember. So, Kitty, you said that you're planning to open a cat café?"

"That's right. In a few months' time, if everything goes according to plan. I understand that you can provide cats specially trained for cat cafés?"

"Absolutely. That's one of the things we do. How many were you thinking of?"

"I'm not sure. I was hoping you might give me some advice on that subject."

"Assuming the café is a standard size — not too large — then ten cats is usually enough. You can always get more later if necessary."

"I don't suppose you have any cats here now that I could see, do you?"

"Absolutely. We actually have a dummy cat café set up at the rear of this building. We use it so that our cats are comfortable in that kind of environment. Follow me."

He led the way into what did indeed look like a cat café — minus the customers. The room was huge and full

275

of cats of all shapes and sizes.

"What do you think?" Felix spread his arms.

"It's very impressive, but what about people? There are no customers in here, so won't the cats freak out when they go into a real café?"

"We have that covered too. Although this isn't a commercial café, it does open its doors once a day just for an hour, during which time we serve drinks and cakes at cost price. That ensures the cats get used to being around people." He checked his watch. "It's due to open in about an hour, at midday. You're welcome to drop by again then if you wish."

"I might do that. What about the cost? How much do you charge per cat?"

"It varies according to the breed. Provided you don't want a pedigree, then you can work on an average of two-hundred pounds per cat. Obviously, the pedigrees are considerably more."

"Wow! I wasn't expecting them to be so expensive."

"You have to factor in that you'd be paying for cats that have experience of living in exactly the type of environment that you'll be offering your customers. If you were to put any old cat in there, the results would be disastrous."

"I guess so. Okay, thanks for showing me around. I might pop back later when the café is open."

"I look forward to seeing you then."

***

To pass the time until Cat City opened the doors to its cat café, I decided to call in at Aunt Lucy's. I wanted to check she'd got over the shock of discovering the truth about her now ex-neighbours.

"I still keep getting flashbacks, Jill. What if I hadn't woken and stopped Lester before he went next door? Who knows what might have happened to him?"

"But you did wake up, and he's fine."

"They seemed such nice young women too. It just goes to show you never can tell."

"I guess the house will be back on the market again."

"Yes, it's a pity Jack isn't a sup. You and he could move in."

"No offence, but there's no way I'd want to live that close to Grandma. Incidentally, Kathy has just bought herself a new house. It's beautiful and much larger than where they're living at present. I've been trying to persuade Jack that we should move house too, but he says we can't afford it."

"Maybe he'll see things differently when you get around to having kids?"

"Maybe."

The sound of paws on the stairs was followed by Barry crashing through the door.

"Are you here to give me my first lesson, Jill?"

"Sorry?"

"You promised you'd teach him to dance," Aunt Lucy reminded me.

"I—err—I don't really have much time at the moment."

"Didn't you just say you had an hour to kill before you went back to that cat place?" Aunt Lucy grinned.

"Please, Jill!" Barry pleaded with those big, sad eyes of his.

"Okay then. What about music?"

"I gave him a CD player," Aunt Lucy said. "He wants to learn disco."

"It just so happens I was quite the disco dancer in my day. I have all the moves."

I followed the excited dog upstairs into the spare bedroom where he switched on the CD player.

"Okay, Barry, watch and learn."

The track was a seventies disco classic, and I had soon lost myself in dance. Barry was staring at me open-mouthed, no doubt in awe of my moves.

"What's that supposed to be?" The laughter knocked me out of my stride.

I paused the music and turned around to find Rhymes in hysterics.

"Is something amusing you?"

"I'm sorry, Jill." He wiped the tears from his eyes. "I've never seen anything quite as bad as that."

What a cheek! And after all I'd done for him. "I suppose you could do better?"

"I happen to be the reigning Tortoise Disco Dancing Champion."

"Of course you are. Go on, then." I restarted the music. "Let's see what you can do."

Much as it pains me to admit it, the tortoise certainly had the moves, but no one likes a show-off.

"Thank you, but we've seen enough." I paused the music again. "If you don't mind, I was in the middle of giving Barry a lesson."

"I think I'd like Rhymes to teach me instead," Barry said.

"A tortoise? You're going to take dancing lessons from a tortoise rather than from me?"

"As long as you don't mind. I don't want to upset you."

"*Mind*? Of course I don't mind. I'm very busy anyway."

"Okay, thanks." He switched on the music, and the two of them got down to the beat.

"How did that go?" Aunt Lucy asked when I got back downstairs.

"Really well. So well, in fact, that Barry said he won't need any more lessons from me."

***

When I'd told Felix Le Chat that I would be returning to check out Cat City's cat café, I hadn't been lying. What I hadn't told him was that I wouldn't be returning as Kitty Sears, or even as Jill Maxwell. Instead, I planned to return as my feline alter ego, Fluffykins.

What? I was more of a Fluffykins than Bruiser would ever be.

And like any experienced undercover cat, I had availed myself of a tiny surveillance camera, which was cleverly hidden under a fur patch. I had Winky to thank for introducing me to that particular invention.

After a quick check to ensure the camera was angled correctly, I slipped quietly into the cat café. I hadn't been inside for more than a couple of minutes before—

"Hello, darling. I've not seen you in here before." The black and white moggy gave me a wink.

"I'm new here."

"I'm Roger. What's your name, sweetlips?"

"Fluffykins."

"What a lovely name. Has anyone ever told you that

279

you have beautiful whiskers?"

"Oh you! You're just saying that."

"I didn't realise they were taking on more staff."

"They just had the one slot free. I was lucky to get it."

"Luck doesn't come into it. I bet they took one look at you and offered you the gig on the spot."

"What's it like, working here?"

"Spot on. Best job I've ever had, and the money is amazing."

"They did explain it in the interview, but to be honest, I'm still not sure exactly how all of this works."

"Don't worry your pretty head about it. I'll be only too pleased to talk you through it, and then maybe you and I can go for a drink later?"

"Maybe."

***

An hour later, having reverted from Fluffykins back to Jill Maxwell, I paid another visit to Cat City.

"Hello again." Felix greeted me with a huge smile and pound signs in his eyes. "Couldn't you make it to the cat café?"

"Yes, I was there."

"Oh? I kept a lookout, but I didn't see you."

"I have a couple more questions about the cats if that's okay?"

"Of course. Fire away."

"I realise this is just hypothetical, but what would happen if, just for argument's sake, some of the cats got out of my café and made their way back here?"

"Back here?" He laughed, nervously. "That would

never happen."

"But if it did?"

"In the unlikely event that it should happen, we'd return the cat to you of course."

"Would you charge me again?"

"For the same cat? No, why would we do that?"

"Then why did you charge my cousins again when their cats ran back here?"

"Sorry? I don't know what you're talking about."

"My cousins Amber and Pearl run Cuppy C. You recently supplied them with cats. Twice now in fact."

"I thought you said you were—"

"Thinking of opening a cat café? Yeah, I kind of lied about that."

"I'm a busy man. I don't have time for this."

"Maybe you'll have more time to talk to the police."

"Why would they want to talk to me? I've done nothing wrong."

"I beg to differ. Take a look at this."

I took out my phone and played the video I'd recorded earlier.

"Okay, Fluffykins," Roger said. "This is how it works. We earn a basic hourly rate, which to be honest isn't all that great. But then we get a bonus every time we make a break for it and come back here."

"Hang on." Fluffykins' voice could be heard off-camera. "Are you saying that we're supposed to run away from whichever café we're placed in?"

"That's right. That's where the real money is."

"Sweet."

"Exactly. Now, about that drink."

"I don't understand." Felix looked suitably stunned.

289

"I think you do. That was one of your cats explaining how your little scam works."

"Who was he talking to?"

"To me, obviously."

"You were Fluffykins?"

"None other."

"Have you called the police already?"

"Not yet, and I won't provided that you agree to my terms."

"What do you want?"

"First, you're going to refund all the money that the twins have paid to you, and you're going to do it today."

"I don't have that kind of money on me."

"You'd better get yourself off to the bank, then."

"Okay, okay. I'll get their money."

"And next, you're going to shut down this scam."

"But this is my livelihood; I'm good at training cats."

"You can continue to supply cats, but you can't incentivise them to run away. Once you've sold a cat, that's it. And if one does make its way back here, you are to return it to its new rightful owner."

"That'll cut my profits in half."

"Would you prefer to go to prison?"

"Okay. I agree. You're a hard woman."

Chapter 27

Getting to the bottom of the Cat City scam had got me thinking.

Lovely, Bruiser and at least two other cats had recently gone missing, and the disappearances had all occurred since the opening of Washbridge's very own cat café. What if something equally sinister was going on right on my own doorstep? What if the owners of the Washbridge cat café had decided to cut costs by stealing cats?

I was on my way to pay them a visit when my phone rang.

"This is James Hattersley. You left a message on my voicemail. Something about my brother?"

"Thanks for calling. Do you know where I can find Paul?"

"Why do you want him? Who are you, anyway?"

"This is something that would probably be best discussed face-to-face. Where are you?"

"In Llandudno."

"That's lucky. I'm just down the road from you, in Colwyn Bay. I could be with you in twenty minutes."

"Can't you just tell me what this is all about?"

"I'd rather not discuss it over the phone. It's a nice day, why don't we meet on the pier?"

"Okay."

"How will I know you?"

"I'm wearing blue overalls. I've only just finished work."

"I'll be with you in twenty minutes."

Obviously, I could have magicked myself there instantly, but I figured that would freak him out. It

291

already required a stretch of the imagination for him to believe that I just happened to be down the road in Colwyn Bay. And besides, the delay would give me time to figure out exactly how to approach this. I didn't think that opening with the line: *I think your brother is a serial killer,* would exactly endear me to James.

***

It had been a few years since I'd last visited Llandudno, but from what I could see it hadn't changed that much. I'd always liked the pier, and according to the plaque I spotted, I wasn't the only one because it had been voted Pier Of The Year in 2005.

It wasn't difficult to pick out James Hattersley because he was the only one wearing overalls, although I would have argued they were closer to turquoise than blue.

"James?"

"Yes. Jill?"

"Shall we take a seat?" I pointed to one of the wooden benches.

"Okay, but what's this all about?"

"I'm a private investigator based in Washbridge."

"How come you were in Colwyn Bay, then?"

"I—err—I'm on a day trip. I'd like to speak to you about your brother and his possible connection to a case I'm working on. He used to work in Washbridge until recently, I believe?"

"What kind of case?"

"My client has been accused of murdering his wife."

"What does that have to do with Paul?"

"Perhaps nothing, but he did visit my client's flat a

couple of weeks before the murder."

"That doesn't mean a thing."

"You're probably right, but the thing is, I've found two similar cases where a man has been convicted of his wife's murder: One in Liverpool and one in Newcastle."

"So what?"

"Your brother visited the properties in question shortly before each of the murders, and then left his job without notice shortly afterwards."

"That could just be a coincidence."

"Quite possibly. Why don't you tell me about your brother?"

He said nothing for the longest time, and I half expected him to stand up and walk away.

"Paul's younger than me by five years. Do you have siblings?"

"An older sister, yeah."

"You'll know what it's like then. The bond, I mean. There's nothing quite like it, is there?"

"I guess not."

"Our parents weren't good people. Drunks, both of them. Drugs too, probably. They should never have had children. Our father was a violent man even when he wasn't drunk. He used to knock my mother about. Us too. Our mum wasn't much better. Instead of protecting us, she took her anger out on Paul and me."

"I can't begin to imagine what that must have been like."

"It only stopped when they locked him up."

"Your father?"

"Yes. He went too far one night and ended up killing our mother. Paul and I were put into care. Thankfully, they kept us together."

"That must have been terrible for you."

"You might have thought so, but actually going into care was the best thing that happened to us. It meant we got away from the beatings."

"An experience like that must have left a psychological mark."

"Of course it did, but more so on Paul, I reckon. Probably because he was younger."

"Do you know where he is now?"

"I've already said too much."

"If you know, you have to tell me. You know you do."

James stood up, and I thought he was going to walk away, but instead he began to pace back and forth, lost in his own thoughts.

"James, please! This isn't something you can simply brush under the carpet."

He stopped pacing, bowed his head, and said in a voice I could barely hear, "Paul's at my place. He moved in a couple of weeks ago. I knew something was wrong. I could sense it."

"Will you take me to see him?"

"Only if you promise to let me do the talking."

"But, I—"

"You have to promise."

"Okay."

We made our way off the pier in silence, and walked to James' van, which he had parked a few streets back from the promenade.

"Is it far?" I asked as we drove away.

"Ten minutes. I'd better warn you: Paul isn't in great shape. He's not been eating properly."

"Okay."

We parked outside a terraced property that, from the exterior at least, had seen better days. I followed James inside, into the small living room which overlooked a tiny garden at the rear of the house. Seated in an old armchair, staring out of the window, was a man who was a shorter version of James. If I hadn't known better, I would have assumed that Paul was the older brother.

"Paul," James said. "I'm back."

His brother didn't seem to be alarmed by my presence. In fact, he didn't register any emotion at all.

"This is Jill." James turned to me. "Take a seat, please."

I took the matching armchair while James sat on the sofa. Paul looked at me but didn't speak.

"Jill is from Washbridge, Paul. She's just been telling me about something bad that happened while you were working there." He waited for a reaction, but there was none, so he continued. "She also told me that something similar happened while you were working in Newcastle and Liverpool. Do you know anything about any of this?"

Paul stared at his brother, but still showed no sign of emotion. This didn't seem to be getting us anywhere, and I was ready to intervene.

"I saved them," Paul said.

"Saved who?" I got in before James had a chance to react.

"Are they okay?" Paul was looking at me now.

Before I could speak again, James said, "Who are you talking about, Paul? Is *who* safe?"

"The children. Are they okay?"

"Yes, Paul." James nodded. "They're safe. How did you

287

save them? What did you do?"

It was a laborious process, but Paul eventually managed to tell us what he'd done. Including the why and the how. By the time he'd finished, he was exhausted. Moments later, his eyes closed, and he drifted off to sleep.

James gestured that I should follow him out of the room, and then said, "What happens now?"

"We have to call the police."

"What will happen to him?"

"He's responsible for the death of three women, and for putting three innocent men in prison."

"But you've seen the state he's in. He didn't know what he was doing."

"That will be for the courts to decide."

"You have to let *me* be the one to contact the police, Jill."

"I'm not sure about that."

"Please. I promise I'll call them as soon as you've left. I want to stay with him."

"I doubt they'll allow you to do that."

"I have to try."

"Okay, but I'll check later, and if you haven't kept your promise, I'll contact the police myself."

"Thank you. I really appreciate this."

I declined James' offer of a lift back to Colwyn Bay. Instead, once I was in an isolated spot, I magicked myself back to Washbridge.

I should have been elated. Laurence Forrest would no doubt soon walk free from prison, as would two more wrongly convicted men. But how could I feel good about what had just happened?

Paul Hattersley was a three-time murderer who had

framed innocent men to cover his tracks. That was inexcusable, and he would no doubt be punished for his crimes. But having listened to the man speak, it was clear that, in his warped mind, he'd believed he was doing good. When Paul's father had murdered his mother, Paul had been taken into care, rescuing him from the abuse he'd suffered at the hands of his parents. Paul believed he was doing the same thing for those children. That was quite obviously wrong on so many levels, not least the fact that these children hadn't been living in abusive homes.

From all accounts, Paul Hattersley had been a model employee. Good at his job, he was diligent and well regarded. In the course of his duties, he had on three separate occasions, in three different cities, found himself in properties where the adults were arguing with one another. Nothing serious, just the kind of arguments all couples have from time to time. But it had been enough to spark terrible memories for Paul. He'd seen it as his mission to rescue the child from that environment, and he'd done that by killing the mother and framing the father. By taking something from the apartment that could later be used as a murder weapon, Paul had been able to return, commit the murder and then leave the incriminating evidence, which would eventually help to convict the innocent husband.

It was impossible to predict how the police and courts would move forward with the case. Had Paul been of sound mind when he committed the murders? The careful planning that had gone into them suggested that he had. But then, to listen to his story, and to hear the way he himself interpreted those actions, might that not cast doubts on his competency to stand trial?

289

I was pleased that I wouldn't be the one who would have to make that decision.

***

Meow!

No, I hadn't turned myself into a cat again. That's where I was: At Meow! Washbridge's new cat café. And I have to be honest, they were fantastic.

No, not the cats. I'm talking about their muffins.

A lot of time and money had been spent on the café, and the results spoke for themselves. The place was packed, and everyone seemed to be having a great time. If it hadn't been for the cats, it would have been perfect. One in particular was really getting on my nerves. It kept trying to grab my muffin.

"Get your own." I tried to shoo it away.

"Give us a bite, lady. Just a small piece."

"No. These are bad for cats. I'm doing you a favour."

"Sorry?" The woman sitting at the next table shot me a confused look. "Were you talking to me?"

"No. To the cat."

"They're all so darling, aren't they?"

"Yeah. Have you been here before?"

"Every day since it opened. I love it here."

"The cats certainly seem to enjoy it."

"They do, but my favourite, Topsy, isn't out today. She's gorgeous."

"Maybe she's poorly?"

"I don't think so. They have lots of cats, but they only allow so many into the café at a time. I suppose they must take turns, so they don't get over-tired."

"Where do they keep the others?"

"Through the back, I believe."

Hmm, interesting.

So far, I hadn't seen Lovely, Bruiser or either of Winky's friends, but maybe they were in the back.

I monitored the staff, and sure enough, every now and then, they would pick up one of the cats, take it through the door at the back of the café, and then a few minutes later, return with a different cat.

When I was sure that all the staff members were out front, and occupied with customers, I slipped quietly into the back. The room was very large and contained dozens of spacious cages, resting on shelves on either side of the room. The sound of meowing in there was deafening, and I could barely hear myself think. Starting at one side of the room, I walked along the row of cages, glancing inside each one, to see if I could spot any of the missing cats.

I had no luck on the first wall, so I crossed the room, and started to make my way back along that side. I'd just reached the last cage—still with no sign of Lovely, Bruiser or the other two—when the door opened.

"What are you doing in here?" the man was carrying a ginger tom.

"I—err—was looking for the toilet."

"It's on the other side of the café."

"Oh? Okay, sorry." I slid past him and scurried away before he could ask any more questions.

***

I'd had a gruelling day, and I couldn't wait to get home. First, though, I needed to nip into the office to feed

Winky.

Mrs V was on the point of leaving as I arrived.

"Any messages, Mrs V?"

"Only the one. A Mrs Rightplace phoned to say she'd tried to find our offices, but she couldn't. I explained about the sign, but she said it didn't matter because she's hired another P.I."

"Great."

"I'd better get going. I'm meeting Armi—we're going to get pizza."

"Very nice. Have a good weekend."

"Don't you pick up your new car tomorrow, Jill?"

"I do. I can't wait."

Winky was looking skywards through his telescope, but he came over to me once I'd put out his salmon.

"I went to the new cat café looking for your two friends, but there was no sign of them."

"They're back."

"Since when?"

"A couple of days ago. It seems they'd gone on a stag night which turned into a stag week and a half. From all accounts, Gemma gave Gavin hell because he hadn't even told her he was going."

"And you didn't think to mention it to me?"

"I thought I had. Sorry."

Chapter 28

I was staring at my bowl of cornflakes and hadn't even heard Jack come into the kitchen.

"Are you okay, Jill?"

"Yeah. Sorry, I was miles away."

"You were quiet last night too. Is something the matter?"

"It's nothing. Just one of the cases I've been working on."

"Do you want to talk about it?"

"Not really."

"I take it that it isn't going well?"

"That depends how you look at it. I've just saved my client's son from being tried for his wife's murder, and if I'm right, two other innocent men will be freed from prison very soon."

"That sounds like a result to me."

"I know, but there's much more to it than that. Anyway, it's the weekend; I don't want to talk about it."

"Fair enough. You get your new car later—that should cheer you up."

Kathy rang.

"Pete and I are taking the kids into Washbridge later. We thought we might as well pop along to see you get your new car. What time is the prize-giving?"

"At eleven."

"At the town hall, right?"

"Yeah."

"Okay, we'll see you there."

***

293

We were going to take Jack's car because I'd be driving my new Jag back home. He was still looking for his favourite scarf when I made my way outside. Before I could get in the car, I spotted Lovely, sitting on next-door's front lawn. Standing next to her was Bruiser.

"Lovely? When did you get back?"

"Hi, Jill. Just now."

"Do Britt and Kit know you're home?"

"Not yet."

"Where have you been? Everyone has been worried sick. And what are you doing with *him*?"

"I think I owe you an apology," Bruiser said. "There's no excuse for the way I acted towards you and—err—Wonky."

"It's Winky."

"I hope you'll both find it in your hearts to forgive me one day."

Was this cat for real? "Hang on. Have you two been somewhere together?"

Looking rather bashful, it was Lovely who responded. "We eloped."

"Are you kidding me? The last I heard, you hated him." I pointed an accusing finger at Bruiser.

"That was before. He's changed, Jill. Ever since the incident with the lion."

"Even so. Isn't this all rather quick?"

"We're in love, aren't we, Fluffykins?" She snuggled up to Bruiser.

"We are, Lovelykins."

Where were the sick bags when you needed them?

"Jill? Are you ready?" Jack, and his favourite scarf, were

standing by the car.

"I'm coming."

"I see the cats have come back," he said, as we drove away. "Where had they been?"

"Getting hitched, apparently."

***

The crowd at the town hall was bigger than I'd expected, and I was just beginning to think we wouldn't be able to find Kathy, Peter and the kids when I heard her call.

"Jill! We're over here."

"You must be excited," Peter said. "I've always fancied a Jag."

"I am. I can't wait to get behind the wheel."

"I've got a rabbit, Auntie Jill," Mikey said.

"He's called Flopsy." Lizzie giggled.

"No, he isn't." Mikey responded indignantly. "That's just what *you* call him. His real name is Jake."

"But he has big floppy ears." Lizzie insisted.

"That's enough, you two." Kathy stepped in.

"I take it you managed to rehome the canary?" I said.

"Yeah, that friend of yours, Dorothy, took him. She said he was just like one she used to have."

"Great. All's well that ends well."

The prize-giving ceremony began promptly at eleven o'clock, and thirty minutes later, they were just getting around to the top three prizes.

"I don't know why they didn't just send out the minor prizes in the post." I sighed.

295

"It won't be long now, "Jack said. "Only two more and then it's your turn.

"No one cares about these other prizes. Everyone is here to find out what the top prize is."

"You could be right. Look." Jack pointed. "It looks like the local TV has only just arrived."

"When they interview me, I must remember to get in a plug for the business."

"And so, citizens of Washbridge," the MC said. "We now come to the top prize. And to award it, please welcome on stage your mayor."

The crowd managed no more than a polite round of applause for the diminutive man, who looked as though he might trip up over his chains of office.

"Hello, everyone." The mayor had the microphone now. "I'm delighted to see such an excellent turnout for Washbridge's inaugural annual lottery. It has raised an incredible amount of money for some very worthy causes. And, as you have already seen, there have been many excellent prizes. None better than the one that it is now my great pleasure to award to Jill Maxwell."

"I'll see you back at the house." I gave Jack a quick peck on the cheek. "I might be a while because I'm going to take her for a spin."

"Jill Maxwell, will you please come on stage to collect — " I was standing next to him before he'd had the chance to finish. "You're very keen, and little wonder." He glanced to the side of the stage to make sure the TV cameras were in place. Satisfied, he continued, "Jill, it gives me great pleasure to present this to you."

As he handed me a white envelope, the cameraman

walked over to us, in order to get a close-up.

"Open it," the mayor encouraged me.

I didn't need telling twice. No doubt this would be the registration documents and the key, although I couldn't feel anything key-shaped inside. But then, weren't all new executive cars keyless these days?

I ripped open the envelope and took out the card.

"What do you think, Jill? I bet you weren't expecting anything as exciting as that, were you?" The mayor was speaking half to me, and half to the camera.

I said nothing. I couldn't. I wanted the ground to open up and swallow me.

"Come on, Jack, let's go." I grabbed him by the arm.

"I thought you might both want to come back to our place," Kathy shouted after us.

"No, thanks. I'm feeling a bit peaky." Back at Jack's car, I slumped into the passenger seat. "Get me out of here."

"Why were you so sure you'd won a car?"

"Because I saw them delivering it, and I asked the man if it had something to do with today, and he said it did."

"I suppose it did, in a way."

"How?"

"Didn't you see the mayor arrive? He was in a Jag, and it looked brand new."

"I've never been so embarrassed."

"Why? You still won first prize."

"A course of lessons at Clown?" I threw the envelope into the back seat. "Are you smirking?"

"No, of course not."

"That looked very much like a smirk to me."

"It wasn't, I promise."

"Just take me home."

We drove back in silence. I should have known better than to think that I could ever win something like a new car. Why had I bragged about it to so many people? They would no doubt all have a good laugh at my expense when they saw what had happened on TV.

We'd just pulled onto our street when Jack stopped the car; he appeared to be staring at our house.

"What's wrong? Why have you stopped here?"

"Your car? It's not on the driveway. Where has it gone?"

"Oh no!"

"What's wrong?"

"I told the breaker's yard that they could come and pick it up. It'll be a heap of scrap metal by now."

"Oh dear." Jack began to laugh so hard that soon there were tears rolling down his cheek.

"It's not funny!"

"Come on, Jill. Surely you can see the funny side."

ALSO BY ADELE ABBOTT

Murder On Account (A Kay Royle Novel)

The Witch P.I. Mysteries
(A Candlefield/Washbridge Series)

Witch Is When... (Books #1 to #12)
Witch Is When It All Began
Witch Is When Life Got Complicated
Witch Is When Everything Went Crazy
Witch Is When Things Fell Apart
Witch Is When The Bubble Burst
Witch Is When The Penny Dropped
Witch Is When The Floodgates Opened
Witch Is When The Hammer Fell
Witch Is When My Heart Broke
Witch Is When I Said Goodbye
Witch Is When Stuff Got Serious
Witch Is When All Was Revealed

Witch Is Why... (Books #13 to #24)
Witch Is Why Time Stood Still
Witch is Why The Laughter Stopped
Witch is Why Another Door Opened
Witch is Why Two Became One
Witch is Why The Moon Disappeared
Witch is Why The Wolf Howled
Witch is Why The Music Stopped
Witch is Why A Pin Dropped

Witch is Why The Owl Returned
Witch is Why The Search Began
Witch is Why Promises Were Broken
Witch is Why It Was Over

Witch Is How... (Books #25 to #36)
Witch is How Things Had Changed
Witch is How Berries Tasted Good
Witch is How The Mirror Lied
Witch is How The Tables Turned
Witch is How The Drought Ended
Witch is How The Dice Fell
Witch is How The Biscuits Disappeared
Witch is How Dreams Became Reality
Witch is How Bells Were Saved
Witch is How To Fool Cats
Witch is How To Lose Big
Witch is How Life Changed Forever

Susan Hall Investigates (A Candlefield/Washbridge Series)
Whoops! Our New Flatmate Is A Human.
Whoops! All The Money Went Missing.
Whoops! Someone Is On Our Case.
Whoops! We're In Big Trouble Now.

Web site: AdeleAbbott.com
Facebook: facebook.com/AdeleAbbottAuthor